MARVEL

ULTIMATE
SPIDER-MAN
VS
THE SINISTER 6

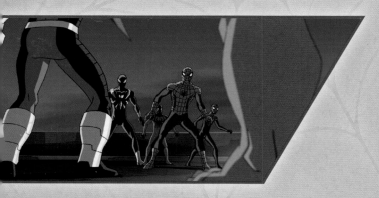

MARVEL UNIVERSE ULTIMATE SPIDER-MAN VS. THE SINISTER SIX VOL. 3. Contains material originally published in magazine form as MARVEL UNIVERSE ULTIMATE SPIDER-MAN VS. THE SINISTER SIX #9-11 and MARVEL UNIVERSE ULTIMATE SPIDER-MAN #1. First printing 2017. ISBN# 978-1-302-90260-5. Published by MARVEL WORLDWIDE, INC., a subsidiary of MARVEL ENTERTAINMENT, LLC. OFFICE OF PUBLICATION: 135 West 50th Street, New York, NY 10020. Copyright © 2017 MARVEL No similarity between any of the names, characters, persons, and/or institutions in this magazine with those of any living or dead person or institution is intended, and any such similarity which may exist is purely coincidental. **Printed in the U.S.A.** DAN BUCKLEY, President, Marvel Entertainment; JOE QUESADA, Chief Creative Officer; TOM BREVOORT, SVP of Publishing; DAVID BOGART, SVP of Business Affairs & Operations, Publishing & Partnership; C.B. CEBULSKI, VP of Brand Management & Development, Asia; DAVID GABRIEL, SVP of Sales & Marketing, Publishing; JEFF YOUNGQUIST, VP of Production & Special Projects; DAN CARR, Executive Director of Publishing Technology; ALEX MORALES, Director of Publishing Operations; SUSAN CRESPI, Production Manager; STAN LEE, Chairman Emeritus. For information regarding advertising in Marvel Comics or on Marvel.com, please contact Vit DeBellis, Integrated Sales Manager, at vdebellis@marvel.com. For Marvel subscription inquiries, please call 888-511-5480. **Manufactured between 5/19/2017 and 6/20/2017 by SHERIDAN, CHELSEA, MI, USA.**

10 9 8 7 6 5 4 3 2 1

MARVEL
ULTIMATE SPIDER-MAN VS THE SINISTER 6

BASED ON THE TV SERIES WRITTEN BY
**GAVIN HIGNIGHT, JACOB SEMAHN,
AND KEVIN BURKE & CHRIS "DOC" WYATT**

DIRECTED BY
ROY BURDINE, YOUNG KI YOON AND JAE WOO KIM

ANIMATION PRODUCED BY
MARVEL ANIMATION STUDIOS WITH **FILM ROMAN**

ADAPTED BY
JOE CARAMAGNA

SPECIAL THANKS TO
HANNAH MacDONALD & PRODUCT FACTORY

EDITOR
CHRISTINA HARRINGTON

SENIOR EDITOR
MARK PANICCIA

SPIDER-MAN CREATED BY **STAN LEE & STEVE DITKO**

Collection Editor: **Jennifer Grünwald**
Assistant Editor: **Caitlin O'Connell**
Associate Managing Editor: **Kateri Woody**
Editor, Special Projects: **Mark D. Beazley**
VP Production & Special Projects: **Jeff Youngquist**
SVP Print, Sales & Marketing: **David Gabriel**
Book Design: **Adam Del Re**

Head of Marvel Television: **Jeph Loeb**

Editor In Chief: **Axel Alonso**
Chief Creative Officer: **Joe Quesada**
President: **Dan Buckley**
Executive Producer: **Alan Fine**

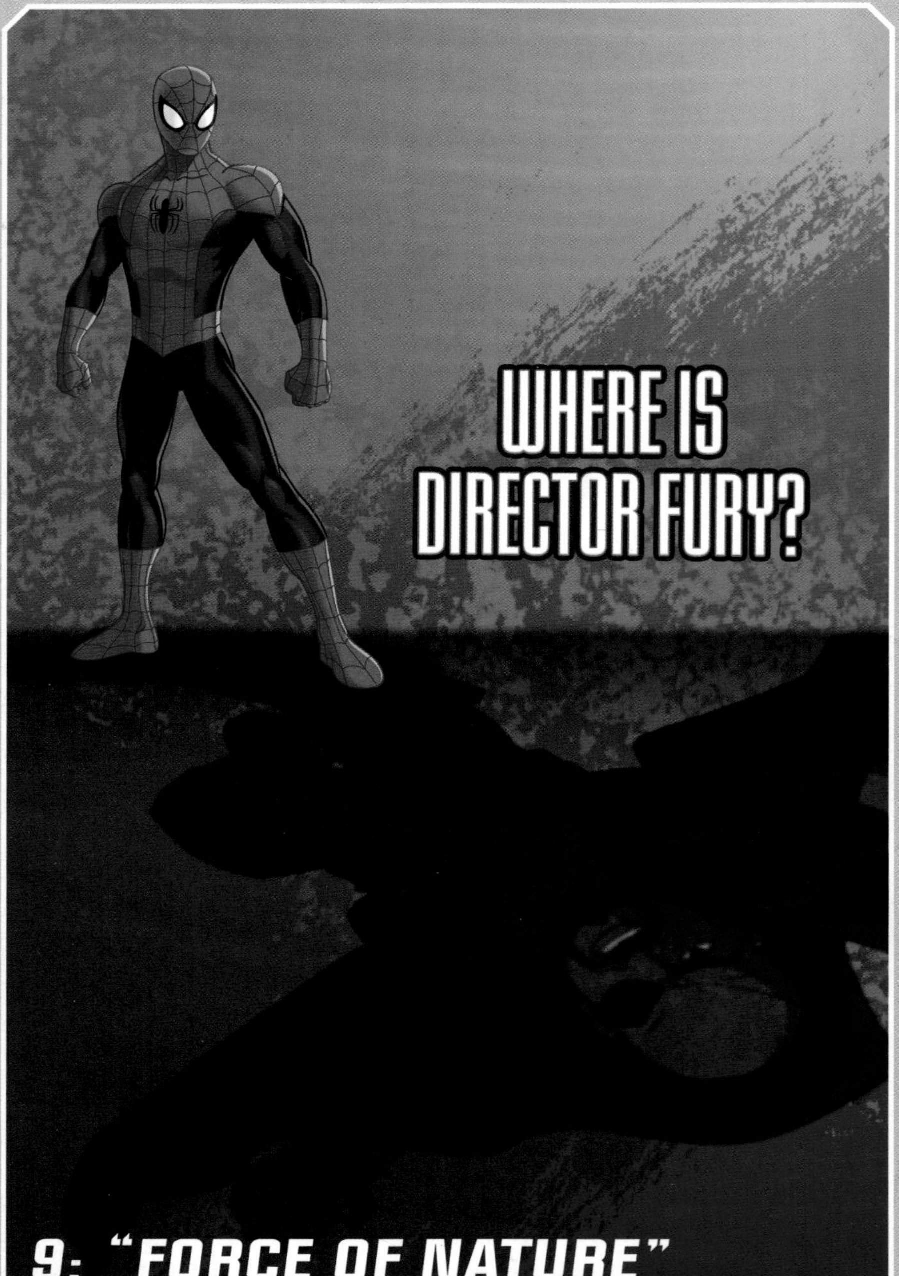
WHERE IS DIRECTOR FURY?

9: "FORCE OF NATURE"

WHILE ATTENDING A RADIOLOGY DEMONSTRATION, HIGH SCHOOL STUDENT PETER PARKER
WAS BITTEN BY A RADIOACTIVE SPIDER AND GAINED THE SPIDER'S POWERS! NOW HE IS
TRAINING WITH THE SUPER-SPY ORGANIZATION CALLED S.H.I.E.L.D. TO BECOME THE...

MARVEL
ULTIMATE
SPIDER-MAN
VS
THE SINISTER 6

Doctor Octopus and his new bestie Arnim Zola conquered S.H.I.E.L.D. and tricked out the
Tricarrier, but the Web-Warriors were able to turn the tables on them and launch their new
"Hydra Island" into space. Unfortunately, S.H.I.E.L.D.'s fearless leader, Nick Fury, was
injured in the siege, and had to be transported to safety by Nova. The problem is that no
one has seen or heard from either one of them since. And with every passing day, we're

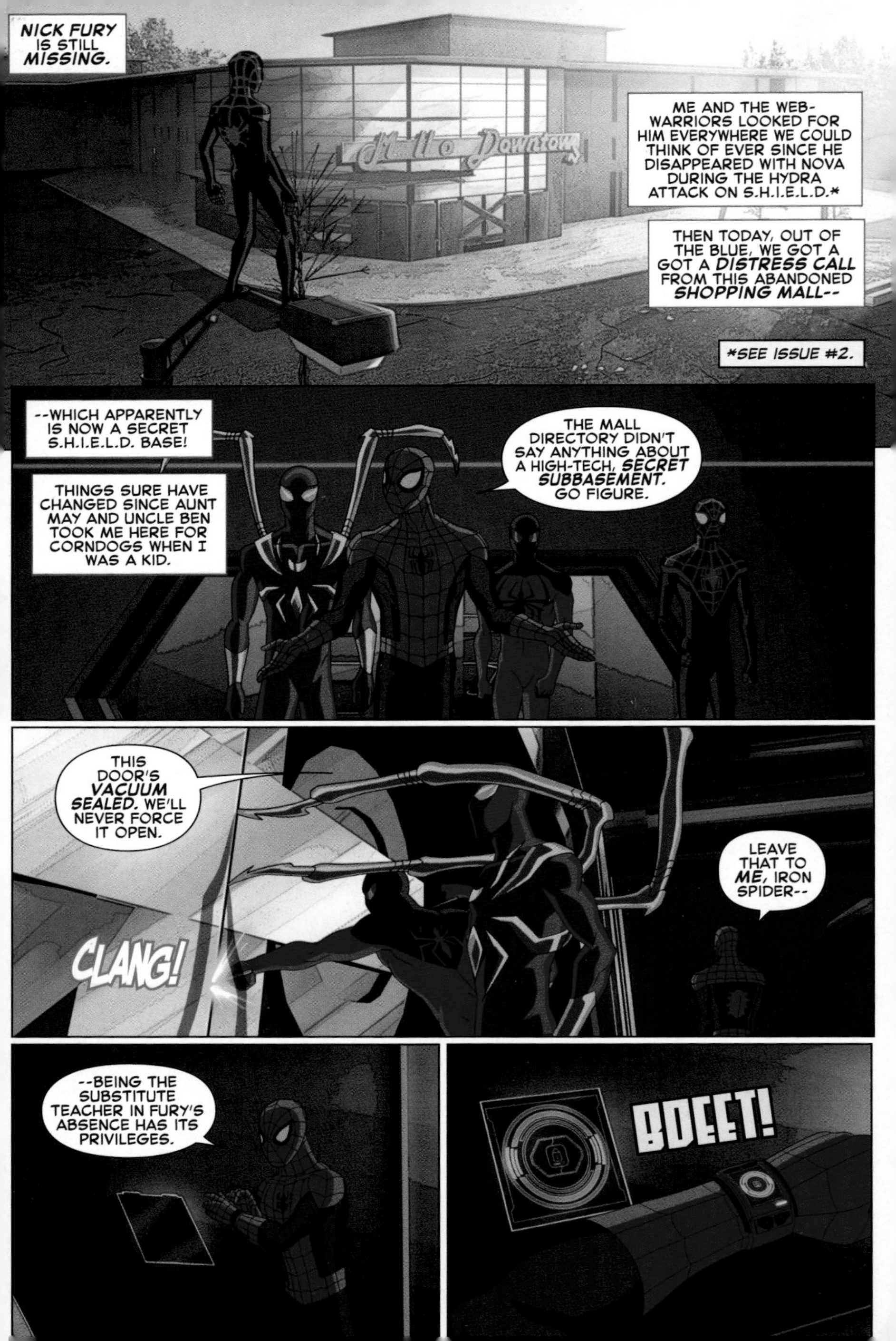
NICK FURY IS STILL MISSING.
ME AND THE WEB-WARRIORS LOOKED FOR HIM EVERYWHERE WE COULD THINK OF EVER SINCE HE DISAPPEARED WITH NOVA DURING THE HYDRA ATTACK ON S.H.I.E.L.D.*
THEN TODAY, OUT OF THE BLUE, WE GOT A GOT A DISTRESS CALL FROM THIS ABANDONED SHOPPING MALL--
*SEE ISSUE #2.
Mall o Downtown
--WHICH APPARENTLY IS NOW A SECRET S.H.I.E.L.D. BASE!
THINGS SURE HAVE CHANGED SINCE AUNT MAY AND UNCLE BEN TOOK ME HERE FOR CORNDOGS WHEN I WAS A KID.
THE MALL DIRECTORY DIDN'T SAY ANYTHING ABOUT A HIGH-TECH, SECRET SUBBASEMENT. GO FIGURE.
THIS DOOR'S VACUUM SEALED. WE'LL NEVER FORCE IT OPEN.
CLANG!
LEAVE THAT TO ME, IRON SPIDER--
--BEING THE SUBSTITUTE TEACHER IN FURY'S ABSENCE HAS ITS PRIVILEGES.
BDEET!

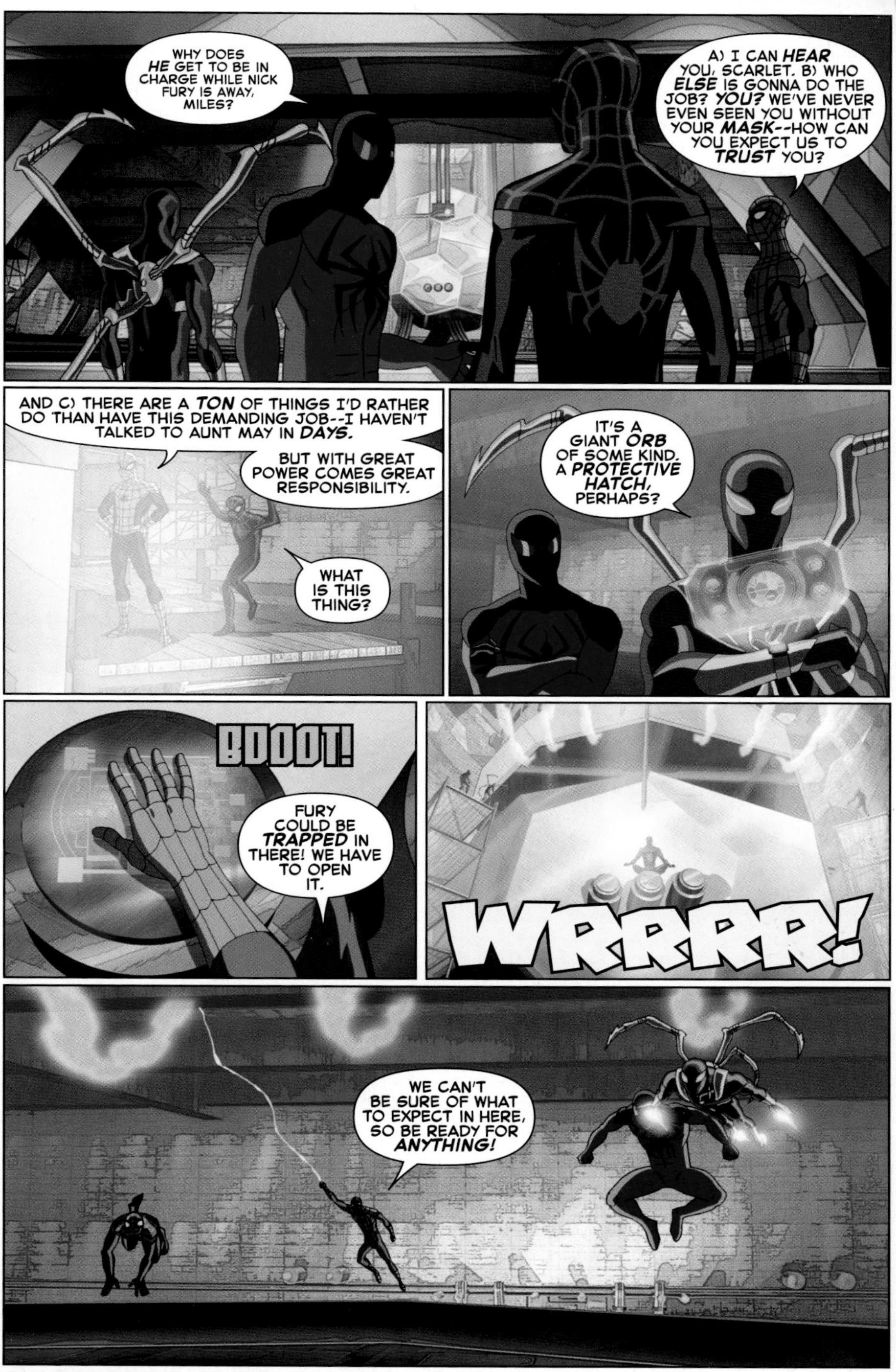
WHY DOES HE GET TO BE IN CHARGE WHILE NICK FURY IS AWAY, MILES?
A) I CAN HEAR YOU, SCARLET. B) WHO ELSE IS GONNA DO THE JOB? YOU? WE'VE NEVER EVEN SEEN YOU WITHOUT YOUR MASK--HOW CAN YOU EXPECT US TO TRUST YOU?
AND C) THERE ARE A TON OF THINGS I'D RATHER DO THAN HAVE THIS DEMANDING JOB--I HAVEN'T TALKED TO AUNT MAY IN DAYS.
BUT WITH GREAT POWER COMES GREAT RESPONSIBILITY.
WHAT IS THIS THING?
IT'S A GIANT ORB OF SOME KIND. A PROTECTIVE HATCH, PERHAPS?
BDOOT!
FURY COULD BE TRAPPED IN THERE! WE HAVE TO OPEN IT.
WRRRR!
WE CAN'T BE SURE OF WHAT TO EXPECT IN HERE, SO BE READY FOR ANYTHING!

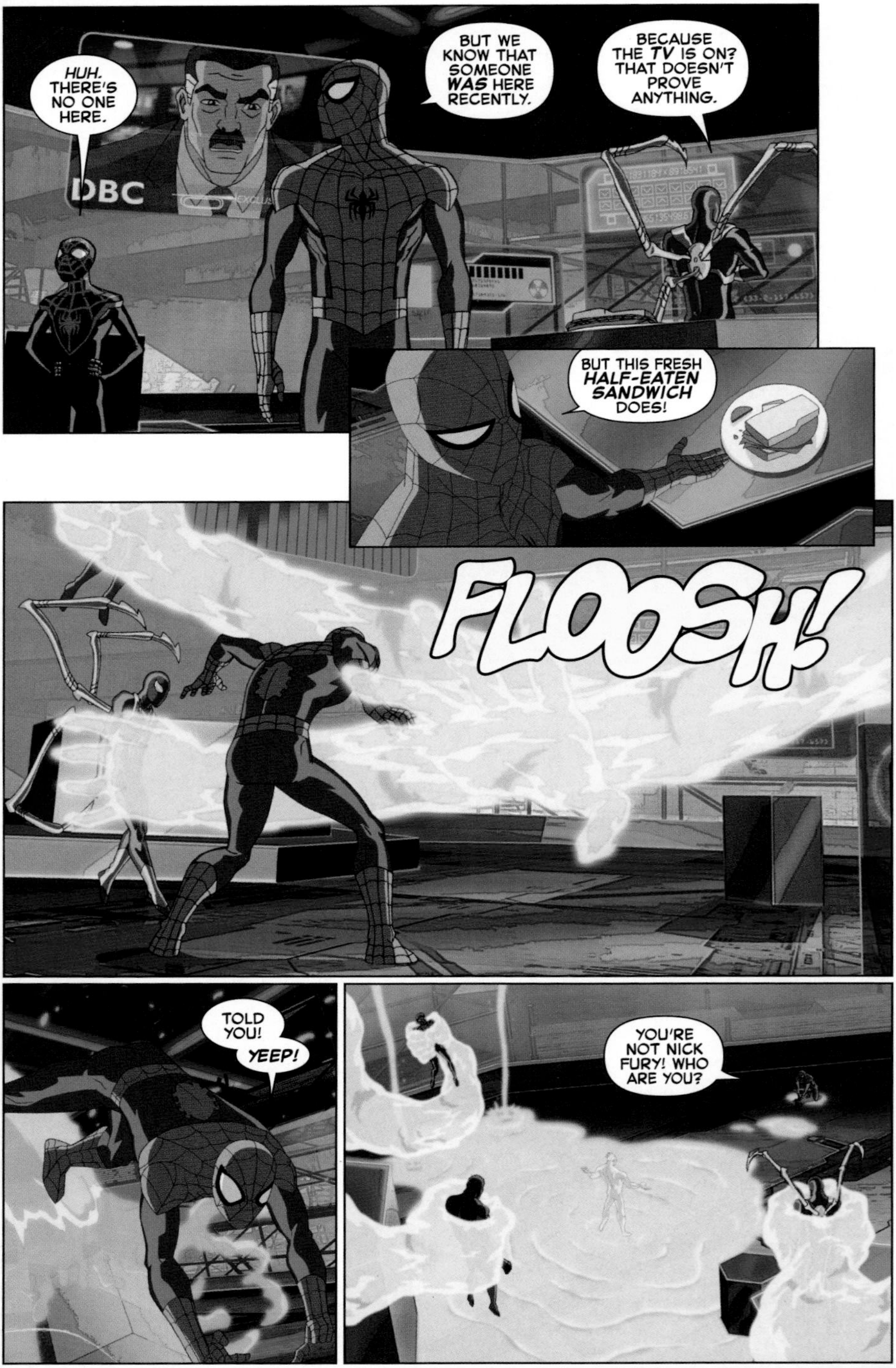
HUH. THERE'S NO ONE HERE.
DBC
BUT WE KNOW THAT SOMEONE WAS HERE RECENTLY.
BECAUSE THE TV IS ON? THAT DOESN'T PROVE ANYTHING.
BUT THIS FRESH HALF-EATEN SANDWICH DOES!
FLOOSH!
TOLD YOU!
YEEP!
YOU'RE NOT NICK FURY! WHO ARE YOU?

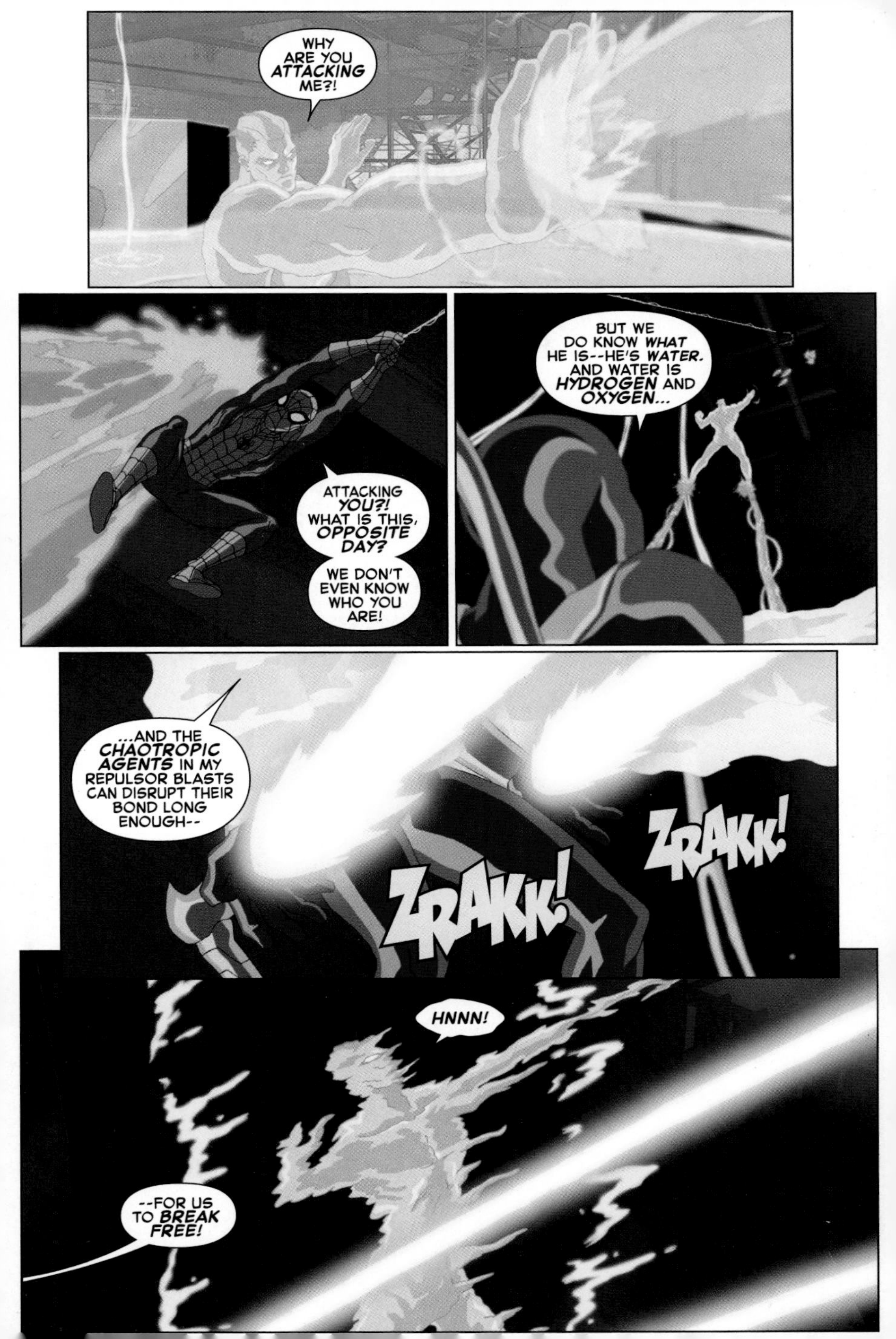
WHY ARE YOU ATTACKING ME?!
ATTACKING YOU?! WHAT IS THIS, OPPOSITE DAY?
WE DON'T EVEN KNOW WHO YOU ARE!
BUT WE DO KNOW WHAT HE IS--HE'S WATER. AND WATER IS HYDROGEN AND OXYGEN...
...AND THE CHAOTROPIC AGENTS IN MY REPULSOR BLASTS CAN DISRUPT THEIR BOND LONG ENOUGH--
ZRAKK!
ZRAKK!
HNNN!
--FOR US TO BREAK FREE!

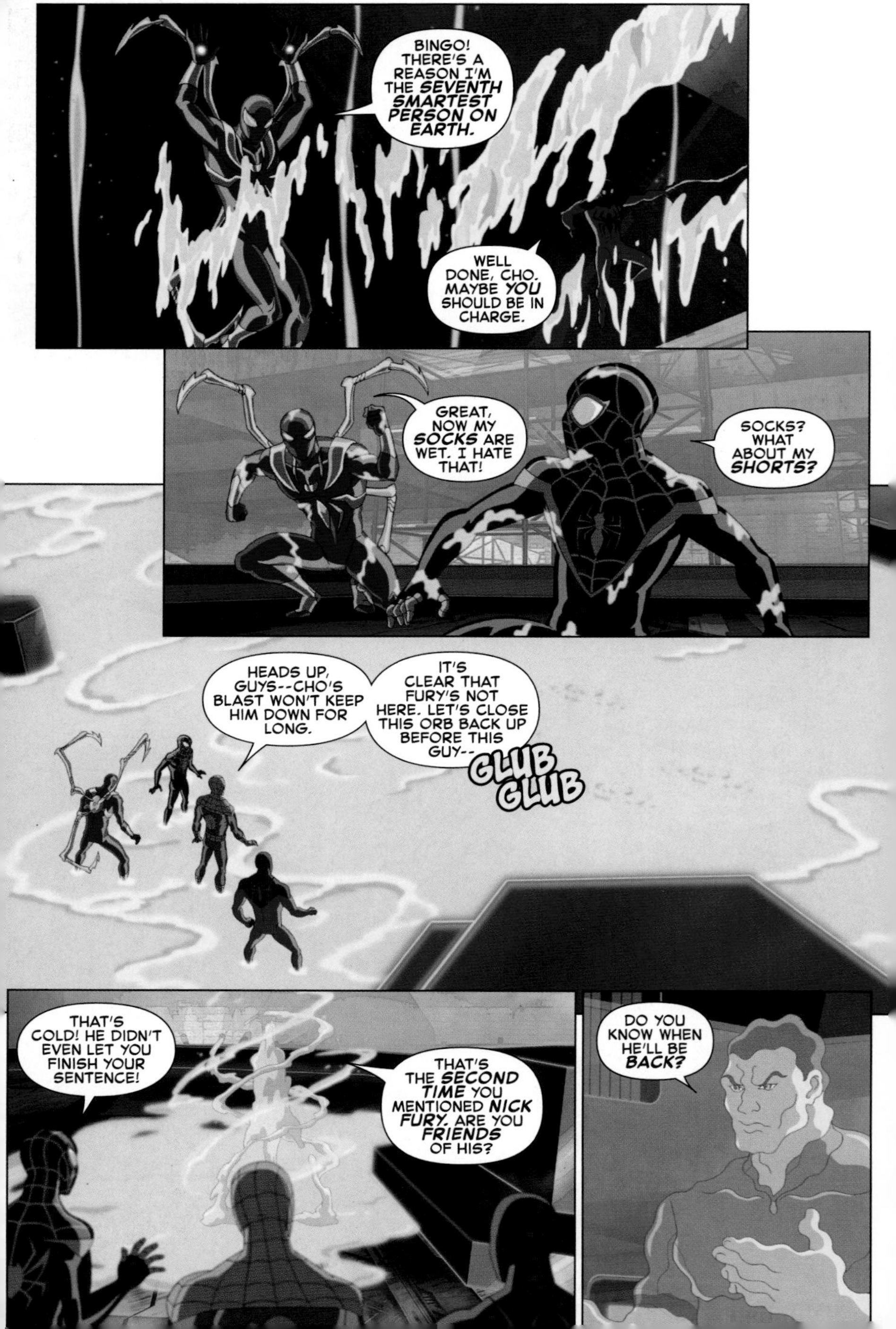
BINGO! THERE'S A REASON I'M THE SEVENTH SMARTEST PERSON ON EARTH.
WELL DONE, CHO. MAYBE YOU SHOULD BE IN CHARGE.
GREAT, NOW MY SOCKS ARE WET. I HATE THAT!
SOCKS? WHAT ABOUT MY SHORTS?
HEADS UP, GUYS--CHO'S BLAST WON'T KEEP HIM DOWN FOR LONG.
IT'S CLEAR THAT FURY'S NOT HERE. LET'S CLOSE THIS ORB BACK UP BEFORE THIS GUY--
GLUB GLUB
THAT'S COLD! HE DIDN'T EVEN LET YOU FINISH YOUR SENTENCE!
THAT'S THE SECOND TIME YOU MENTIONED NICK FURY. ARE YOU FRIENDS OF HIS?
DO YOU KNOW WHEN HE'LL BE BACK?

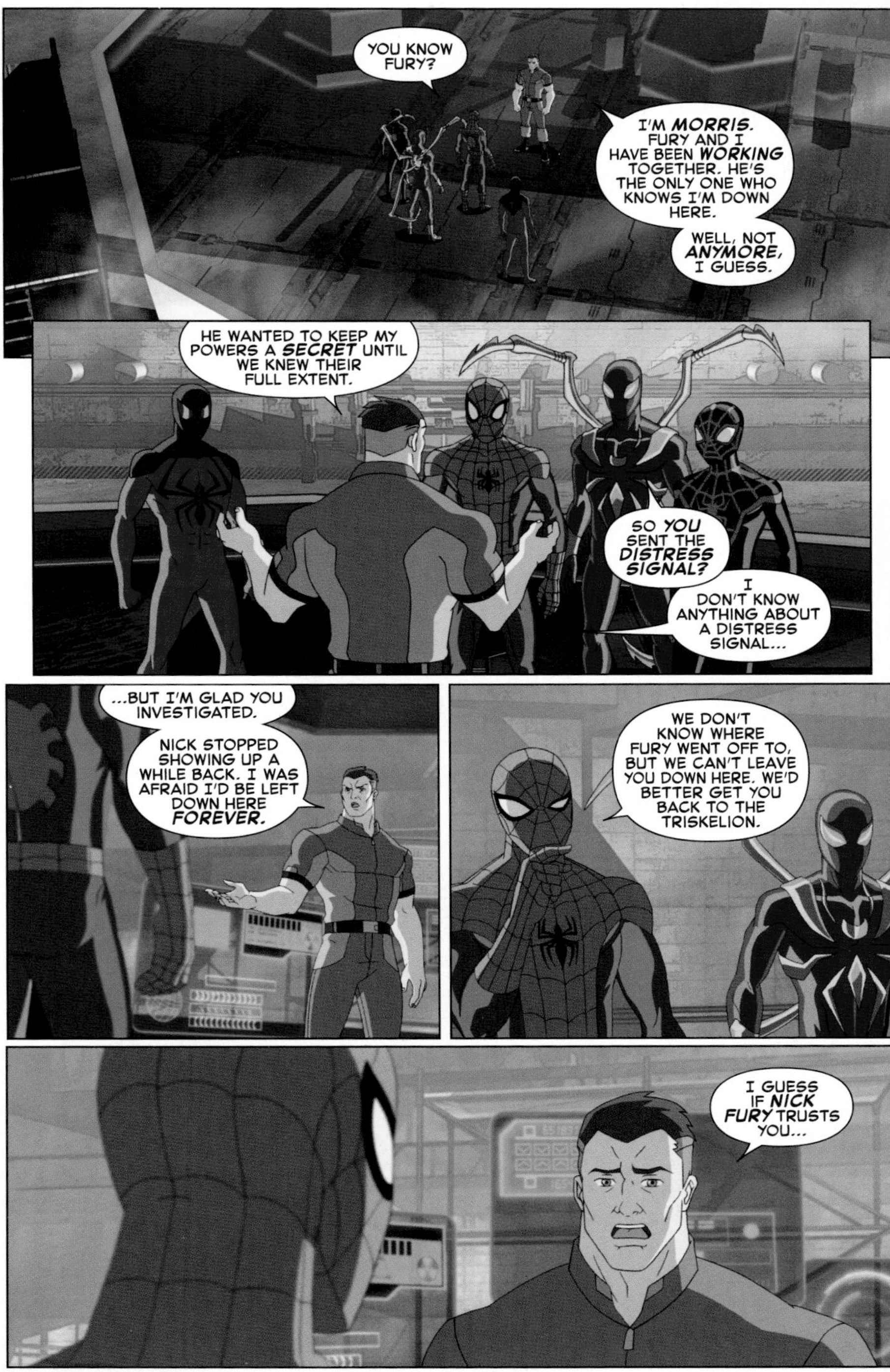
YOU KNOW FURY?
I'M MORRIS. FURY AND I HAVE BEEN WORKING TOGETHER. HE'S THE ONLY ONE WHO KNOWS I'M DOWN HERE.
WELL, NOT ANYMORE, I GUESS.
HE WANTED TO KEEP MY POWERS A SECRET UNTIL WE KNEW THEIR FULL EXTENT.
SO YOU SENT THE DISTRESS SIGNAL?
I DON'T KNOW ANYTHING ABOUT A DISTRESS SIGNAL...
...BUT I'M GLAD YOU INVESTIGATED.
NICK STOPPED SHOWING UP A WHILE BACK. I WAS AFRAID I'D BE LEFT DOWN HERE FOREVER.
WE DON'T KNOW WHERE FURY WENT OFF TO, BUT WE CAN'T LEAVE YOU DOWN HERE. WE'D BETTER GET YOU BACK TO THE TRISKELION.
I GUESS IF NICK FURY TRUSTS YOU...

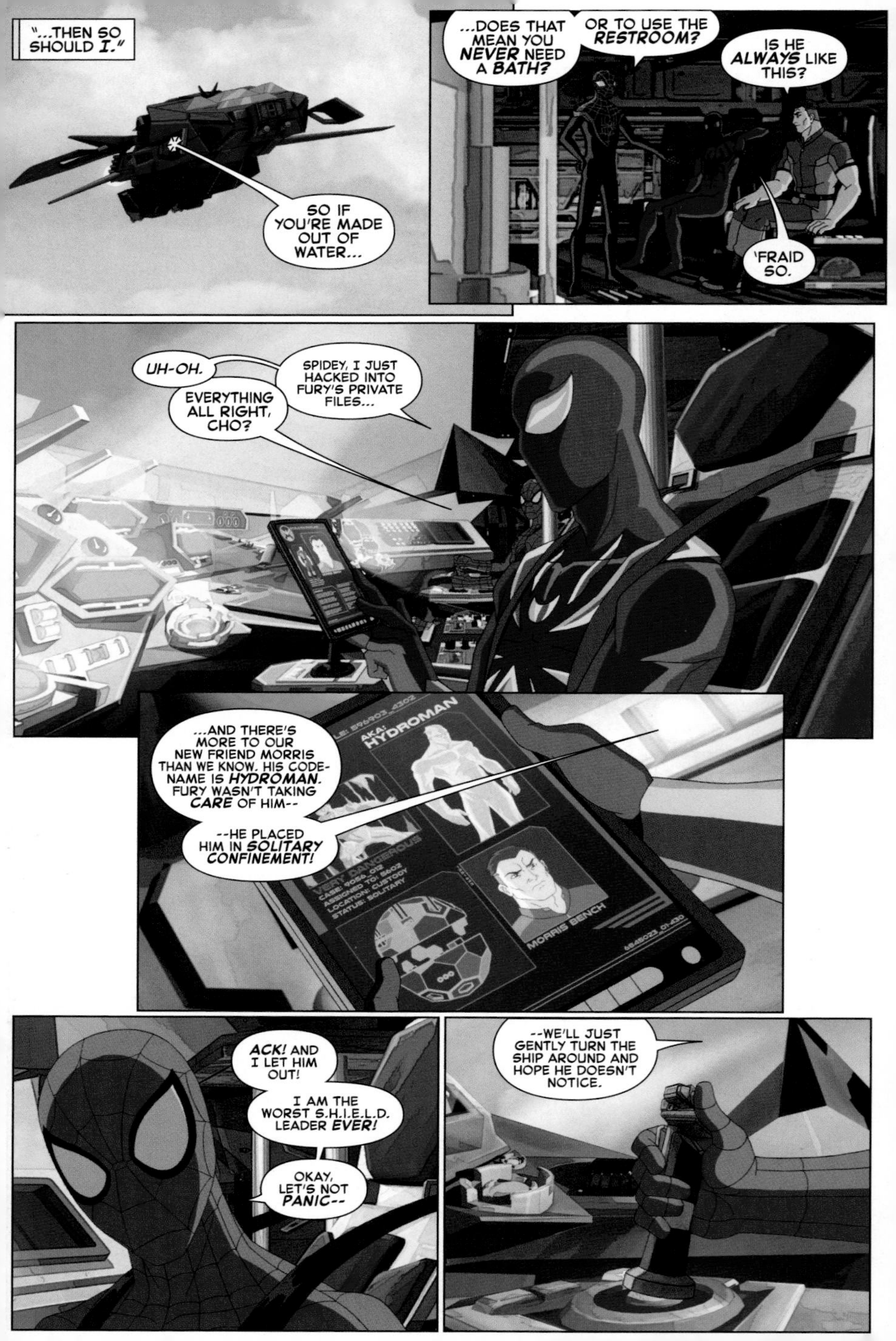
"...THEN SO SHOULD I."
SO IF YOU'RE MADE OUT OF WATER...
...DOES THAT MEAN YOU NEVER NEED A BATH?
OR TO USE THE RESTROOM?
IS HE ALWAYS LIKE THIS?
'FRAID SO.
SPIDEY, I JUST HACKED INTO FURY'S PRIVATE FILES...
UH-OH.
EVERYTHING ALL RIGHT, CHO?
...AND THERE'S MORE TO OUR NEW FRIEND MORRIS THAN WE KNOW. HIS CODE-NAME IS HYDROMAN. FURY WASN'T TAKING CARE OF HIM--
--HE PLACED HIM IN SOLITARY CONFINEMENT!
AKA: HYDROMAN
VERY DANGEROUS
MORRIS BENCH
ACK! AND I LET HIM OUT!
I AM THE WORST S.H.I.E.L.D. LEADER EVER!
OKAY, LET'S NOT PANIC--
--WE'LL JUST GENTLY TURN THE SHIP AROUND AND HOPE HE DOESN'T NOTICE.

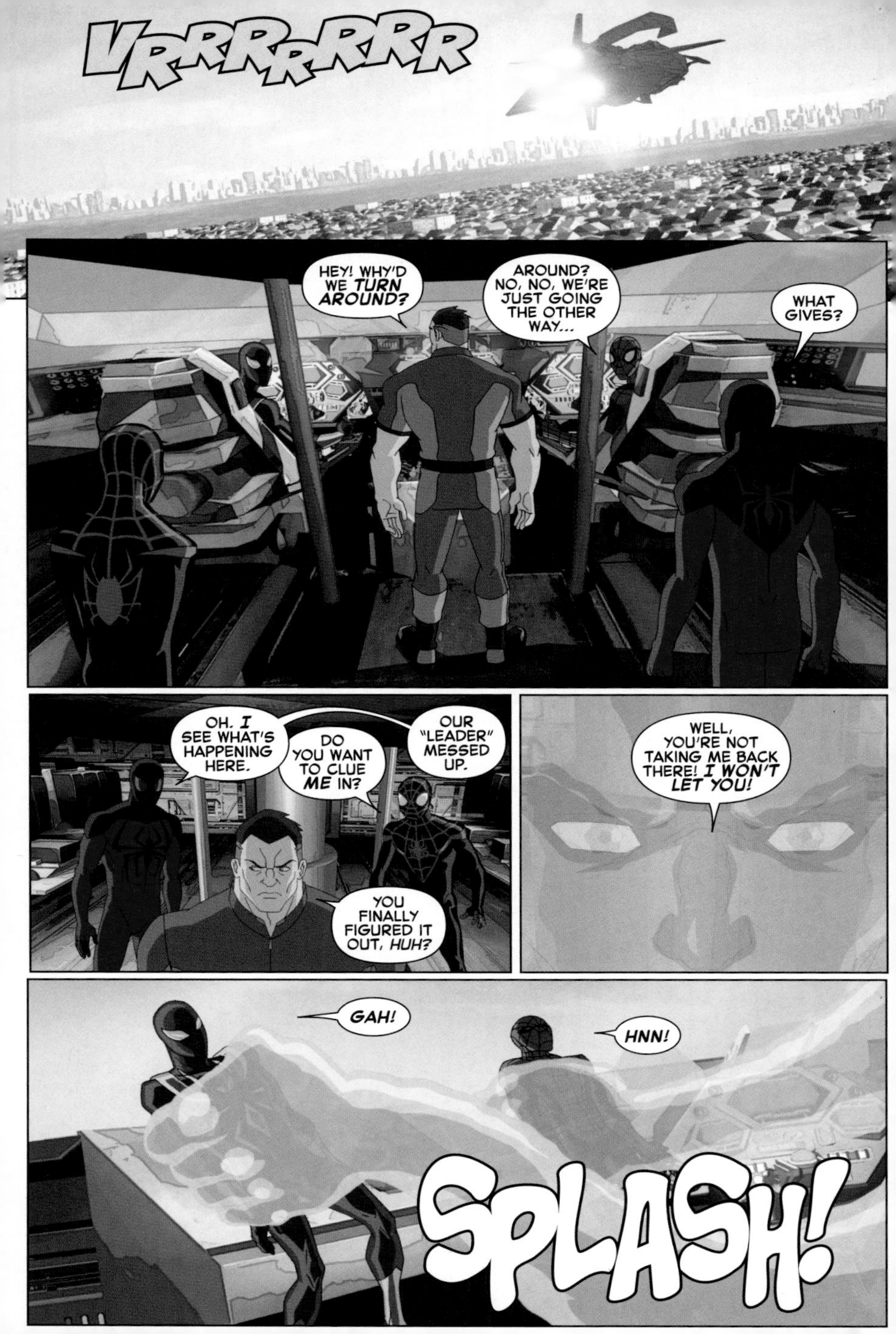
VRRRRRRRR
HEY! WHY'D WE *TURN AROUND?*
AROUND? NO, NO, WE'RE JUST GOING THE OTHER WAY...
WHAT GIVES?
OH. *I* SEE WHAT'S HAPPENING HERE.
DO YOU WANT TO CLUE *ME* IN?
OUR "LEADER" MESSED UP.
YOU FINALLY FIGURED IT OUT, *HUH?*
WELL, YOU'RE NOT TAKING ME BACK THERE! *I WON'T LET YOU!*
GAH!
HNN!
SPLASH!

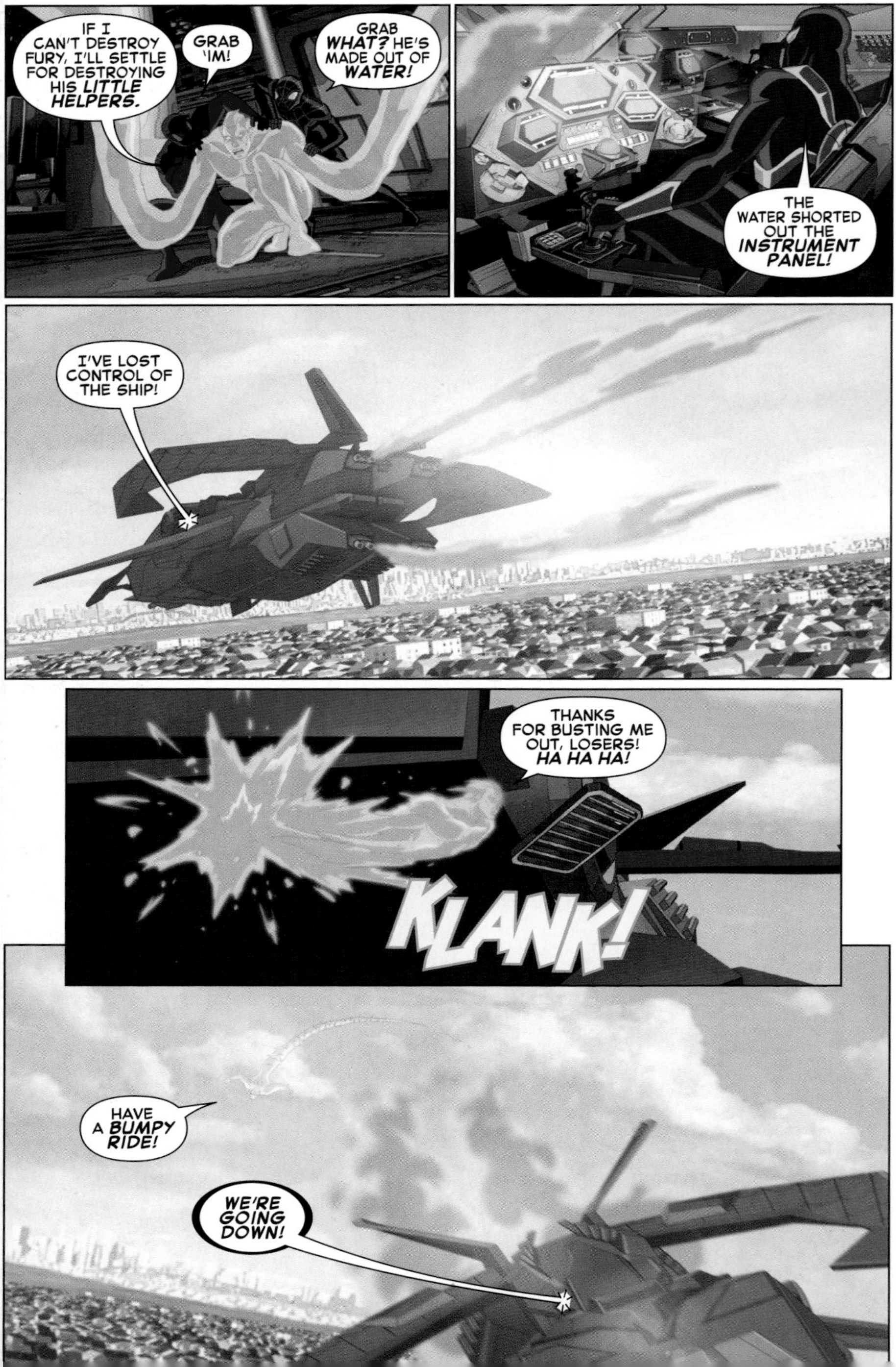

IF I CAN'T DESTROY FURY, I'LL SETTLE FOR DESTROYING HIS LITTLE HELPERS.
GRAB 'IM!
GRAB WHAT? HE'S MADE OUT OF WATER!
THE WATER SHORTED OUT THE INSTRUMENT PANEL!
I'VE LOST CONTROL OF THE SHIP!
THANKS FOR BUSTING ME OUT, LOSERS! HA HA HA!
KLANK!
HAVE A BUMPY RIDE!
WE'RE GOING DOWN!

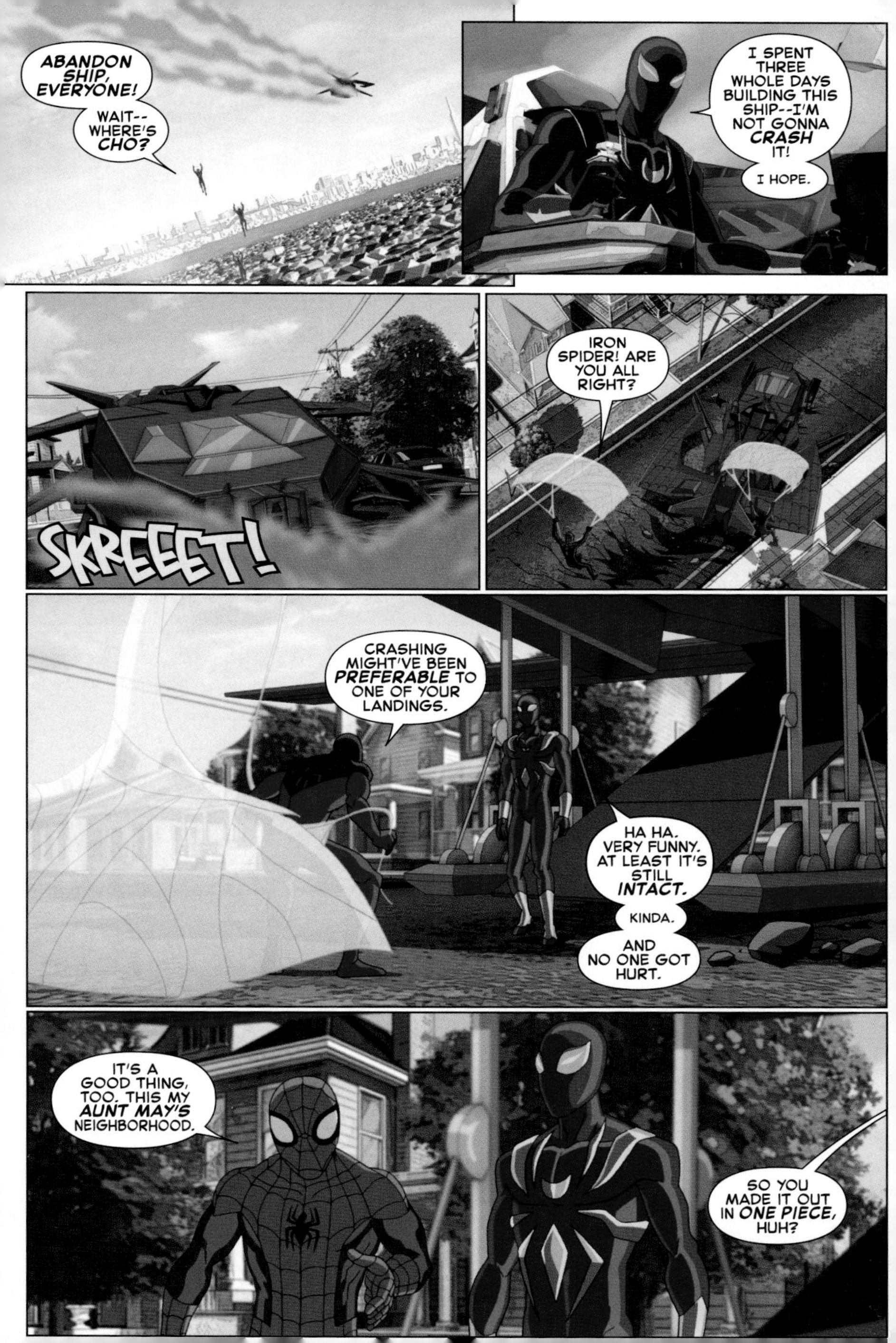
ABANDON SHIP, EVERYONE!
WAIT-- WHERE'S CHO?
I SPENT THREE WHOLE DAYS BUILDING THIS SHIP--I'M NOT GONNA CRASH IT!
I HOPE.
SKREEEET!
IRON SPIDER! ARE YOU ALL RIGHT?
CRASHING MIGHT'VE BEEN PREFERABLE TO ONE OF YOUR LANDINGS.
HA HA. VERY FUNNY. AT LEAST IT'S STILL INTACT.
KINDA.
AND NO ONE GOT HURT.
IT'S A GOOD THING, TOO. THIS MY AUNT MAY'S NEIGHBORHOOD.
SO YOU MADE IT OUT IN ONE PIECE, HUH?

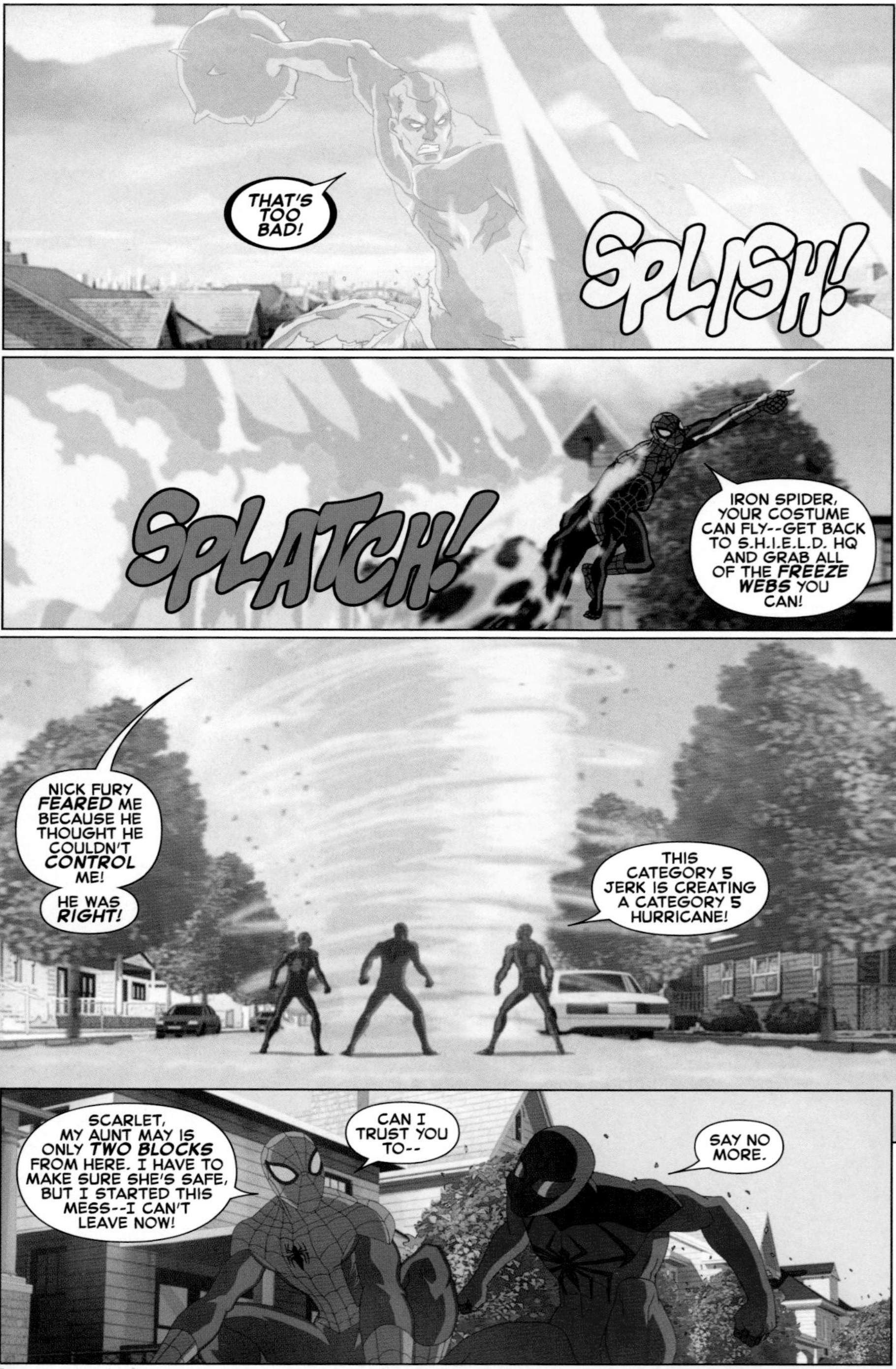
THAT'S TOO BAD!
SPLISH!
SPLATCH!
IRON SPIDER, YOUR COSTUME CAN FLY--GET BACK TO S.H.I.E.L.D. HQ AND GRAB ALL OF THE FREEZE WEBS YOU CAN!
NICK FURY FEARED ME BECAUSE HE THOUGHT HE COULDN'T CONTROL ME!
HE WAS RIGHT!
THIS CATEGORY 5 JERK IS CREATING A CATEGORY 5 HURRICANE!
SCARLET, MY AUNT MAY IS ONLY TWO BLOCKS FROM HERE. I HAVE TO MAKE SURE SHE'S SAFE, BUT I STARTED THIS MESS--I CAN'T LEAVE NOW!
CAN I TRUST YOU TO--
SAY NO MORE.

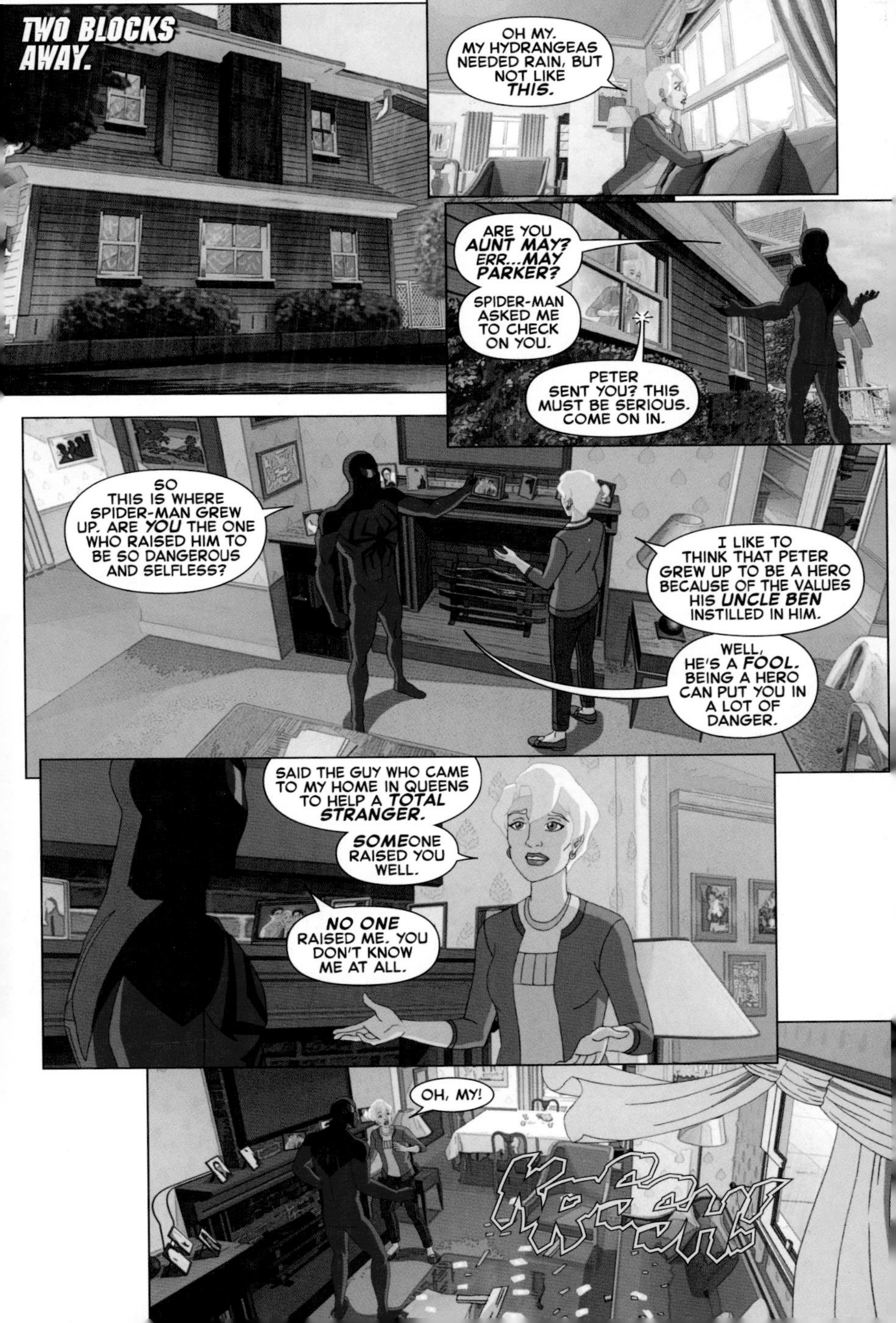
TWO BLOCKS AWAY.
OH MY. MY HYDRANGEAS NEEDED RAIN, BUT NOT LIKE THIS.
ARE YOU AUNT MAY? ERR...MAY PARKER?
SPIDER-MAN ASKED ME TO CHECK ON YOU.
PETER SENT YOU? THIS MUST BE SERIOUS. COME ON IN.
SO THIS IS WHERE SPIDER-MAN GREW UP. ARE YOU THE ONE WHO RAISED HIM TO BE SO DANGEROUS AND SELFLESS?
I LIKE TO THINK THAT PETER GREW UP TO BE A HERO BECAUSE OF THE VALUES HIS UNCLE BEN INSTILLED IN HIM.
WELL, HE'S A FOOL. BEING A HERO CAN PUT YOU IN A LOT OF DANGER.
SAID THE GUY WHO CAME TO MY HOME IN QUEENS TO HELP A TOTAL STRANGER.
SOMEONE RAISED YOU WELL.
NO ONE RAISED ME. YOU DON'T KNOW ME AT ALL.
OH, MY!

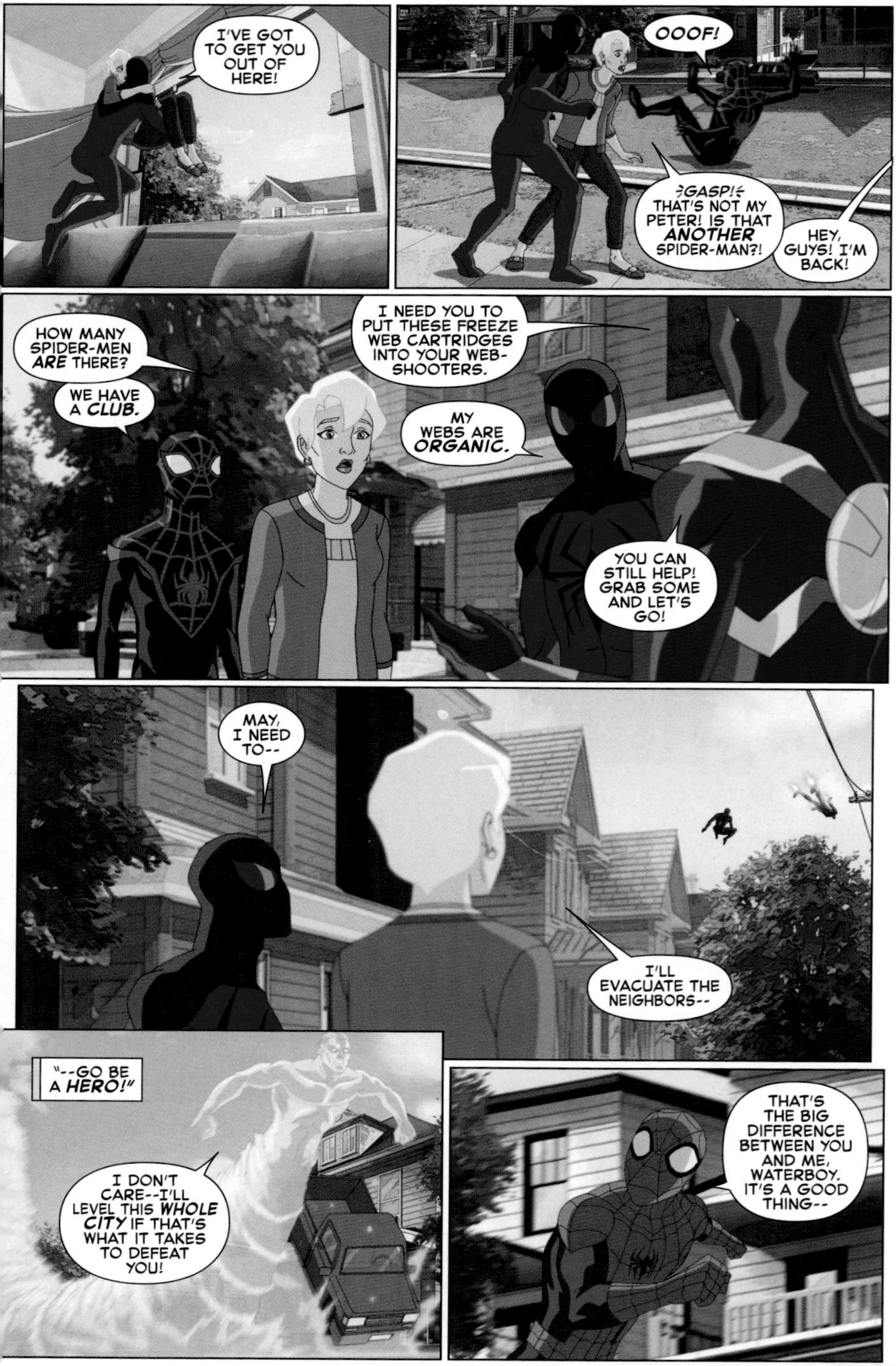
I'VE GOT TO GET YOU OUT OF HERE!
OOOF!
⸗GASP!⸗ THAT'S NOT MY PETER! IS THAT ANOTHER SPIDER-MAN?!
HEY, GUYS! I'M BACK!
HOW MANY SPIDER-MEN ARE THERE?
WE HAVE A CLUB.
I NEED YOU TO PUT THESE FREEZE WEB CARTRIDGES INTO YOUR WEB-SHOOTERS.
MY WEBS ARE ORGANIC.
YOU CAN STILL HELP! GRAB SOME AND LET'S GO!
MAY, I NEED TO--
I'LL EVACUATE THE NEIGHBORS--
"--GO BE A HERO!"
I DON'T CARE--I'LL LEVEL THIS WHOLE CITY IF THAT'S WHAT IT TAKES TO DEFEAT YOU!
THAT'S THE BIG DIFFERENCE BETWEEN YOU AND ME, WATERBOY. IT'S A GOOD THING--

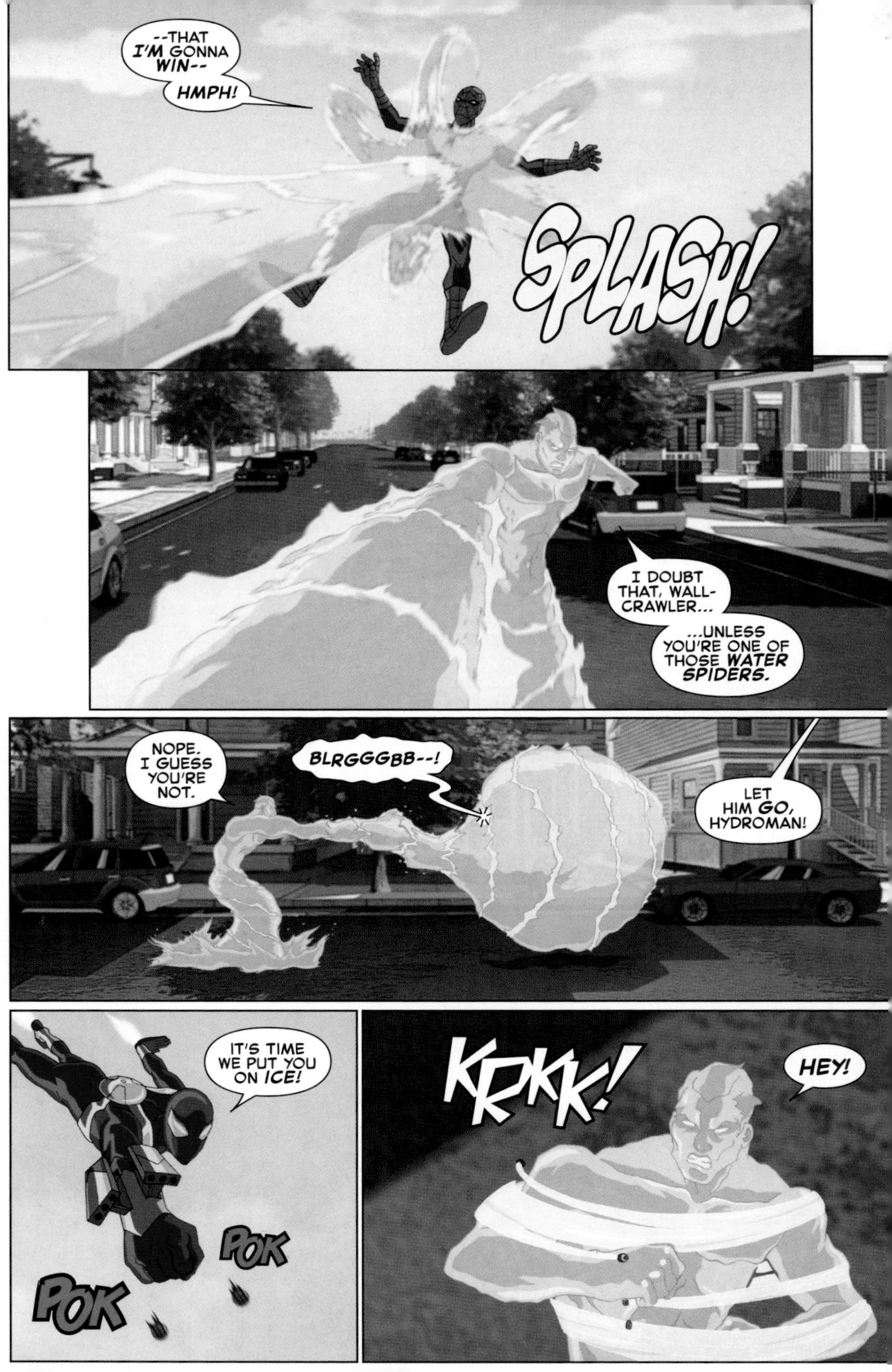
--THAT I'M GONNA WIN--
HMPH!
SPLASH!
I DOUBT THAT, WALL-CRAWLER...
...UNLESS YOU'RE ONE OF THOSE WATER SPIDERS.
NOPE. I GUESS YOU'RE NOT.
BLRGGGBB--!
LET HIM GO, HYDROMAN!
IT'S TIME WE PUT YOU ON ICE!
POK
POK
KRKK!
HEY!

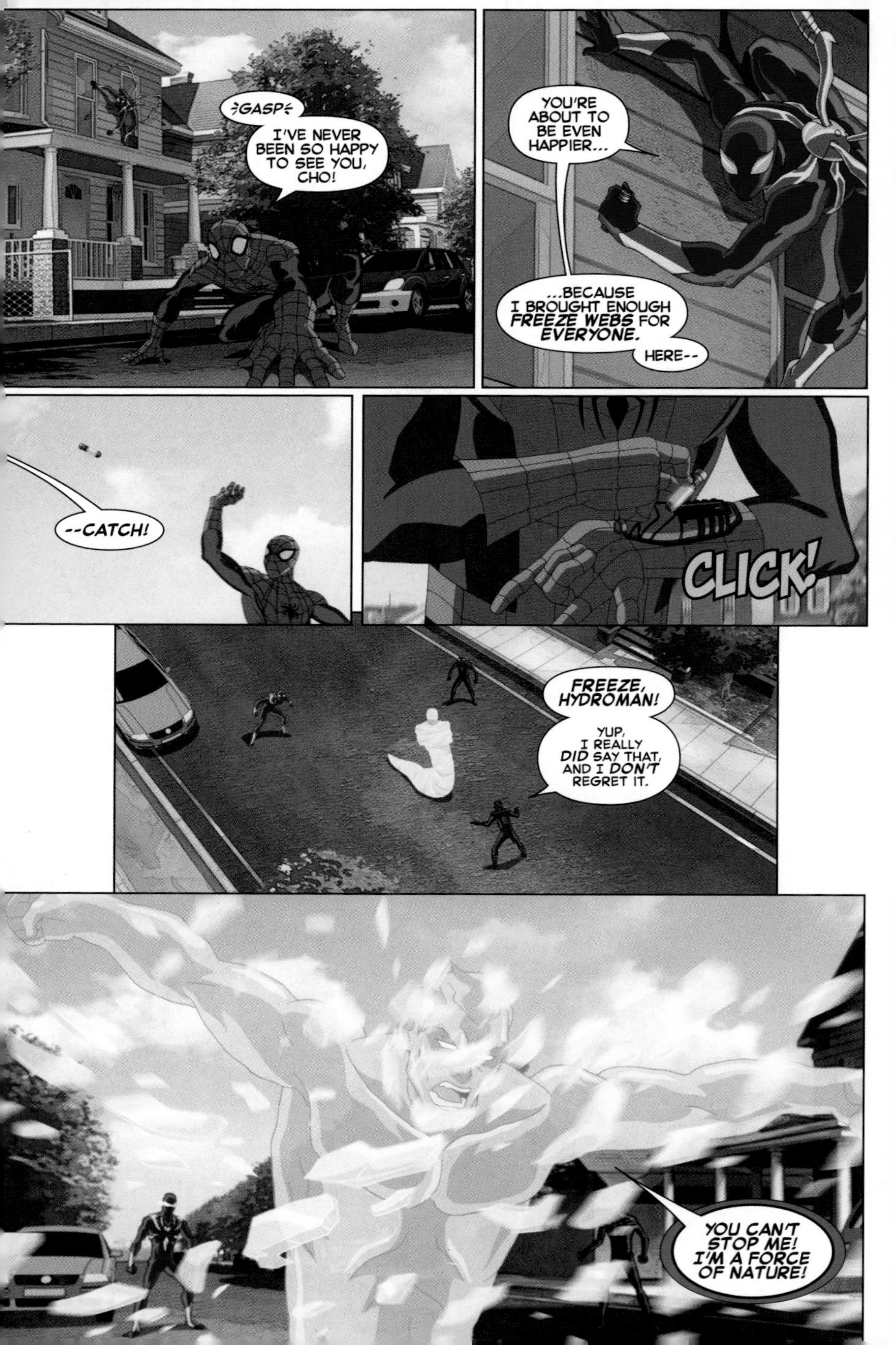

⩴GASP⩵
I'VE NEVER BEEN SO HAPPY TO SEE YOU, CHO!
YOU'RE ABOUT TO BE EVEN HAPPIER...
...BECAUSE I BROUGHT ENOUGH FREEZE WEBS FOR EVERYONE.
HERE--
--CATCH!
CLICK!
FREEZE, HYDROMAN!
YUP, I REALLY DID SAY THAT, AND I DON'T REGRET IT.
YOU CAN'T STOP ME! I'M A FORCE OF NATURE!

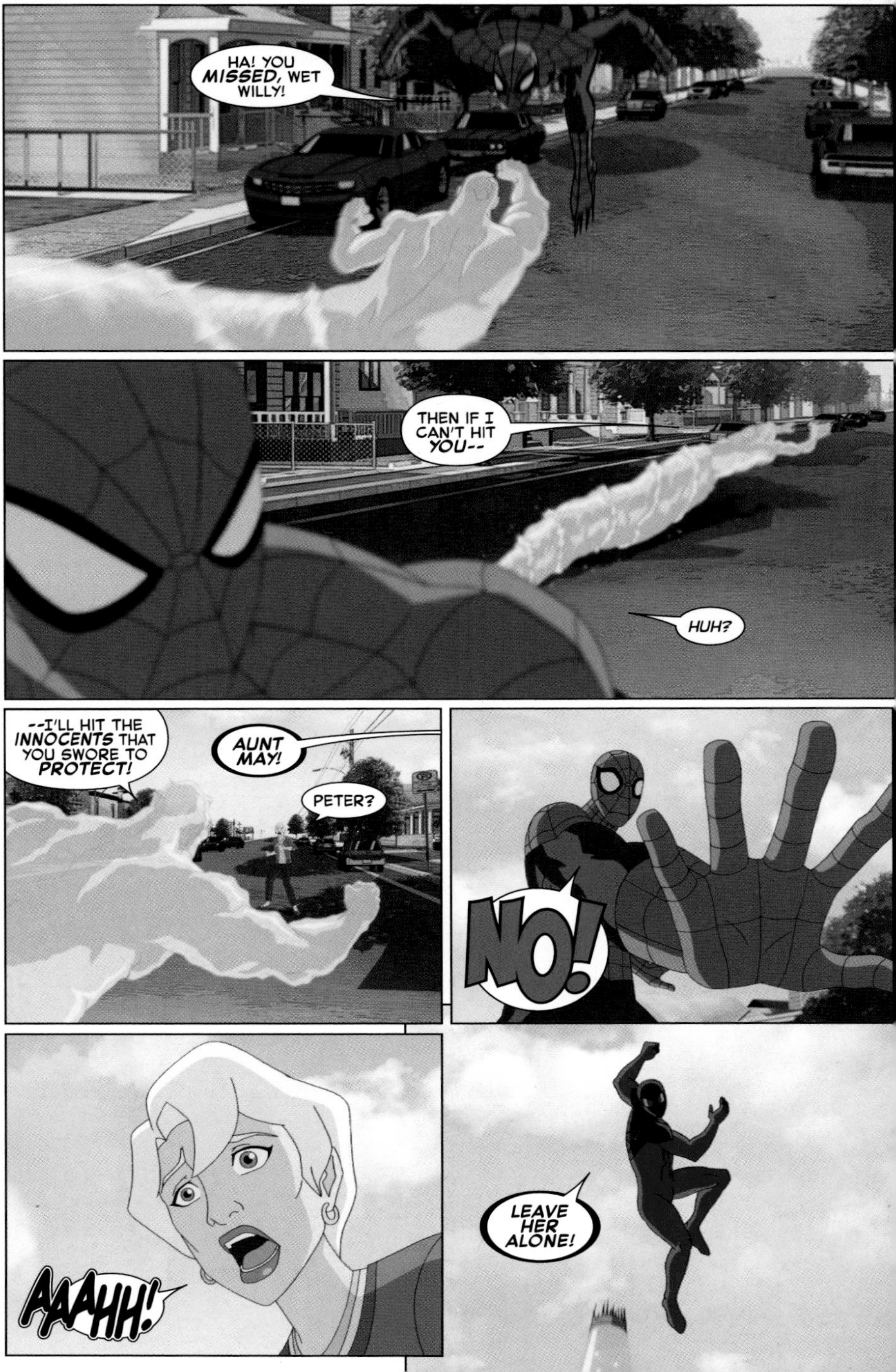
HA! YOU MISSED, WET WILLY!
THEN IF I CAN'T HIT YOU--
HUH?
--I'LL HIT THE INNOCENTS THAT YOU SWORE TO PROTECT!
AUNT MAY!
PETER?
NO!
AAAHH!
LEAVE HER ALONE!

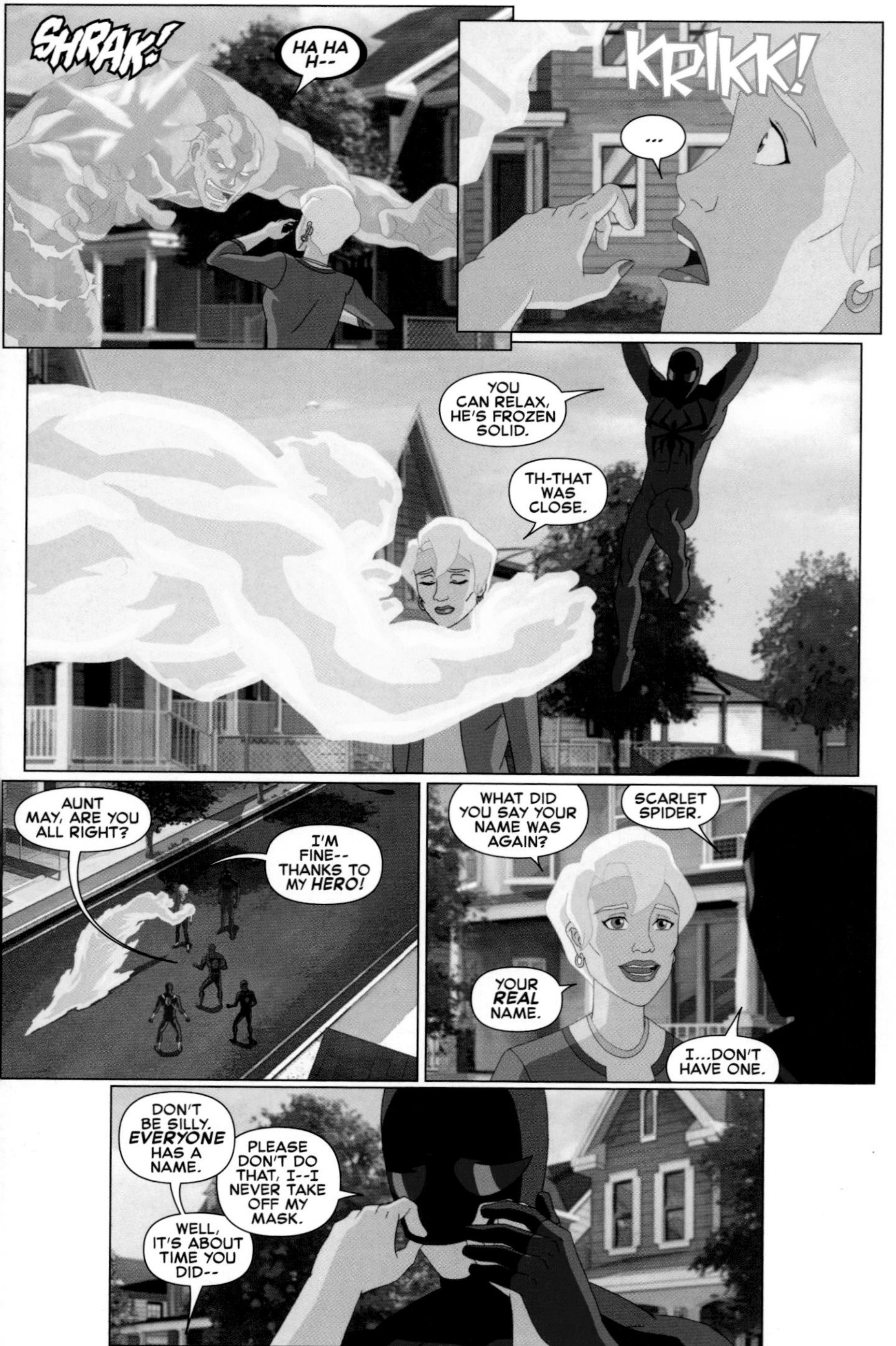
SHRAK!
HA HA H--
KRIKK!
...
YOU CAN RELAX, HE'S FROZEN SOLID.
TH-THAT WAS CLOSE.
AUNT MAY, ARE YOU ALL RIGHT?
I'M FINE-- THANKS TO MY HERO!
WHAT DID YOU SAY YOUR NAME WAS AGAIN?
SCARLET SPIDER.
YOUR REAL NAME.
I...DON'T HAVE ONE.
DON'T BE SILLY. EVERYONE HAS A NAME.
PLEASE DON'T DO THAT, I--I NEVER TAKE OFF MY MASK.
WELL, IT'S ABOUT TIME YOU DID--

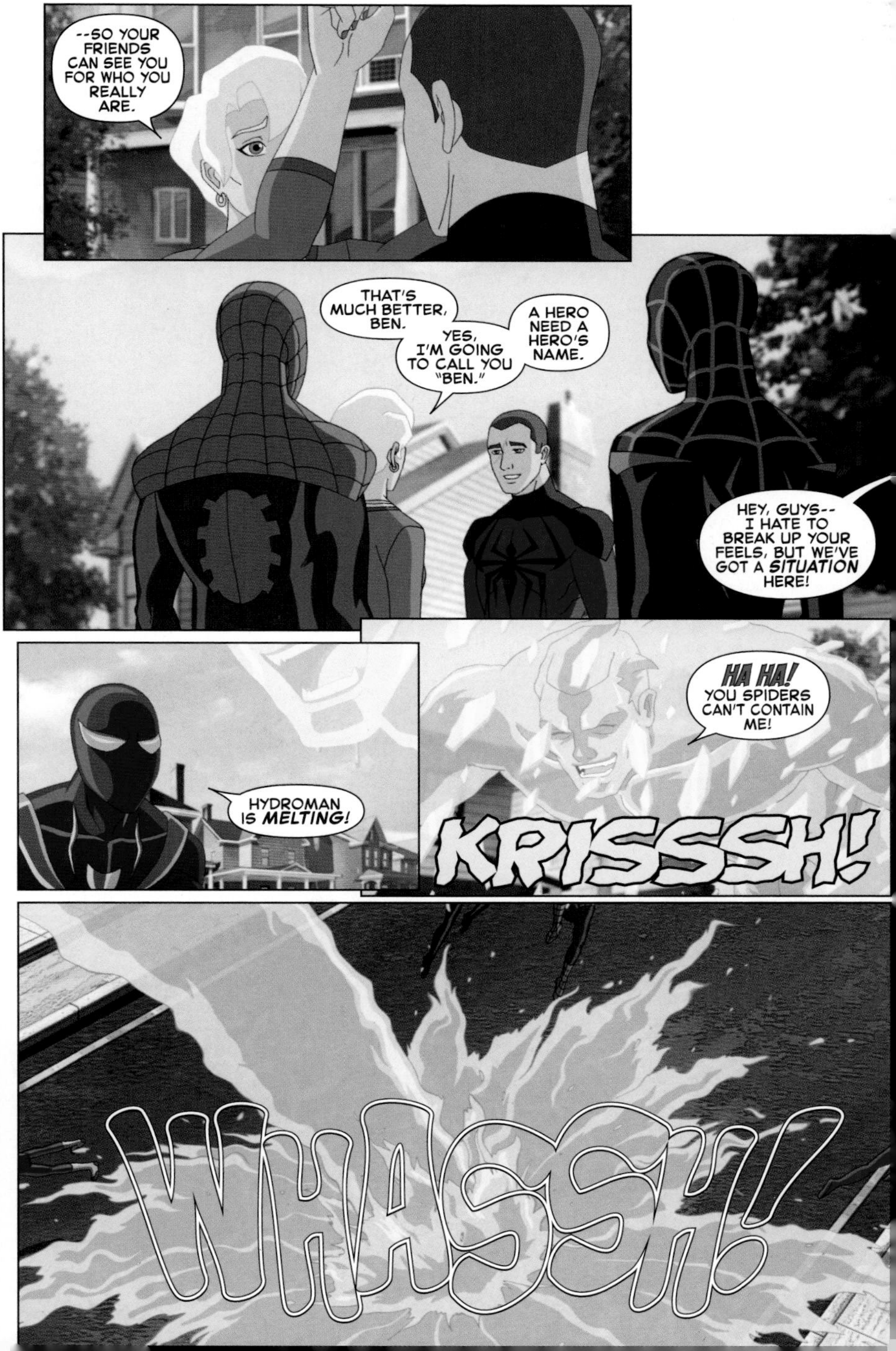
--SO YOUR FRIENDS CAN SEE YOU FOR WHO YOU REALLY ARE.
THAT'S MUCH BETTER, BEN.
YES, I'M GOING TO CALL YOU "BEN."
A HERO NEED A HERO'S NAME.
HEY, GUYS-- I HATE TO BREAK UP YOUR FEELS, BUT WE'VE GOT A SITUATION HERE!
HYDROMAN IS MELTING!
HA HA! YOU SPIDERS CAN'T CONTAIN ME!
KRISSSH!
WHASSH!

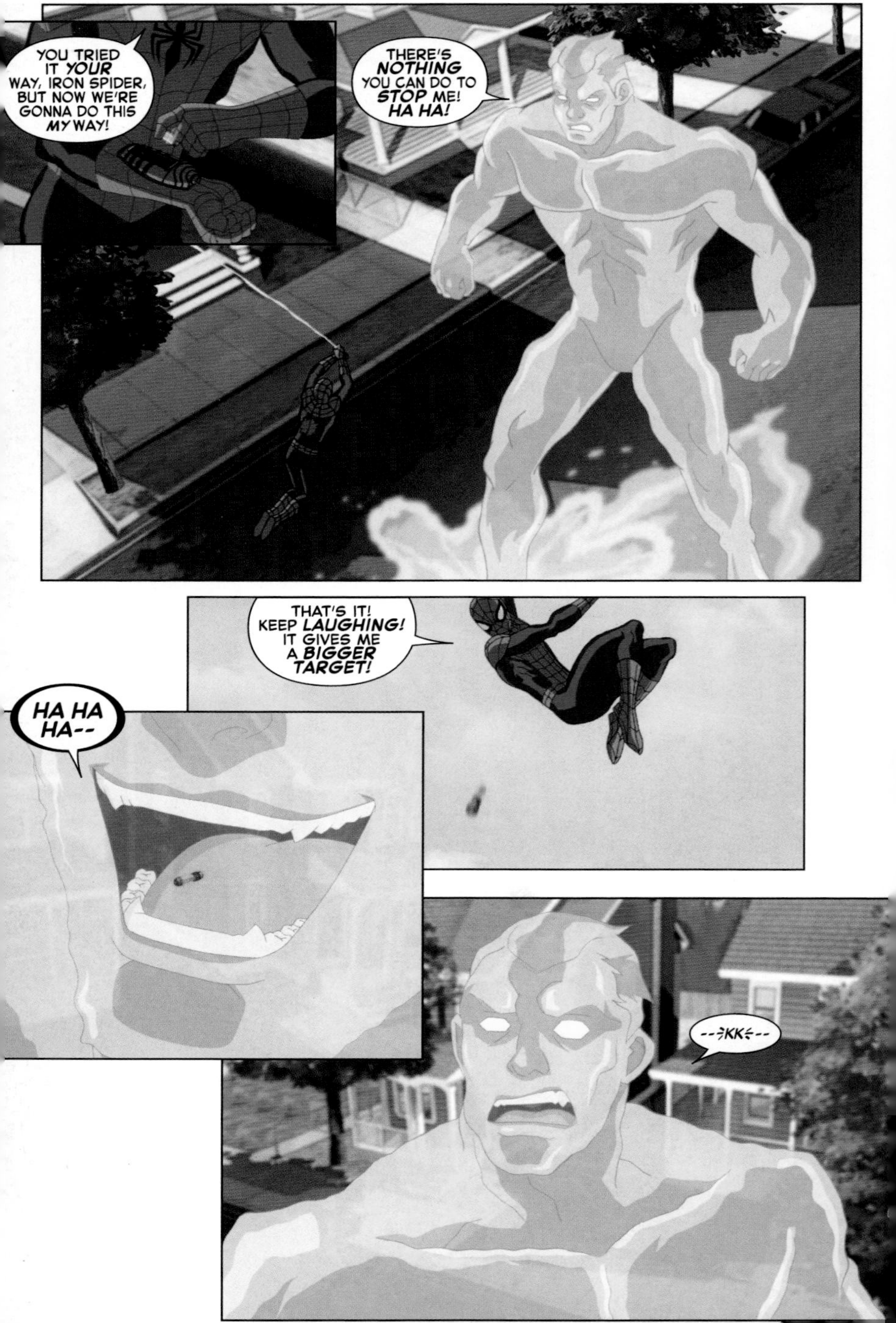
YOU TRIED IT YOUR WAY, IRON SPIDER, BUT NOW WE'RE GONNA DO THIS MY WAY!
THERE'S NOTHING YOU CAN DO TO STOP ME! HA HA!
THAT'S IT! KEEP LAUGHING! IT GIVES ME A BIGGER TARGET!
HA HA HA--
--KK--

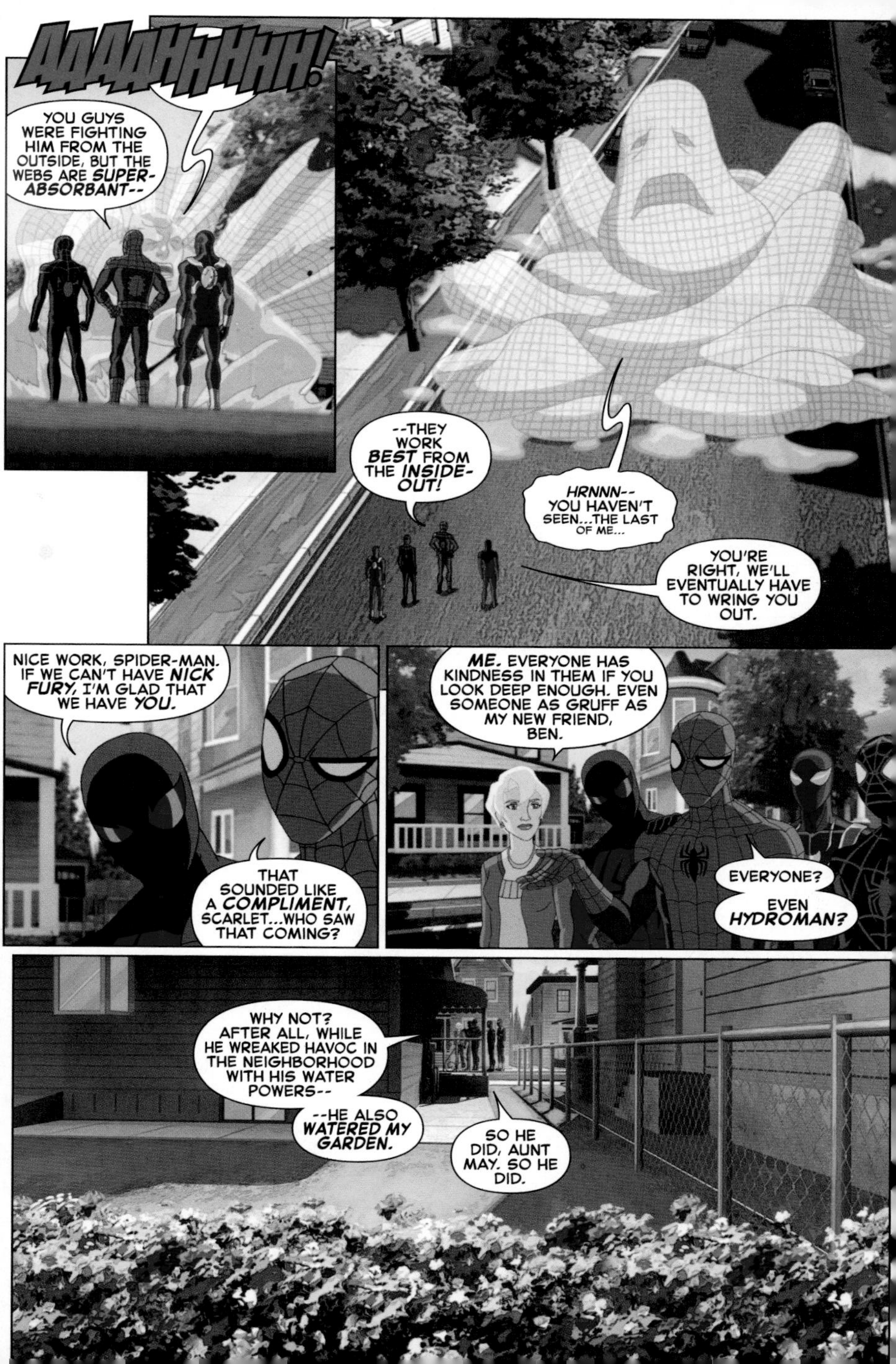
AAAAAHHHHH!
YOU GUYS WERE FIGHTING HIM FROM THE OUTSIDE, BUT THE WEBS ARE SUPER-ABSORBANT--
--THEY WORK BEST FROM THE INSIDE-OUT!
HRNNN-- YOU HAVEN'T SEEN...THE LAST OF ME...
YOU'RE RIGHT, WE'LL EVENTUALLY HAVE TO WRING YOU OUT.
NICE WORK, SPIDER-MAN. IF WE CAN'T HAVE NICK FURY, I'M GLAD THAT WE HAVE YOU.
THAT SOUNDED LIKE A COMPLIMENT, SCARLET...WHO SAW THAT COMING?
ME. EVERYONE HAS KINDNESS IN THEM IF YOU LOOK DEEP ENOUGH. EVEN SOMEONE AS GRUFF AS MY NEW FRIEND, BEN.
EVERYONE?
EVEN HYDROMAN?
WHY NOT? AFTER ALL, WHILE HE WREAKED HAVOC IN THE NEIGHBORHOOD WITH HIS WATER POWERS--
--HE ALSO WATERED MY GARDEN.
SO HE DID, AUNT MAY. SO HE DID.

10: "THE NEW SINISTER SIX"
PART ONE

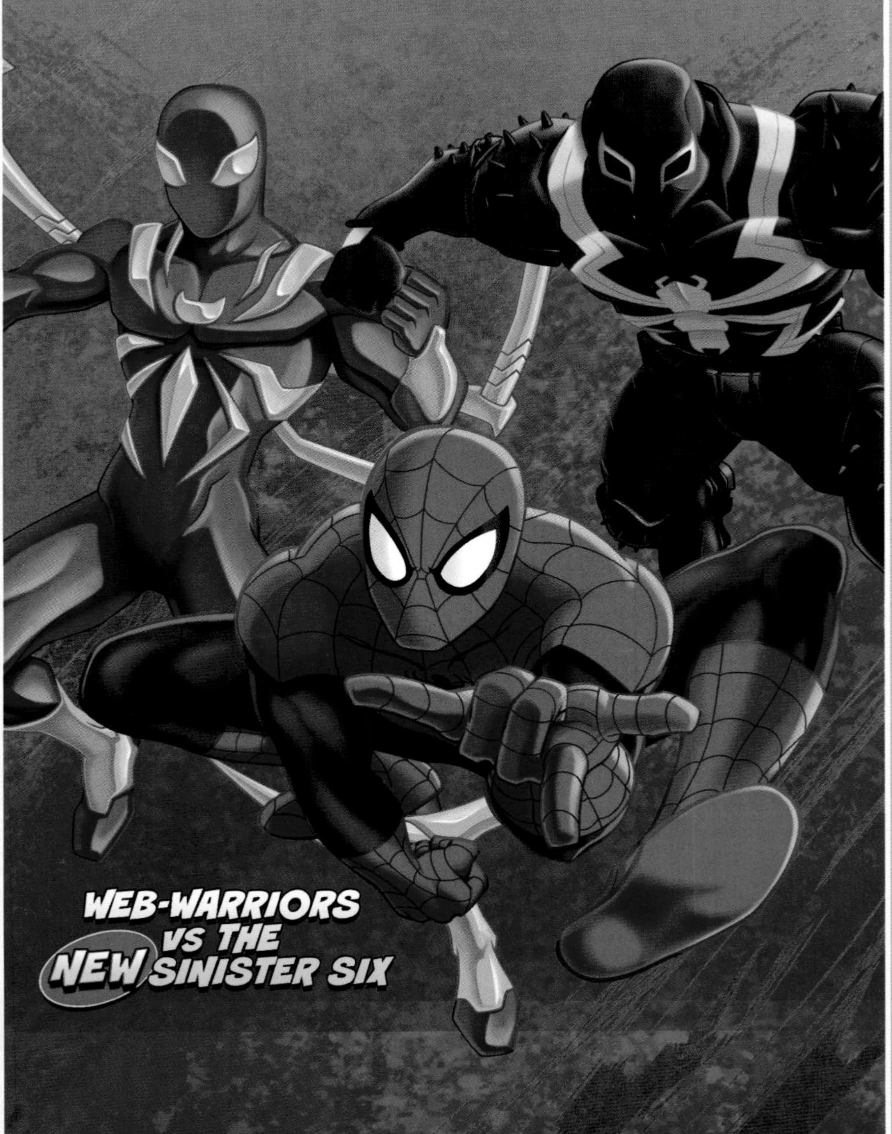
WEB-WARRIORS
VS THE
NEW SINISTER SIX

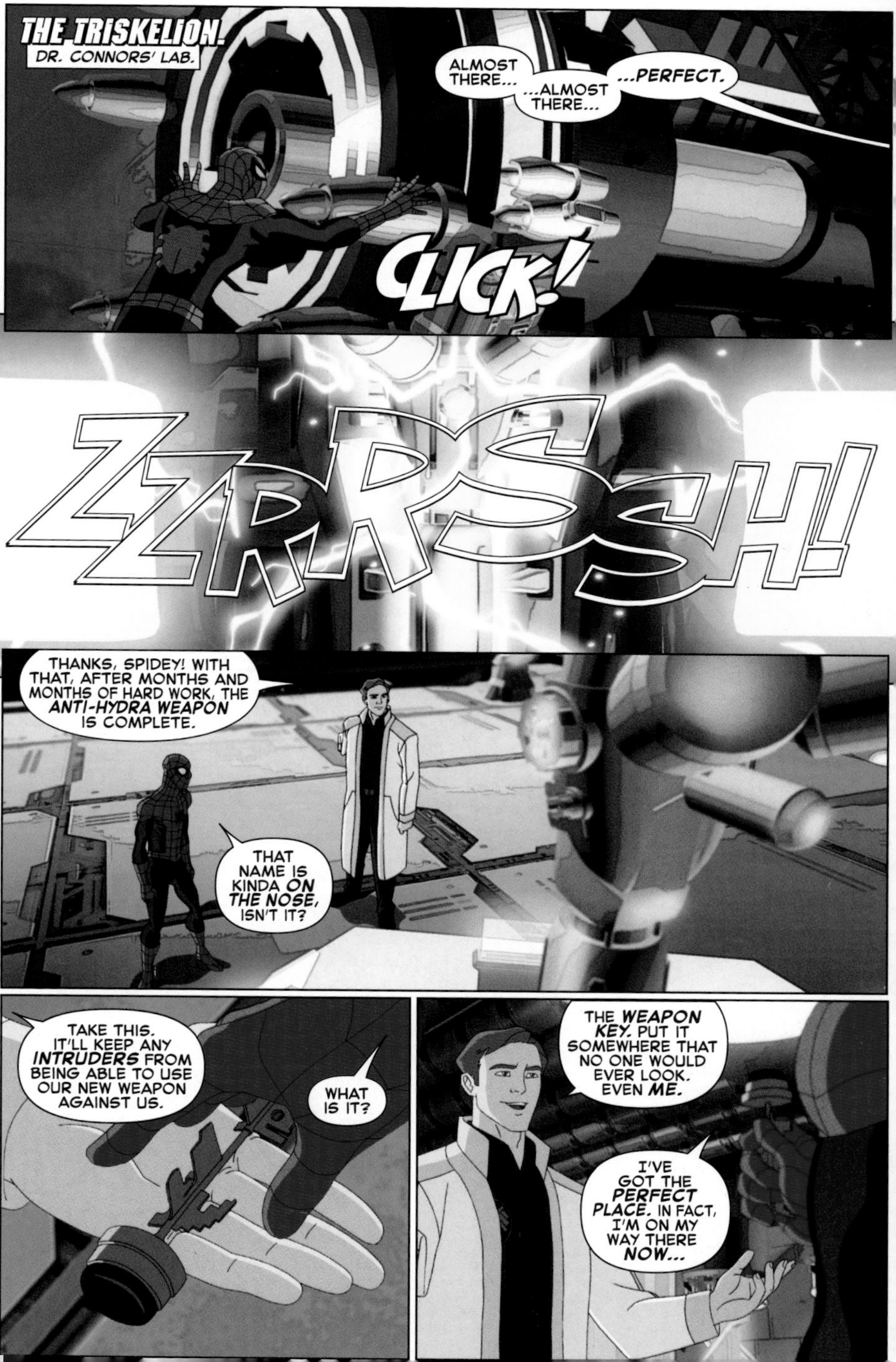
THE TRISKELION!
DR. CONNORS' LAB.
ALMOST THERE...
...ALMOST THERE...
...PERFECT.
CLICK!
ZZRRSSH!
THANKS, SPIDEY! WITH THAT, AFTER MONTHS AND MONTHS OF HARD WORK, THE ANTI-HYDRA WEAPON IS COMPLETE.
THAT NAME IS KINDA ON THE NOSE, ISN'T IT?
TAKE THIS. IT'LL KEEP ANY INTRUDERS FROM BEING ABLE TO USE OUR NEW WEAPON AGAINST US.
WHAT IS IT?
THE WEAPON KEY. PUT IT SOMEWHERE THAT NO ONE WOULD EVER LOOK. EVEN ME.
I'VE GOT THE PERFECT PLACE. IN FACT, I'M ON MY WAY THERE NOW...

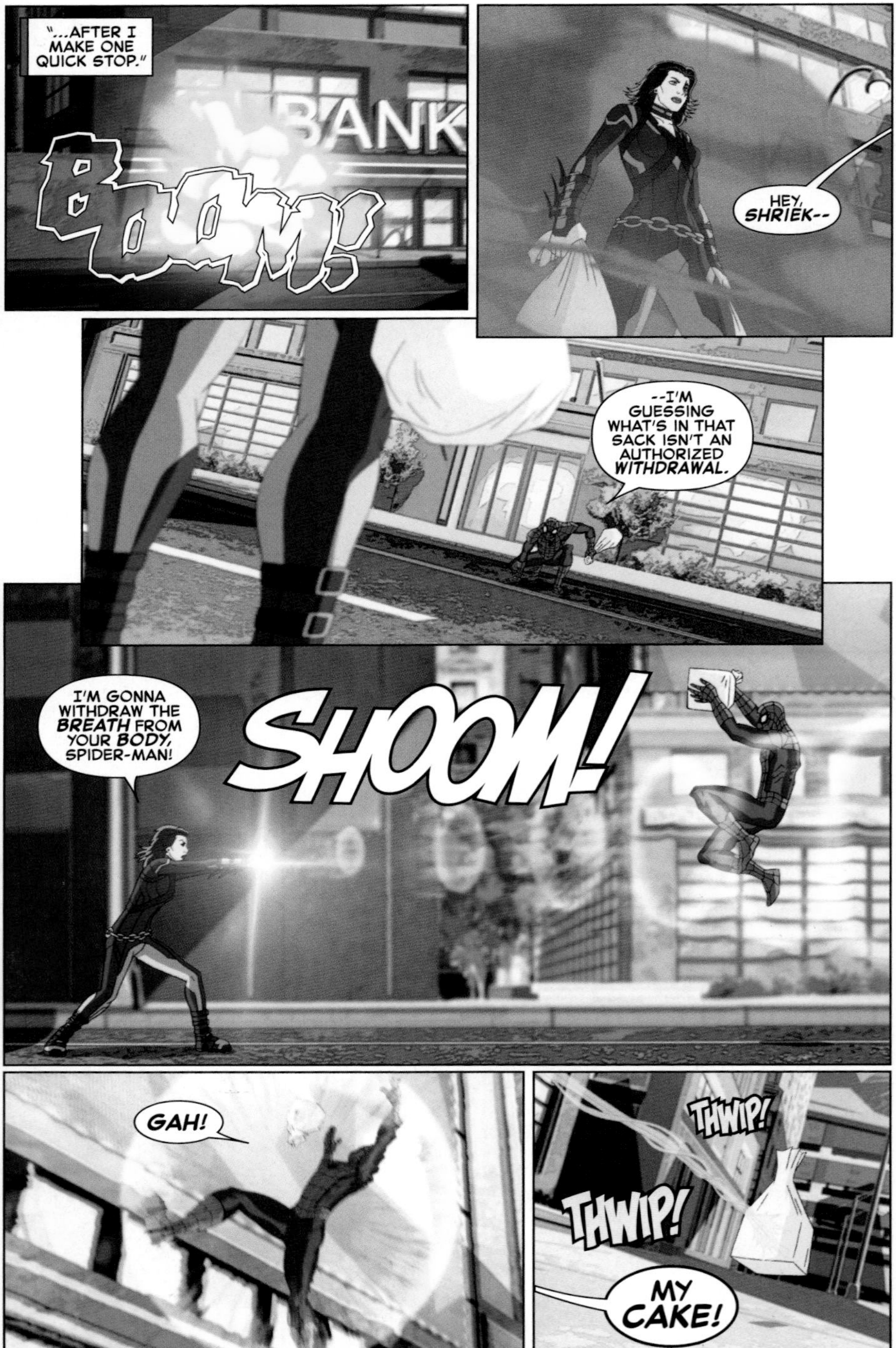
"...AFTER I MAKE ONE QUICK STOP."
BANK
BOOM!
HEY, SHRIEK--
--I'M GUESSING WHAT'S IN THAT SACK ISN'T AN AUTHORIZED WITHDRAWAL.
I'M GONNA WITHDRAW THE BREATH FROM YOUR BODY, SPIDER-MAN!
SHOOM!
GAH!
THWIP!
THWIP!
MY CAKE!

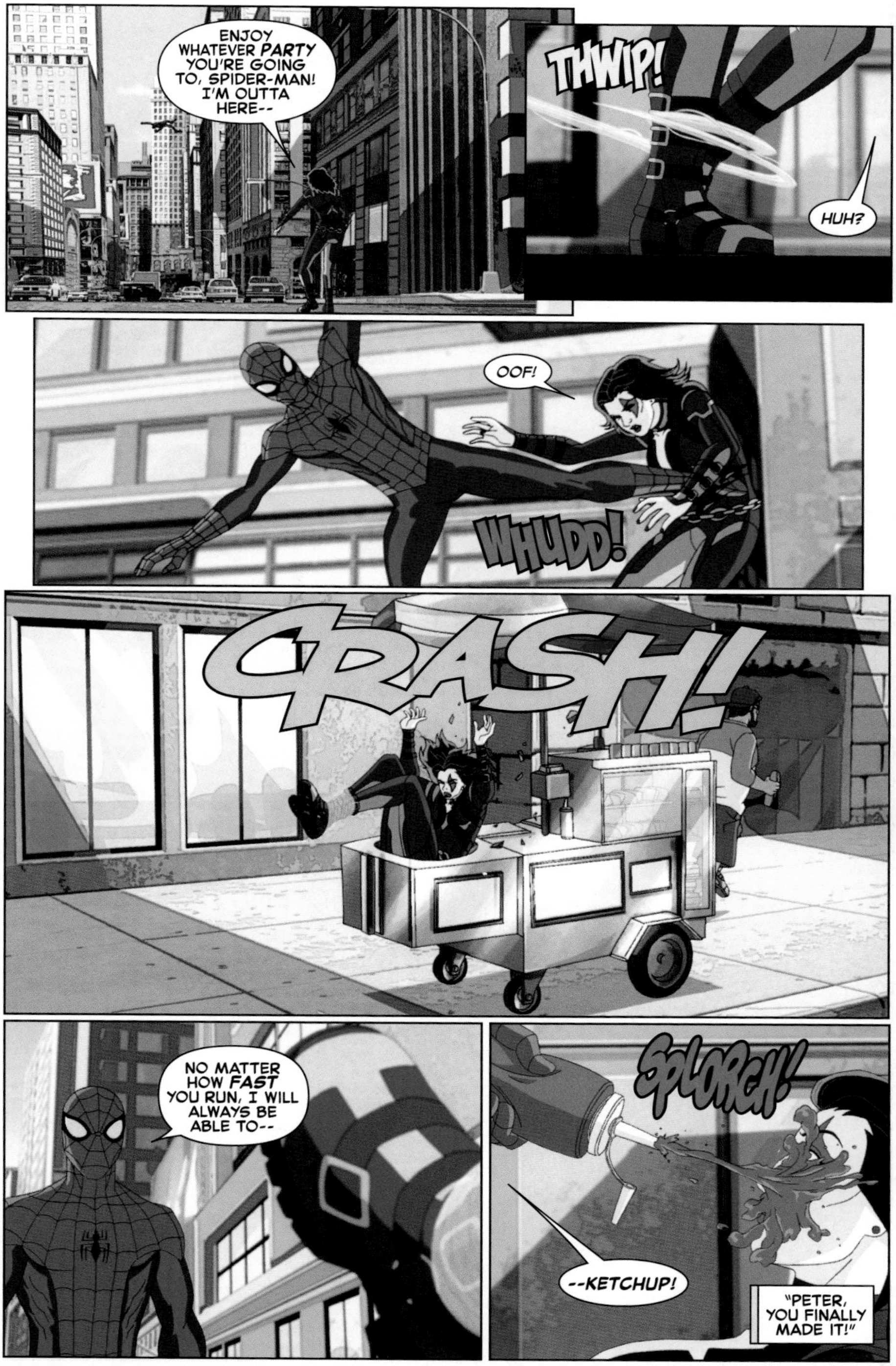
ENJOY WHATEVER PARTY YOU'RE GOING TO, SPIDER-MAN! I'M OUTTA HERE--
THWIP!
HUH?
OOF!
WHUDD!
CRASH!
NO MATTER HOW FAST YOU RUN, I WILL ALWAYS BE ABLE TO--
SPLORCH!
--KETCHUP!
"PETER, YOU FINALLY MADE IT!"

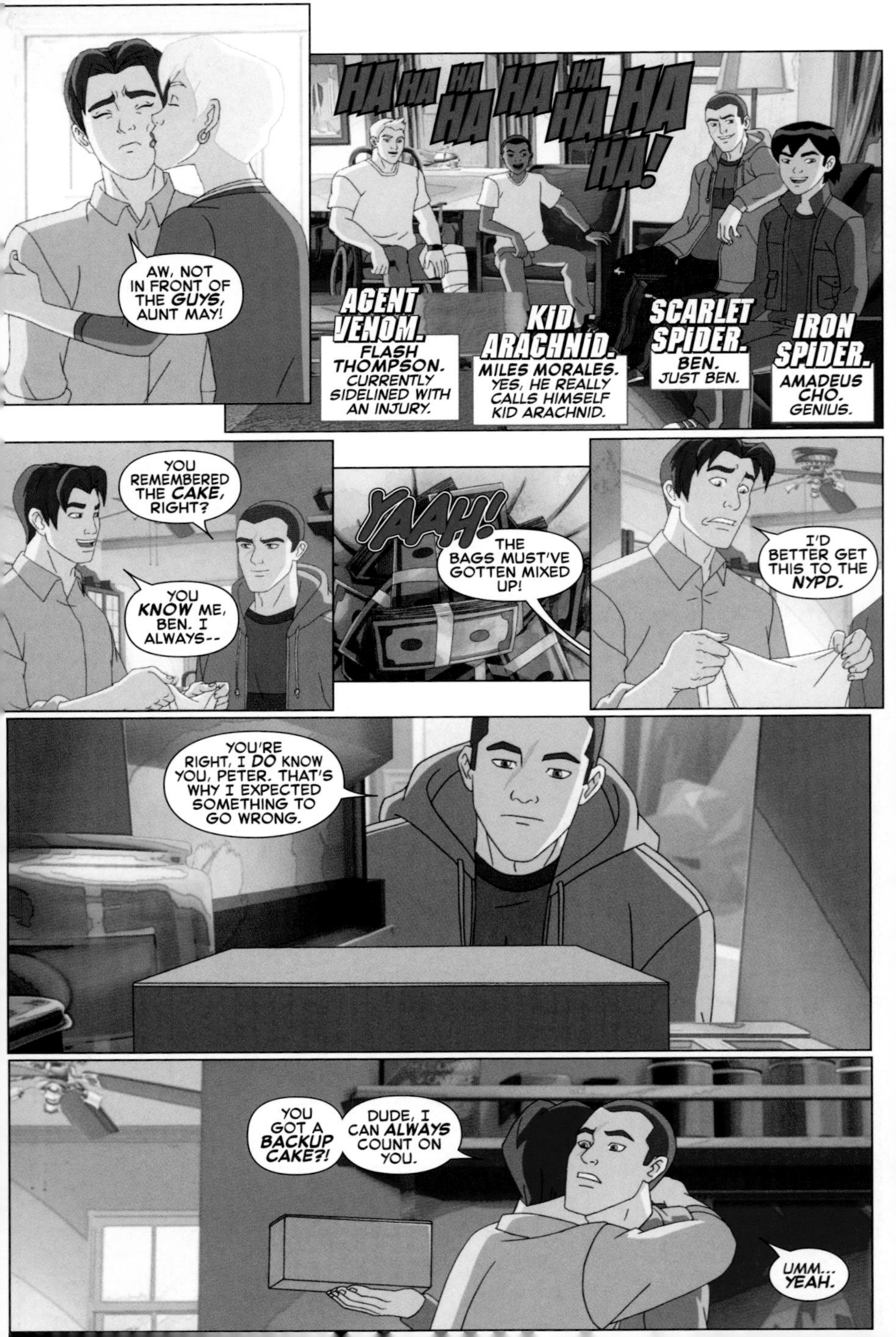
AW, NOT IN FRONT OF THE GUYS, AUNT MAY!
HA HA HA HA HA HA HA HA HA HA!
AGENT VENOM.
FLASH THOMPSON. CURRENTLY SIDELINED WITH AN INJURY.
KID ARACHNID.
MILES MORALES. YES, HE REALLY CALLS HIMSELF KID ARACHNID.
SCARLET SPIDER.
BEN. JUST BEN.
IRON SPIDER.
AMADEUS CHO. GENIUS.
YOU REMEMBERED THE CAKE, RIGHT?
YOU KNOW ME, BEN. I ALWAYS--
YAAAH!
THE BAGS MUST'VE GOTTEN MIXED UP!
I'D BETTER GET THIS TO THE NYPD.
YOU'RE RIGHT, I DO KNOW YOU, PETER. THAT'S WHY I EXPECTED SOMETHING TO GO WRONG.
YOU GOT A BACKUP CAKE?!
DUDE, I CAN ALWAYS COUNT ON YOU.
UMM... YEAH.

HAPPY BIRTHDAY, AUNT MAY!

THANKS FOR ALWAYS BEING THERE FOR US. FOR *ALL* OF US.

I *LOVE* IT, BOYS!

AND DR. CONNORS AT S.H.I.E.L.D. GOT YOU A GIFT, TOO.

OH! HOW... *NICE.* WHAT IS IT?

IT'S... *ART!*

KEEP IT SOMEWHERE SAFE.

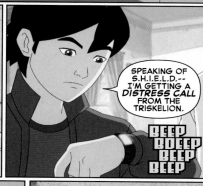

SPEAKING OF S.H.I.E.L.D.-- I'M GETTING A *DISTRESS CALL* FROM THE TRISKELION.

BEEP BOEEP BEEP BEEP

WHAT ARE YOU WAITING FOR? GO BE *HEROES!*

THE PARTY CAN WAIT.

YOU'RE THE BEST, AUNT MAY.

I GUESS I'LL HAVE TO SIT THIS ONE OUT.

DON'T WORRY, FLASH--

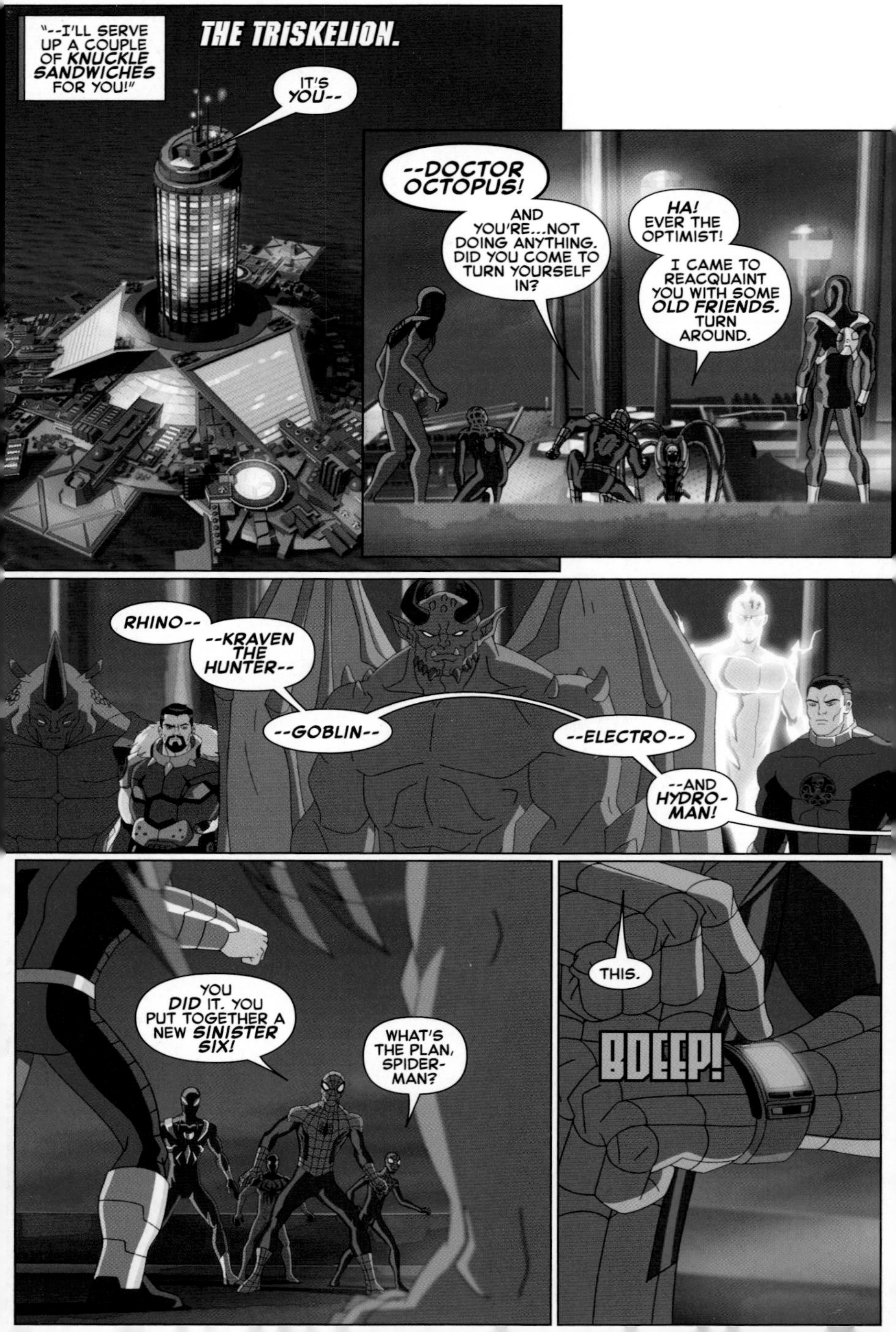
"--I'LL SERVE UP A COUPLE OF KNUCKLE SANDWICHES FOR YOU!"
THE TRISKELION.
IT'S YOU--
--DOCTOR OCTOPUS!
AND YOU'RE...NOT DOING ANYTHING. DID YOU COME TO TURN YOURSELF IN?
HA! EVER THE OPTIMIST!
I CAME TO REACQUAINT YOU WITH SOME OLD FRIENDS. TURN AROUND.
RHINO--
--KRAVEN THE HUNTER--
--GOBLIN--
--ELECTRO--
--AND HYDRO-MAN!
YOU DID IT. YOU PUT TOGETHER A NEW SINISTER SIX!
WHAT'S THE PLAN, SPIDER-MAN?
THIS.
BDEEP!

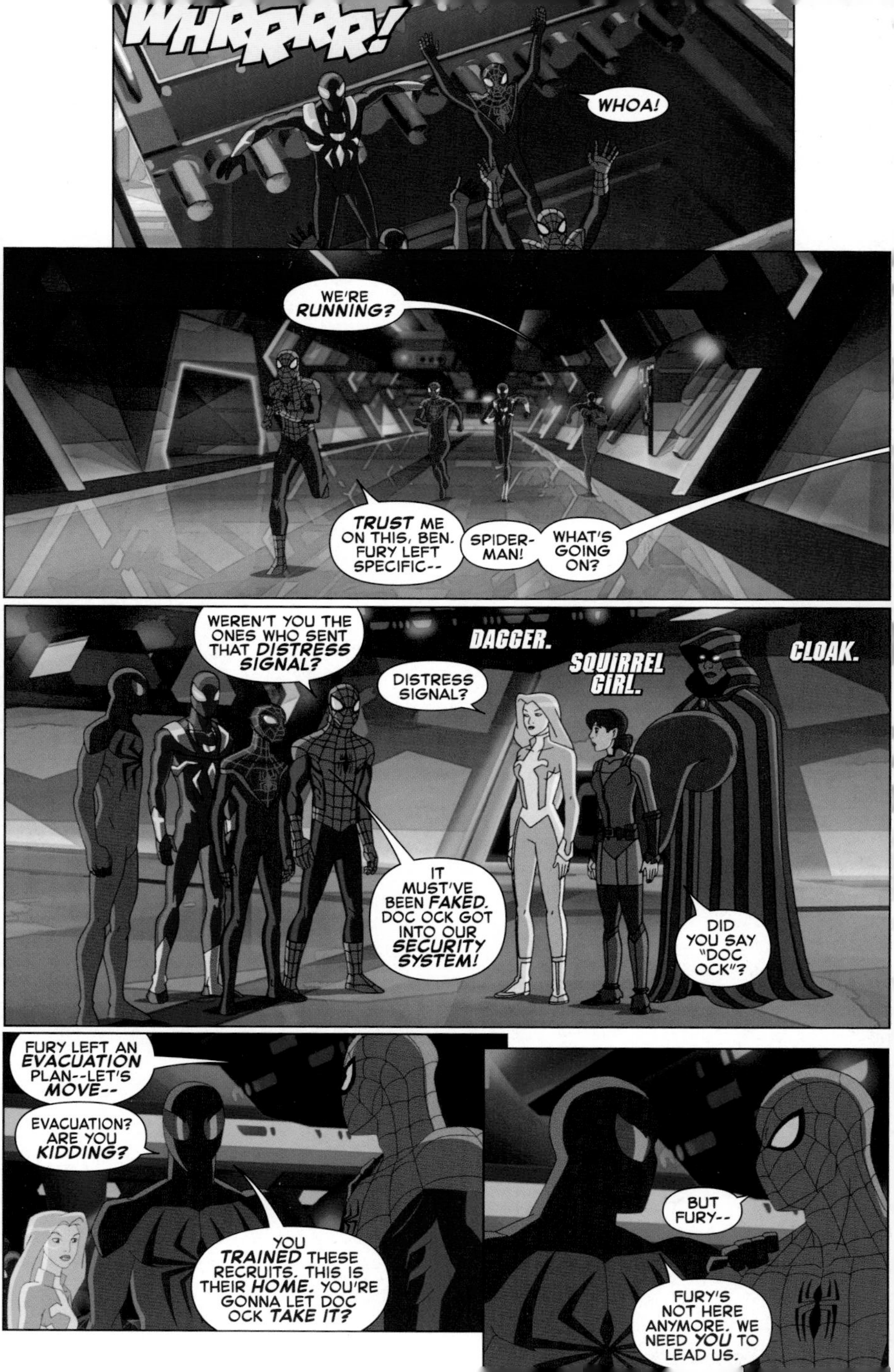
WHRRRR!
WHOA!
WE'RE RUNNING?
TRUST ME ON THIS, BEN. FURY LEFT SPECIFIC--
SPIDER-MAN!
WHAT'S GOING ON?
WEREN'T YOU THE ONES WHO SENT THAT DISTRESS SIGNAL?
DISTRESS SIGNAL?
DAGGER.
SQUIRREL GIRL.
CLOAK.
IT MUST'VE BEEN FAKED. DOC OCK GOT INTO OUR SECURITY SYSTEM!
DID YOU SAY "DOC OCK"?
FURY LEFT AN EVACUATION PLAN--LET'S MOVE--
EVACUATION? ARE YOU KIDDING?
YOU TRAINED THESE RECRUITS. THIS IS THEIR HOME. YOU'RE GONNA LET DOC OCK TAKE IT?
BUT FURY--
FURY'S NOT HERE ANYMORE. WE NEED YOU TO LEAD US.

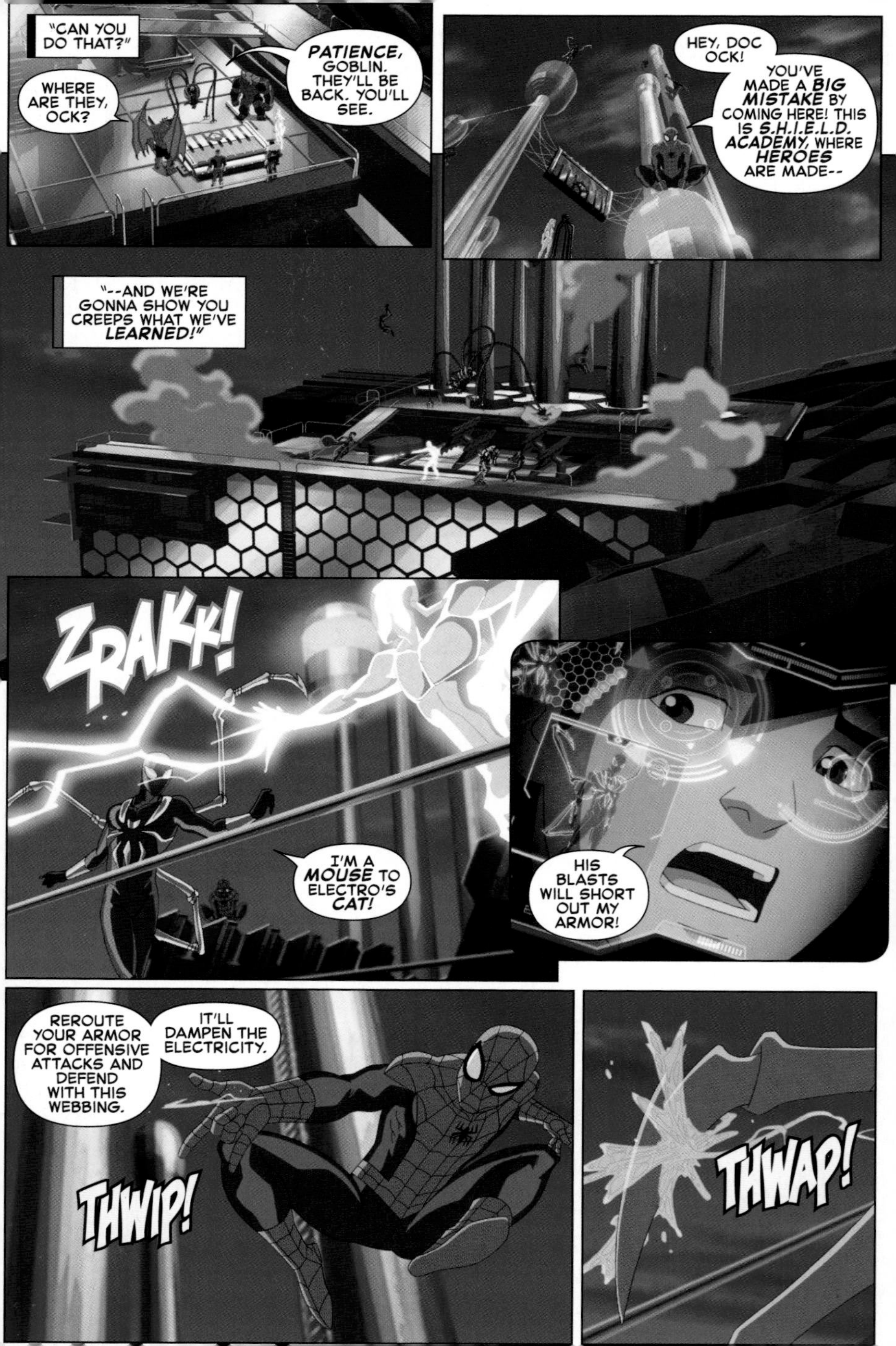
"CAN YOU DO THAT?"
WHERE ARE THEY, OCK?
PATIENCE, GOBLIN. THEY'LL BE BACK. YOU'LL SEE.
HEY, DOC OCK!
YOU'VE MADE A BIG MISTAKE BY COMING HERE! THIS IS S.H.I.E.L.D. ACADEMY, WHERE HEROES ARE MADE--
"--AND WE'RE GONNA SHOW YOU CREEPS WHAT WE'VE LEARNED!"
ZRAKK!
I'M A MOUSE TO ELECTRO'S CAT!
HIS BLASTS WILL SHORT OUT MY ARMOR!
REROUTE YOUR ARMOR FOR OFFENSIVE ATTACKS AND DEFEND WITH THIS WEBBING.
IT'LL DAMPEN THE ELECTRICITY.
THWIP!
THWAP!

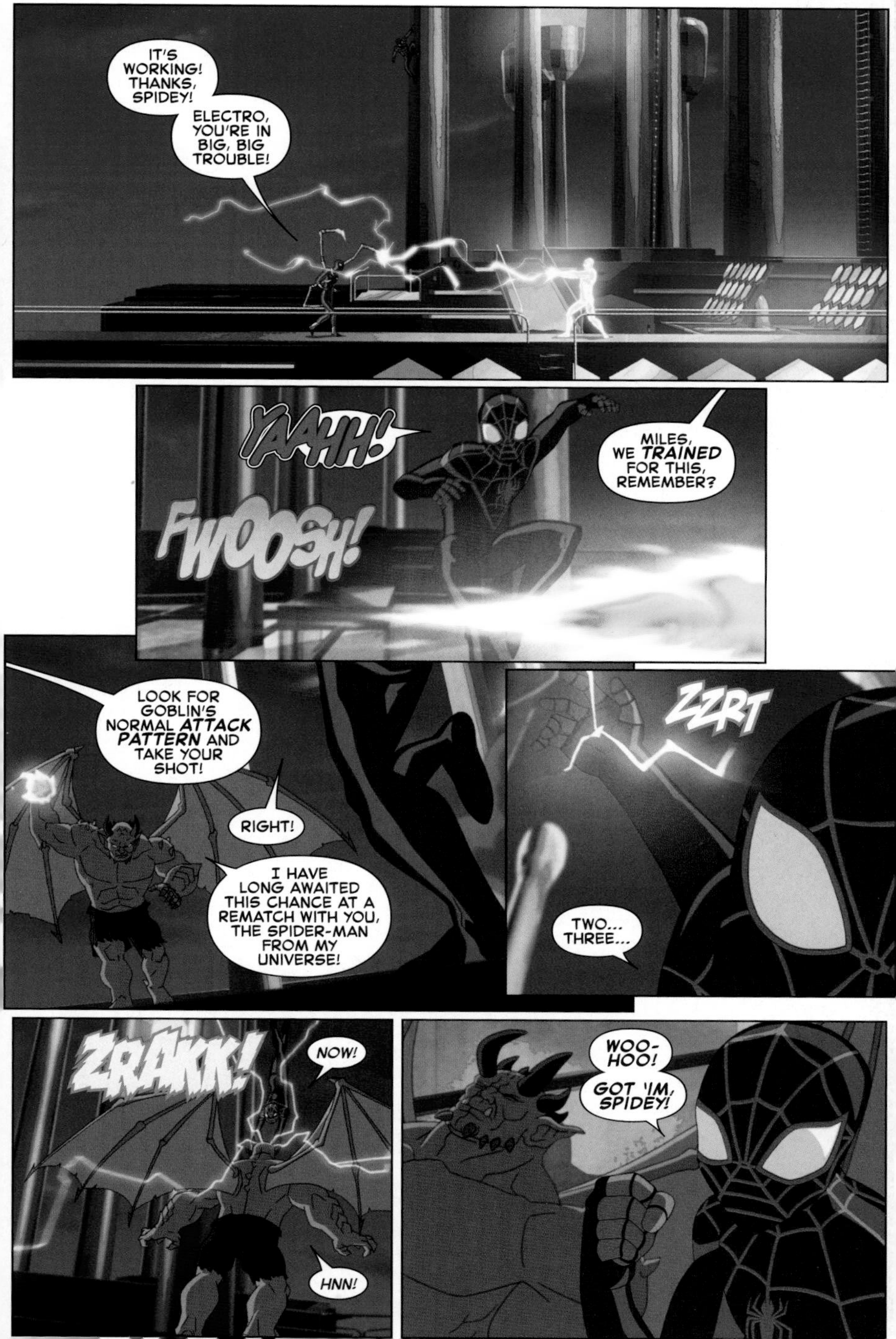
IT'S WORKING! THANKS, SPIDEY!
ELECTRO, YOU'RE IN BIG, BIG TROUBLE!
YAAHH!
MILES, WE TRAINED FOR THIS, REMEMBER?
FWOOSH!
LOOK FOR GOBLIN'S NORMAL ATTACK PATTERN AND TAKE YOUR SHOT!
RIGHT!
I HAVE LONG AWAITED THIS CHANCE AT A REMATCH WITH YOU, THE SPIDER-MAN FROM MY UNIVERSE!
ZZRT
TWO... THREE...
ZRAKK!
NOW!
HNN!
WOO-HOO!
GOT 'IM, SPIDEY!

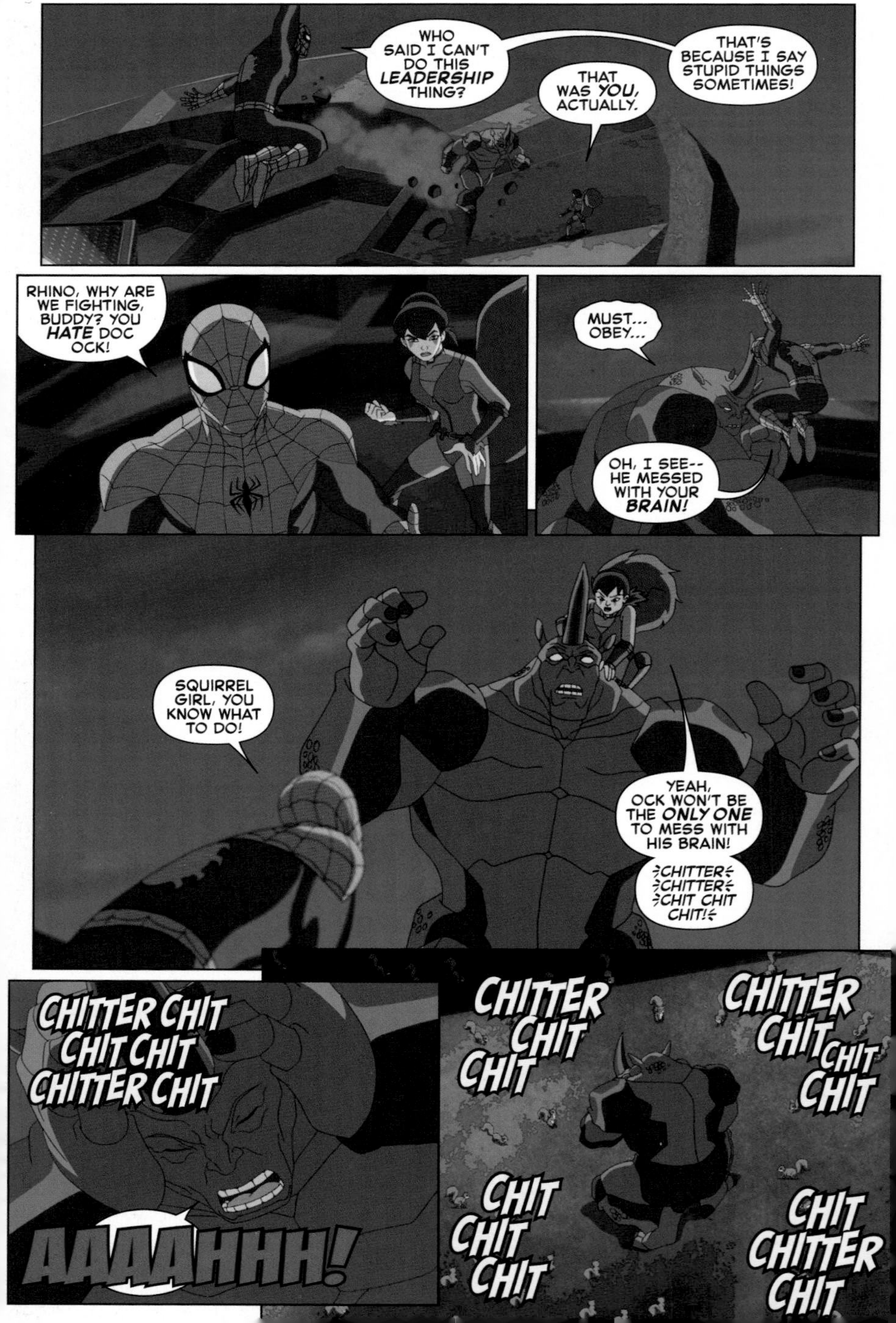
WHO SAID I CAN'T DO THIS LEADERSHIP THING?
THAT'S BECAUSE I SAY STUPID THINGS SOMETIMES!
THAT WAS YOU, ACTUALLY.
RHINO, WHY ARE WE FIGHTING, BUDDY? YOU HATE DOC OCK!
MUST... OBEY...
OH, I SEE-- HE MESSED WITH YOUR BRAIN!
SQUIRREL GIRL, YOU KNOW WHAT TO DO!
YEAH, OCK WON'T BE THE ONLY ONE TO MESS WITH HIS BRAIN!
CHITTER CHITTER CHIT CHIT CHIT!
CHITTER CHIT CHIT CHIT CHITTER CHIT
AAAAHHH!
CHITTER CHIT CHIT
CHITTER CHIT CHIT CHIT
CHIT CHIT CHIT
CHIT CHITTER CHIT

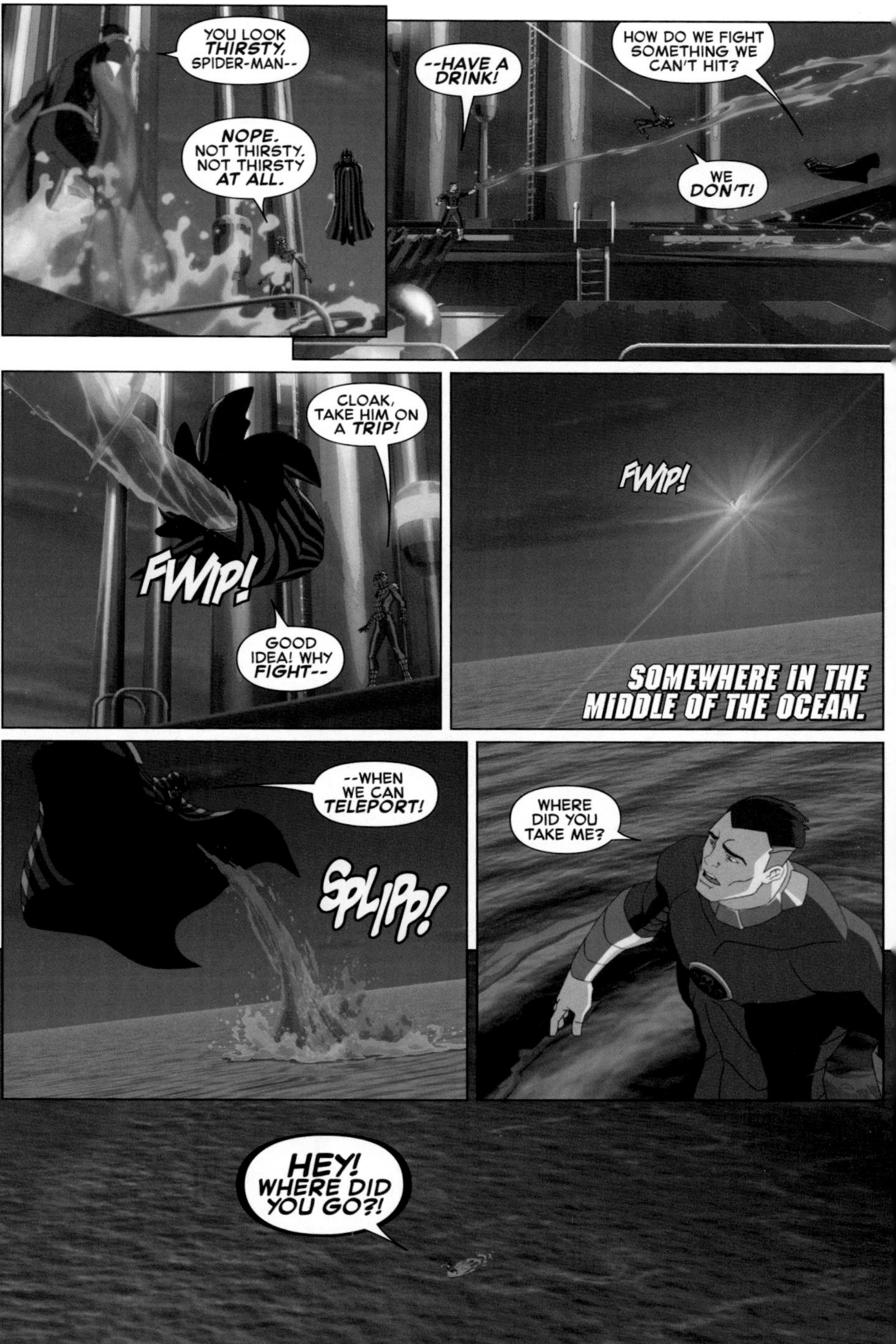
YOU LOOK THIRSTY, SPIDER-MAN--
NOPE. NOT THIRSTY. NOT THIRSTY AT ALL.
--HAVE A DRINK!
HOW DO WE FIGHT SOMETHING WE CAN'T HIT?
WE DON'T!
CLOAK, TAKE HIM ON A TRIP!
FWIP!
GOOD IDEA! WHY FIGHT--
FWIP!
SOMEWHERE IN THE MIDDLE OF THE OCEAN.
--WHEN WE CAN TELEPORT!
SPLIPP!
WHERE DID YOU TAKE ME?
HEY! WHERE DID YOU GO?!

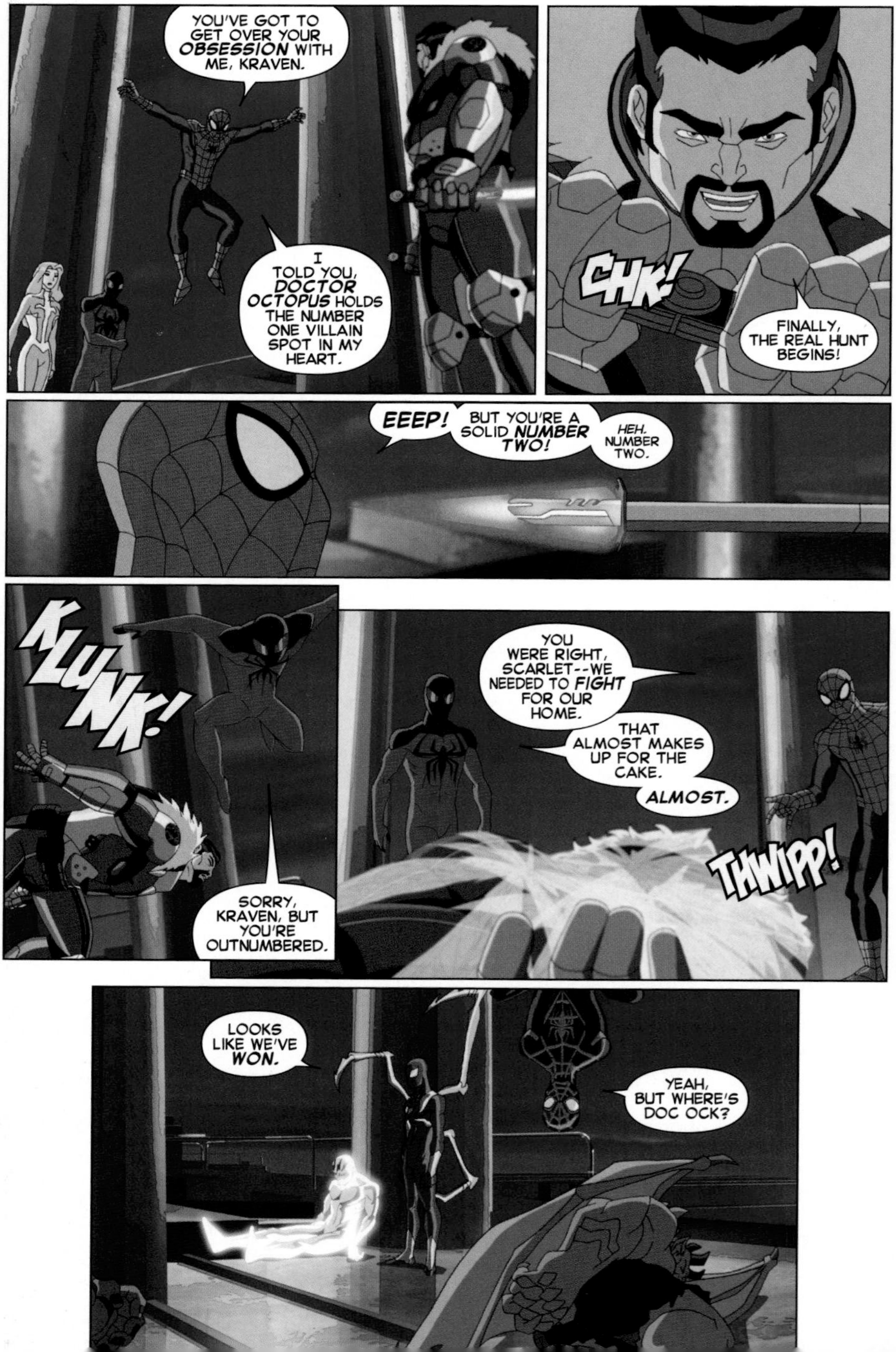
YOU'VE GOT TO GET OVER YOUR OBSESSION WITH ME, KRAVEN.
I TOLD YOU, DOCTOR OCTOPUS HOLDS THE NUMBER ONE VILLAIN SPOT IN MY HEART.
CHK!
FINALLY, THE REAL HUNT BEGINS!
EEEP!
BUT YOU'RE A SOLID NUMBER TWO!
HEH. NUMBER TWO.
KLUNK!
SORRY, KRAVEN, BUT YOU'RE OUTNUMBERED.
YOU WERE RIGHT, SCARLET--WE NEEDED TO FIGHT FOR OUR HOME.
THAT ALMOST MAKES UP FOR THE CAKE.
ALMOST.
THWIPP!
LOOKS LIKE WE'VE WON.
YEAH, BUT WHERE'S DOC OCK?

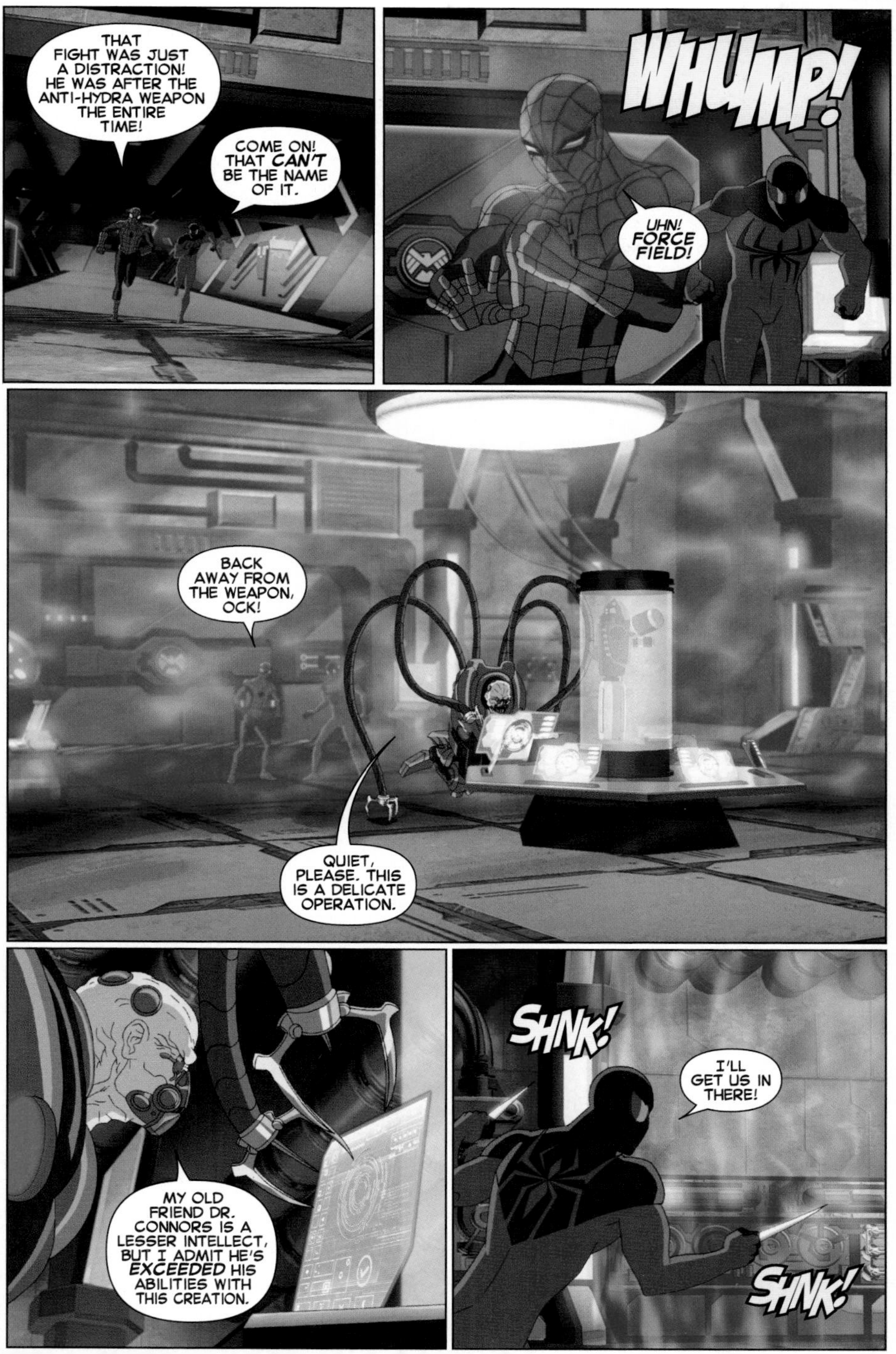
THAT FIGHT WAS JUST A DISTRACTION! HE WAS AFTER THE ANTI-HYDRA WEAPON THE ENTIRE TIME!
COME ON! THAT CAN'T BE THE NAME OF IT.
WHUMP!
UHN! FORCE FIELD!
BACK AWAY FROM THE WEAPON, OCK!
QUIET, PLEASE. THIS IS A DELICATE OPERATION.
MY OLD FRIEND DR. CONNORS IS A LESSER INTELLECT, BUT I ADMIT HE'S EXCEEDED HIS ABILITIES WITH THIS CREATION.
SHNK!
I'LL GET US IN THERE!
SHNK!

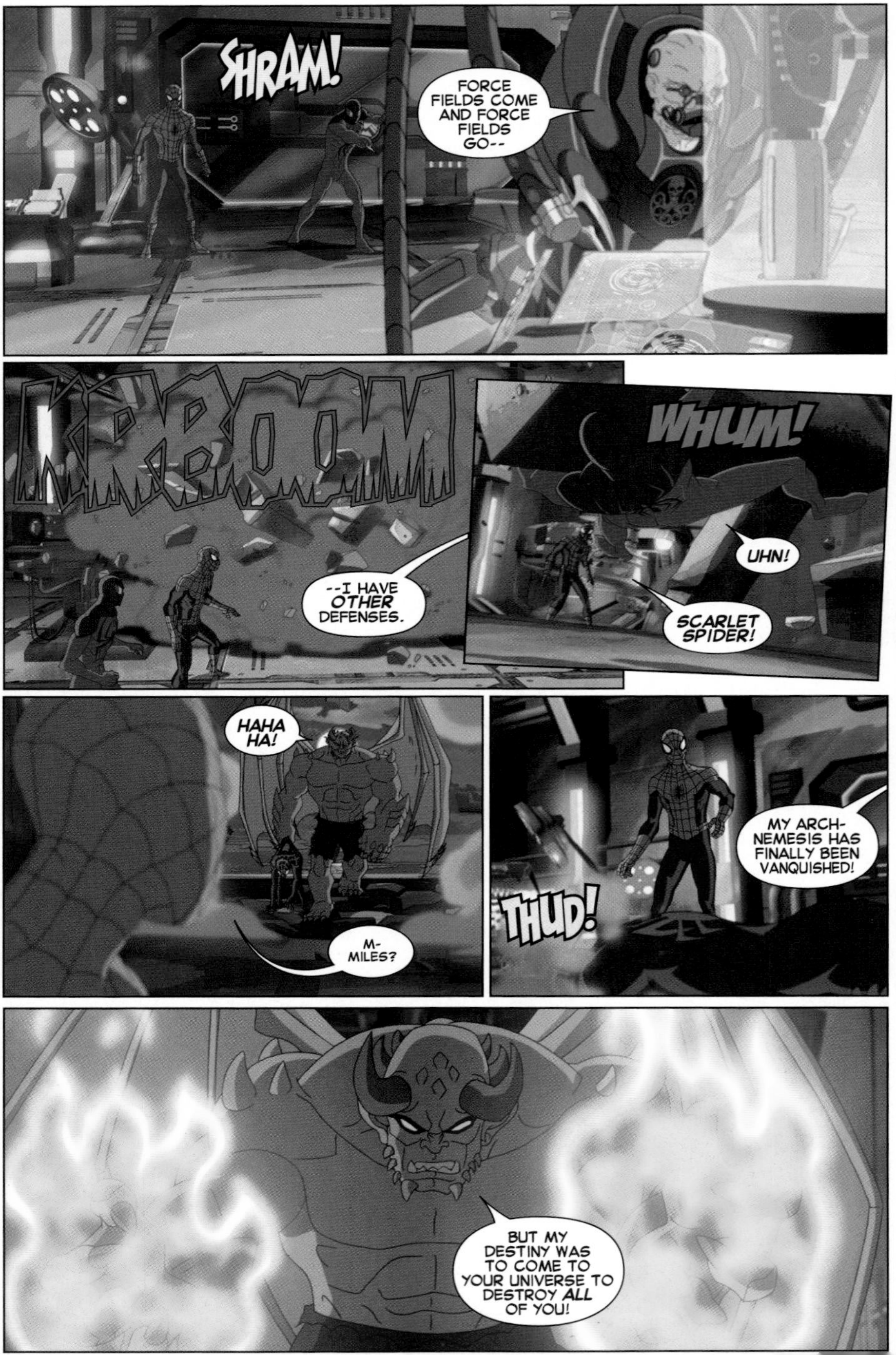
SHRAM!
FORCE FIELDS COME AND FORCE FIELDS GO--
KRBOOM
--I HAVE OTHER DEFENSES.
WHUM!
UHN!
SCARLET SPIDER!
HAHA HA!
M-MILES?
MY ARCH-NEMESIS HAS FINALLY BEEN VANQUISHED!
THUD!
BUT MY DESTINY WAS TO COME TO YOUR UNIVERSE TO DESTROY ALL OF YOU!

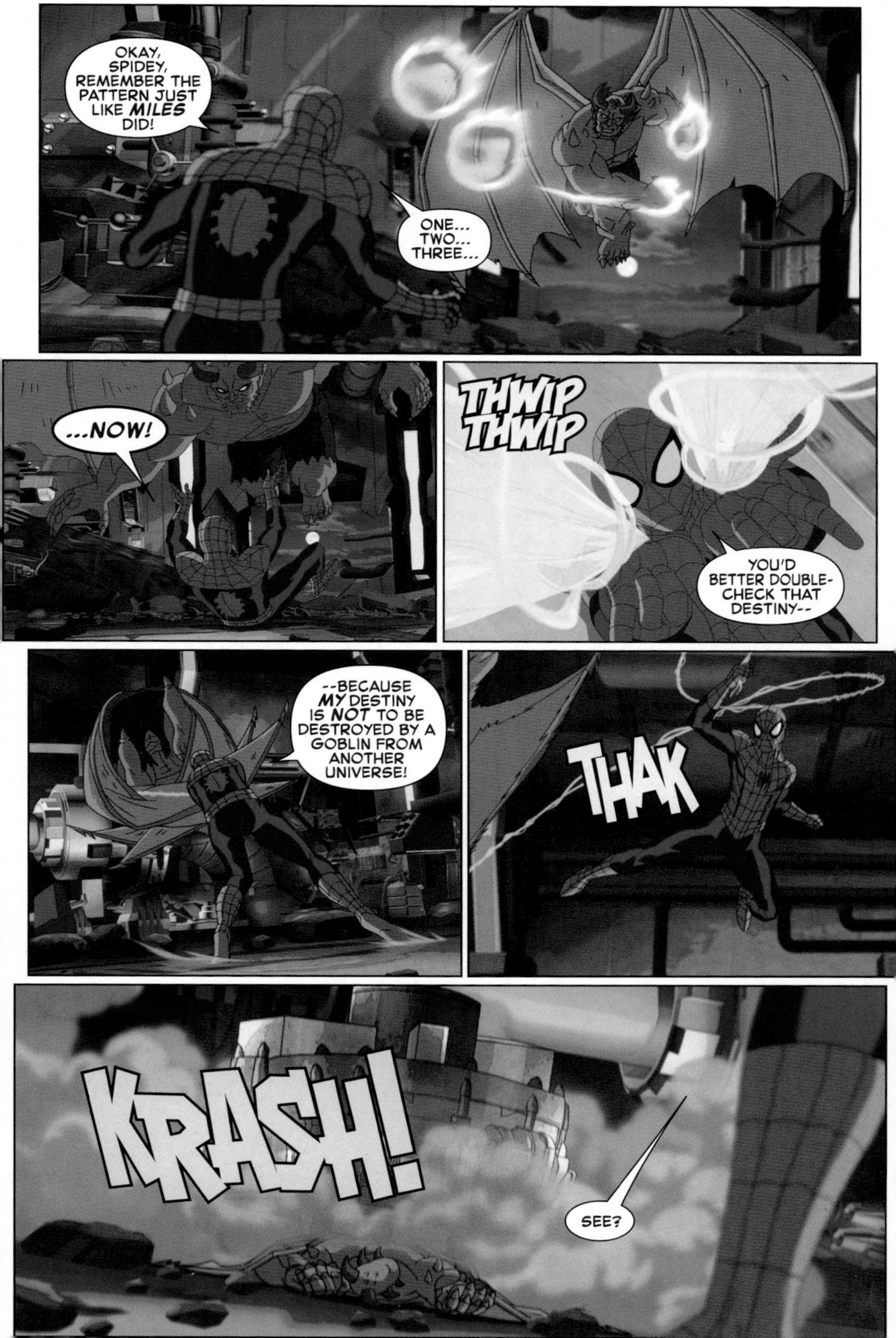
OKAY, SPIDEY, REMEMBER THE PATTERN JUST LIKE MILES DID!
ONE... TWO... THREE...
...NOW!
THWIP THWIP
YOU'D BETTER DOUBLE-CHECK THAT DESTINY--
--BECAUSE MY DESTINY IS NOT TO BE DESTROYED BY A GOBLIN FROM ANOTHER UNIVERSE!
THAK
KRASH!
SEE?

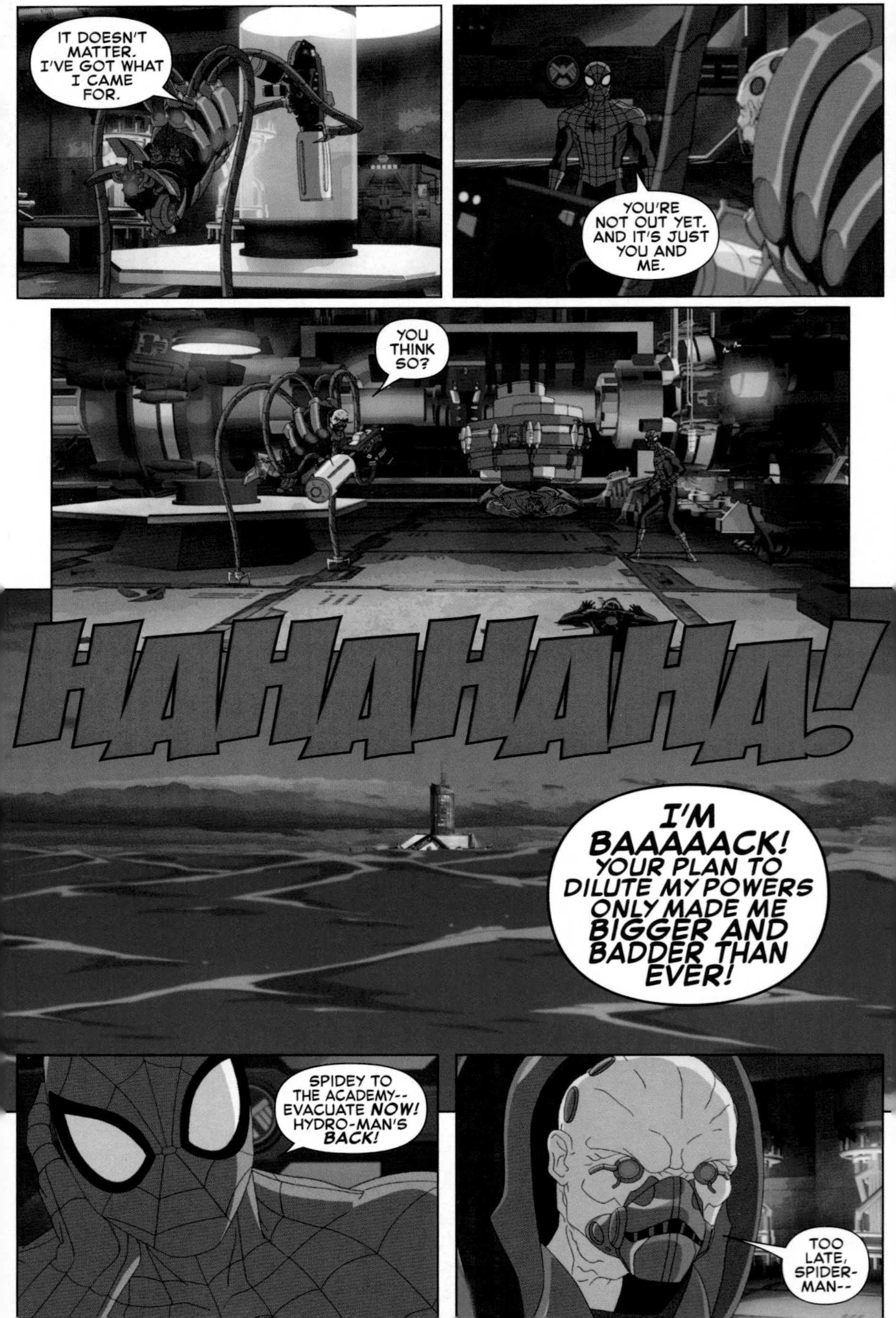
IT DOESN'T MATTER. I'VE GOT WHAT I CAME FOR.
YOU'RE NOT OUT YET. AND IT'S JUST YOU AND ME.
YOU THINK SO?
HAHAHAHA!
I'M BAAAAACK! YOUR PLAN TO DILUTE MY POWERS ONLY MADE ME BIGGER AND BADDER THAN EVER!
SPIDEY TO THE ACADEMY-- EVACUATE NOW! HYDRO-MAN'S BACK!
TOO LATE, SPIDER-MAN--

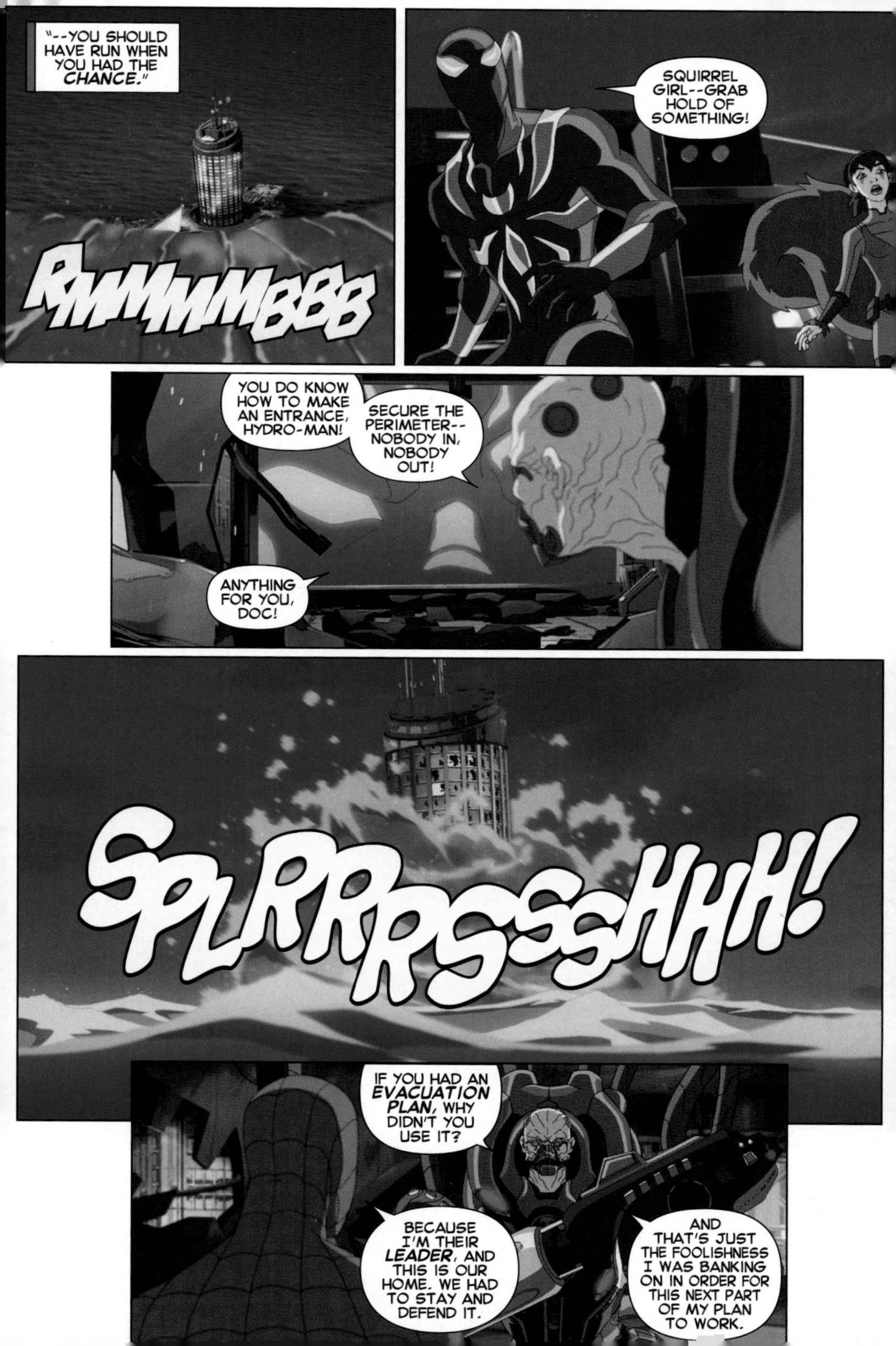
"--YOU SHOULD HAVE RUN WHEN YOU HAD THE *CHANCE.*"
RMMMMBBB
SQUIRREL GIRL--GRAB HOLD OF SOMETHING!
YOU DO KNOW HOW TO MAKE AN ENTRANCE, HYDRO-MAN!
SECURE THE PERIMETER--NOBODY IN, NOBODY OUT!
ANYTHING FOR YOU, DOC!
SPLRRRSSSHHH!
IF YOU HAD AN *EVACUATION PLAN*, WHY DIDN'T YOU USE IT?
BECAUSE I'M THEIR *LEADER*, AND THIS IS OUR HOME. WE HAD TO STAY AND DEFEND IT.
AND THAT'S JUST THE FOOLISHNESS I WAS BANKING ON IN ORDER FOR THIS NEXT PART OF MY PLAN TO WORK.

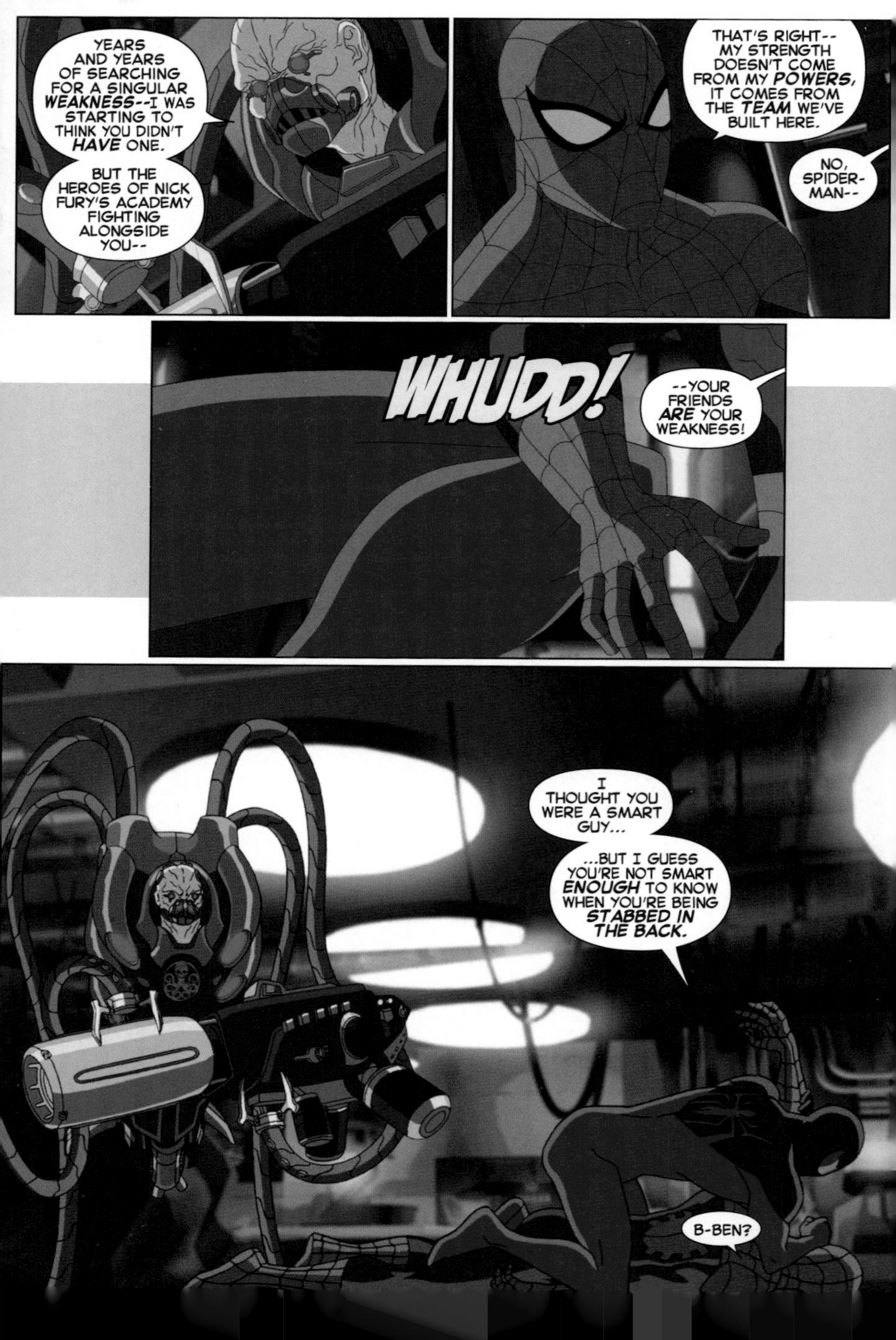
YEARS AND YEARS OF SEARCHING FOR A SINGULAR WEAKNESS--I WAS STARTING TO THINK YOU DIDN'T HAVE ONE.
BUT THE HEROES OF NICK FURY'S ACADEMY FIGHTING ALONGSIDE YOU--
THAT'S RIGHT-- MY STRENGTH DOESN'T COME FROM MY POWERS, IT COMES FROM THE TEAM WE'VE BUILT HERE.
NO, SPIDER-MAN--
WHUDD!
--YOUR FRIENDS ARE YOUR WEAKNESS!
I THOUGHT YOU WERE A SMART GUY...
...BUT I GUESS YOU'RE NOT SMART ENOUGH TO KNOW WHEN YOU'RE BEING STABBED IN THE BACK.
B-BEN?

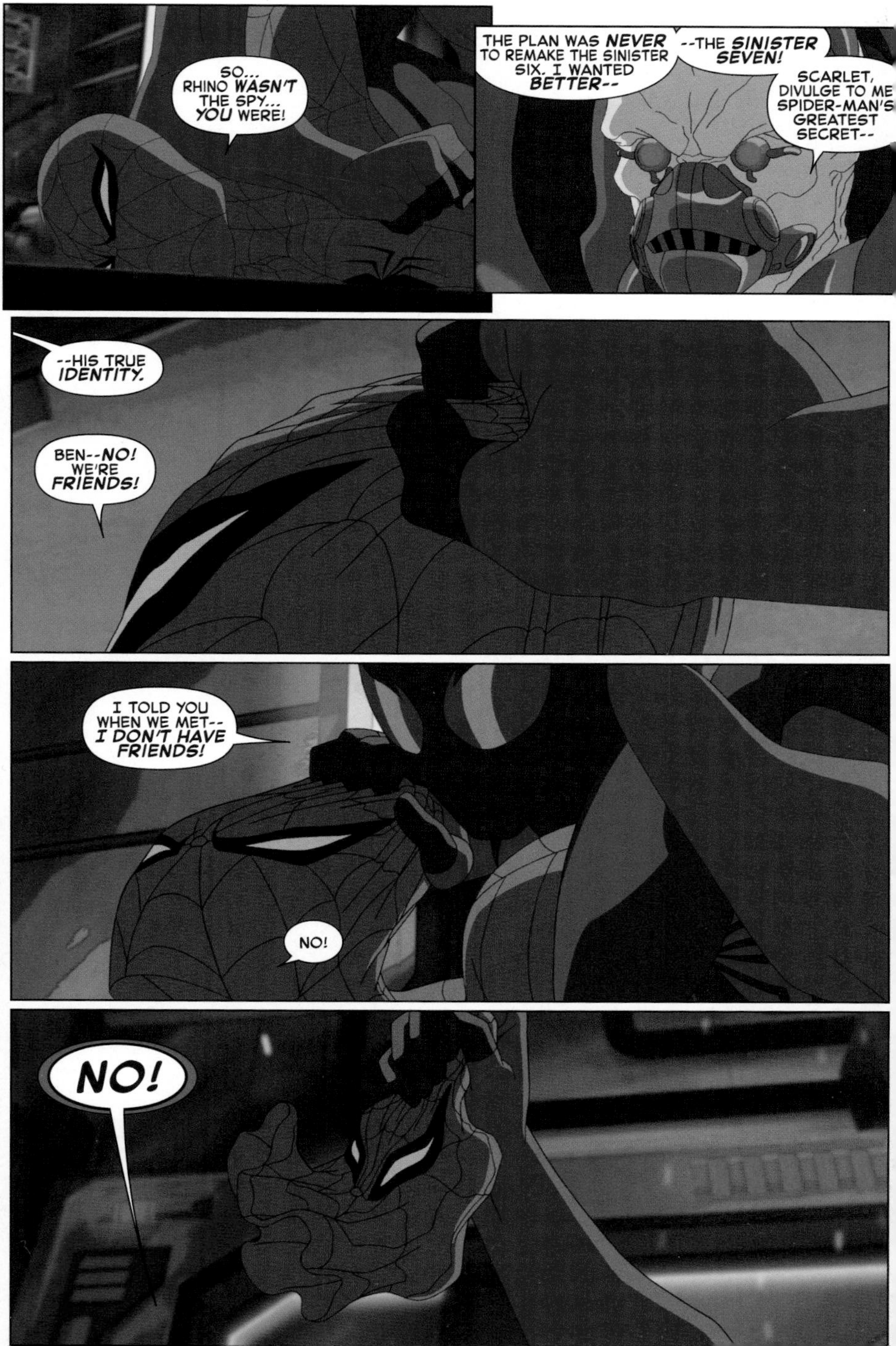
SO... RHINO WASN'T THE SPY... YOU WERE!
THE PLAN WAS NEVER TO REMAKE THE SINISTER SIX. I WANTED BETTER--
--THE SINISTER SEVEN!
SCARLET, DIVULGE TO ME SPIDER-MAN'S GREATEST SECRET--
--HIS TRUE IDENTITY.
BEN--NO! WE'RE FRIENDS!
I TOLD YOU WHEN WE MET-- I DON'T HAVE FRIENDS!
NO!
NO!

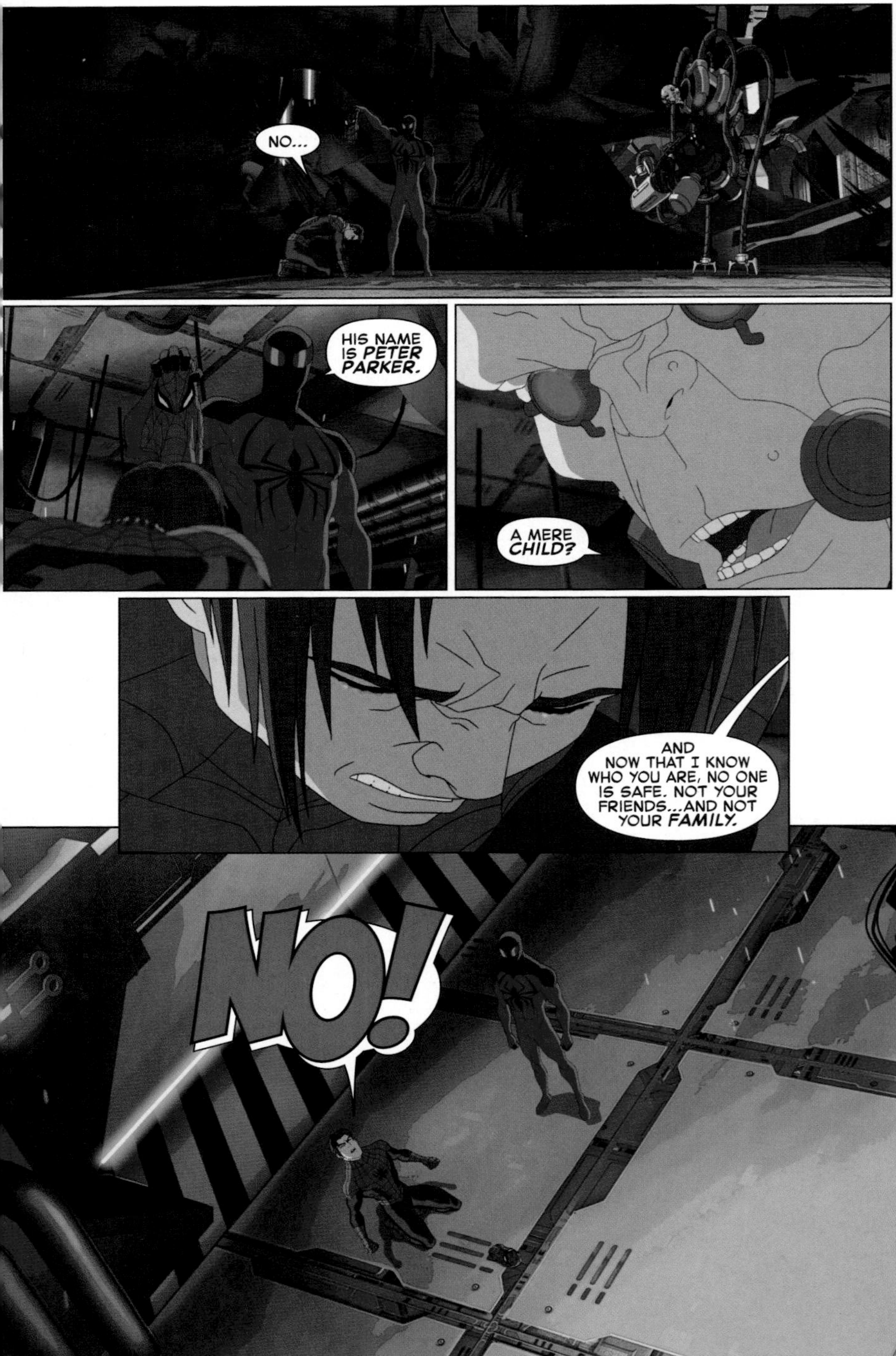
NO...
HIS NAME IS PETER PARKER.
A MERE CHILD?
AND NOW THAT I KNOW WHO YOU ARE, NO ONE IS SAFE. NOT YOUR FRIENDS...AND NOT YOUR FAMILY.
NO!

11: "THE NEW SINISTER SIX"
PART TWO

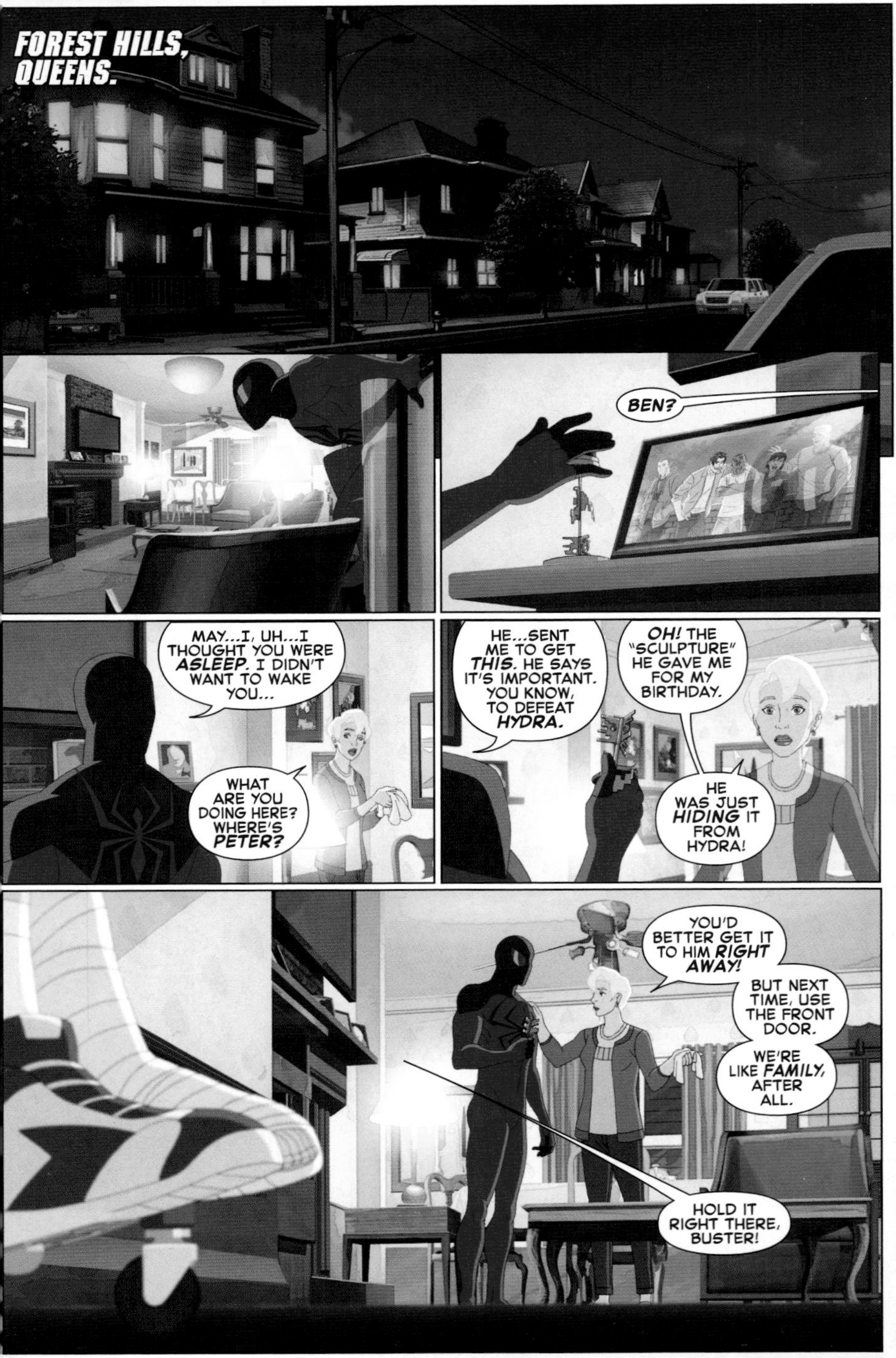
FOREST HILLS, QUEENS.
BEN?
MAY...I, UH...I THOUGHT YOU WERE ASLEEP. I DIDN'T WANT TO WAKE YOU...
WHAT ARE YOU DOING HERE? WHERE'S PETER?
HE...SENT ME TO GET THIS. HE SAYS IT'S IMPORTANT. YOU KNOW, TO DEFEAT HYDRA.
OH! THE "SCULPTURE" HE GAVE ME FOR MY BIRTHDAY.
HE WAS JUST HIDING IT FROM HYDRA!
YOU'D BETTER GET IT TO HIM RIGHT AWAY!
BUT NEXT TIME, USE THE FRONT DOOR.
WE'RE LIKE FAMILY, AFTER ALL.
HOLD IT RIGHT THERE, BUSTER!

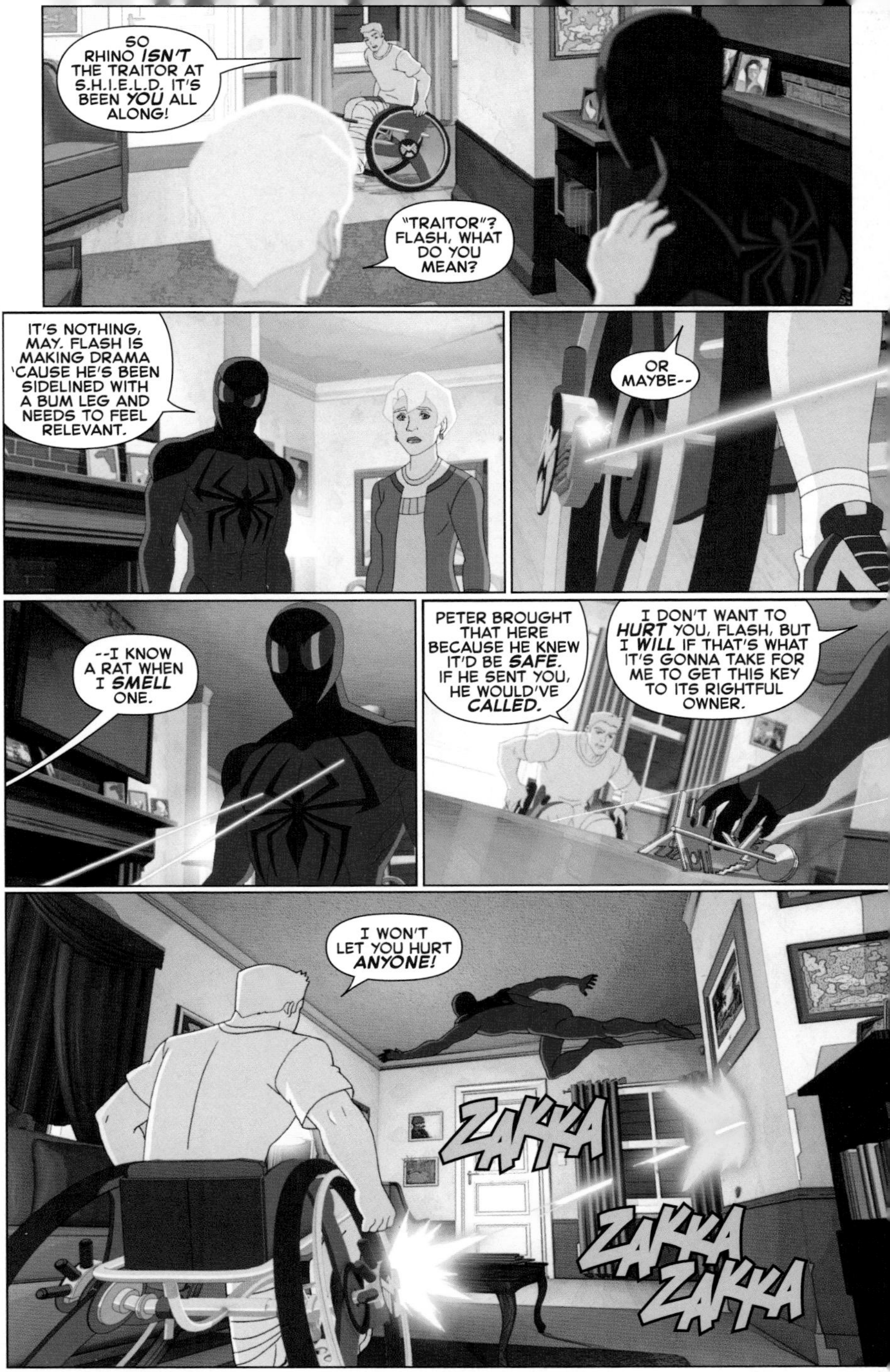
SO RHINO ISN'T THE TRAITOR AT S.H.I.E.L.D. IT'S BEEN YOU ALL ALONG!
"TRAITOR"? FLASH, WHAT DO YOU MEAN?
IT'S NOTHING, MAY. FLASH IS MAKING DRAMA 'CAUSE HE'S BEEN SIDELINED WITH A BUM LEG AND NEEDS TO FEEL RELEVANT.
OR MAYBE--
--I KNOW A RAT WHEN I SMELL ONE.
PETER BROUGHT THAT HERE BECAUSE HE KNEW IT'D BE SAFE. IF HE SENT YOU, HE WOULD'VE CALLED.
I DON'T WANT TO HURT YOU, FLASH, BUT I WILL IF THAT'S WHAT IT'S GONNA TAKE FOR ME TO GET THIS KEY TO ITS RIGHTFUL OWNER.
I WON'T LET YOU HURT ANYONE!
ZAKKA
ZAKKA
ZAKKA

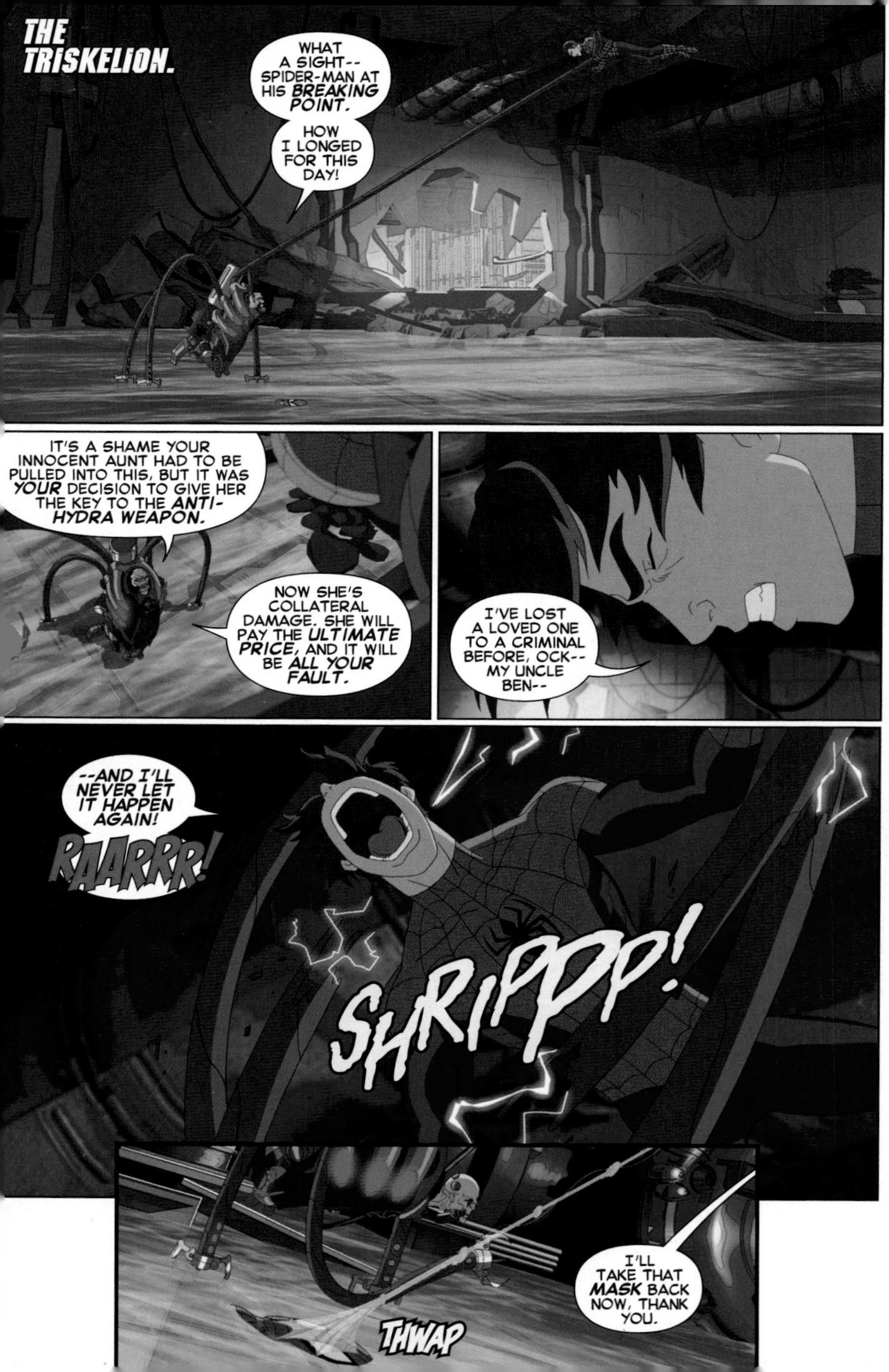
THE TRISKELION.
WHAT A SIGHT-- SPIDER-MAN AT HIS BREAKING POINT.
HOW I LONGED FOR THIS DAY!
IT'S A SHAME YOUR INNOCENT AUNT HAD TO BE PULLED INTO THIS, BUT IT WAS YOUR DECISION TO GIVE HER THE KEY TO THE ANTI-HYDRA WEAPON.
NOW SHE'S COLLATERAL DAMAGE. SHE WILL PAY THE ULTIMATE PRICE, AND IT WILL BE ALL YOUR FAULT.
I'VE LOST A LOVED ONE TO A CRIMINAL BEFORE, OCK-- MY UNCLE BEN--
--AND I'LL NEVER LET IT HAPPEN AGAIN!
RAARRR!
SHRIPPP!
I'LL TAKE THAT MASK BACK NOW, THANK YOU.
THWAP

YOU'D BETTER HOPE NOTHING'S HAPPENED TO AUNT MAY!

IF YOU THINK YOU'VE PUSHED SPIDER-MAN TO HIS LIMIT, WAIT'LL YOU SEE WHAT *PETER PARKER* IS CAPABLE OF!

HAHA!

WHERE DO YOU THINK *YOU'RE* GOING?

DO YOU REALLY THINK YOU CAN GET AROUND *ME*?

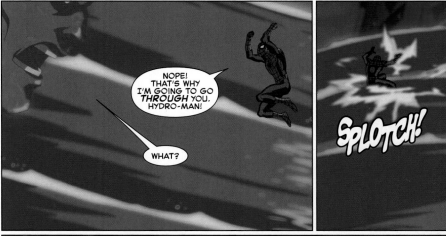

NOPE! THAT'S WHY I'M GOING TO GO *THROUGH* YOU, HYDRO-MAN!

WHAT?

SPLOTCH!

WUMP!

S-SEE...?

HRNNN...

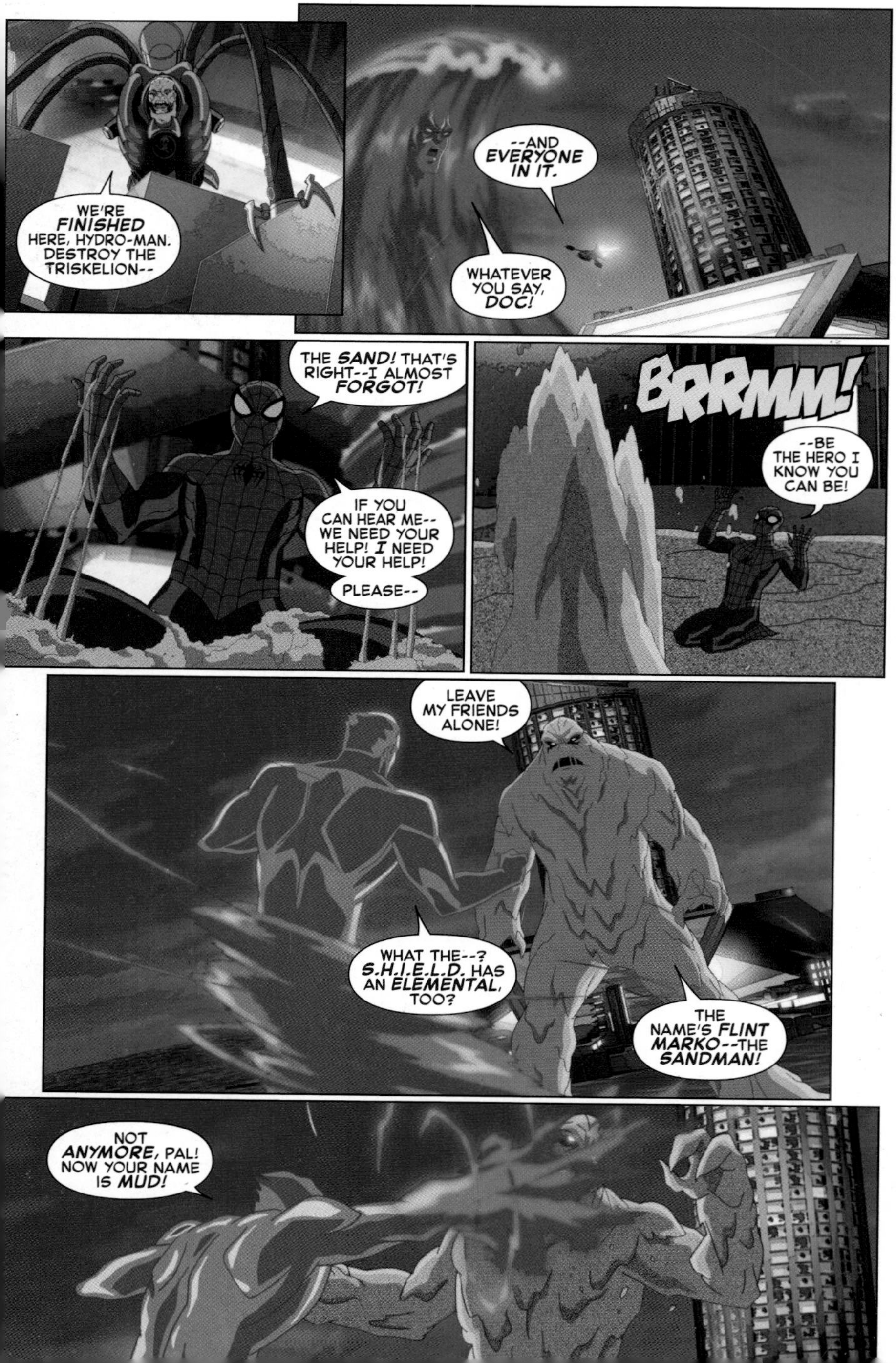
WE'RE FINISHED HERE, HYDRO-MAN. DESTROY THE TRISKELION--
--AND EVERYONE IN IT.
WHATEVER YOU SAY, DOC!
THE SAND! THAT'S RIGHT--I ALMOST FORGOT!
IF YOU CAN HEAR ME--WE NEED YOUR HELP! I NEED YOUR HELP!
PLEASE--
BRRMM!
--BE THE HERO I KNOW YOU CAN BE!
LEAVE MY FRIENDS ALONE!
WHAT THE--? S.H.I.E.L.D. HAS AN ELEMENTAL, TOO?
THE NAME'S FLINT MARKO--THE SANDMAN!
NOT ANYMORE, PAL! NOW YOUR NAME IS MUD!

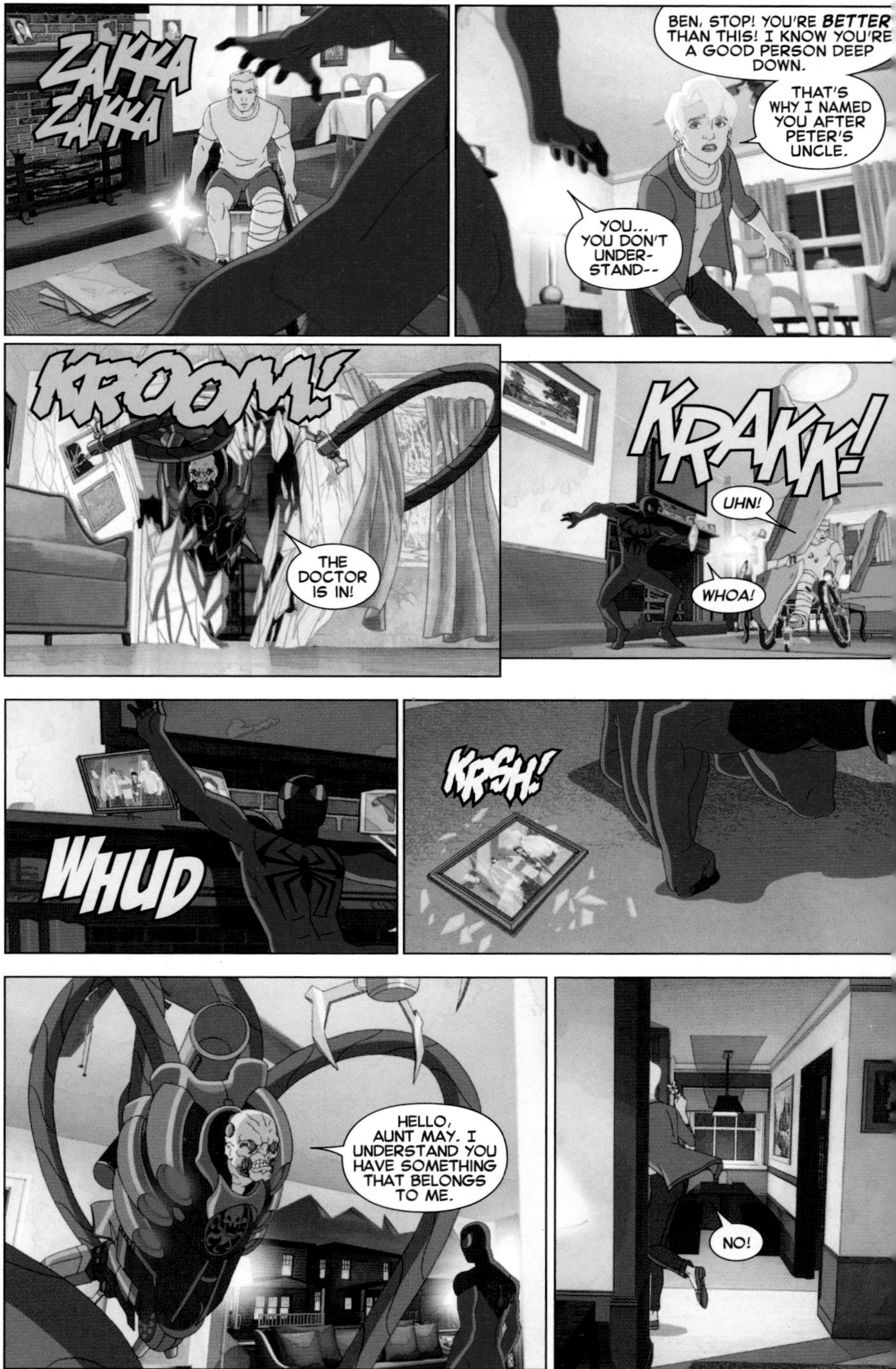
ZAKKA ZAKKA
BEN, STOP! YOU'RE BETTER THAN THIS! I KNOW YOU'RE A GOOD PERSON DEEP DOWN.
THAT'S WHY I NAMED YOU AFTER PETER'S UNCLE.
YOU... YOU DON'T UNDER-STAND--
KROOM!
THE DOCTOR IS IN!
KRAKK!
UHN!
WHOA!
WHUD
KRSH!
HELLO, AUNT MAY. I UNDERSTAND YOU HAVE SOMETHING THAT BELONGS TO ME.
NO!

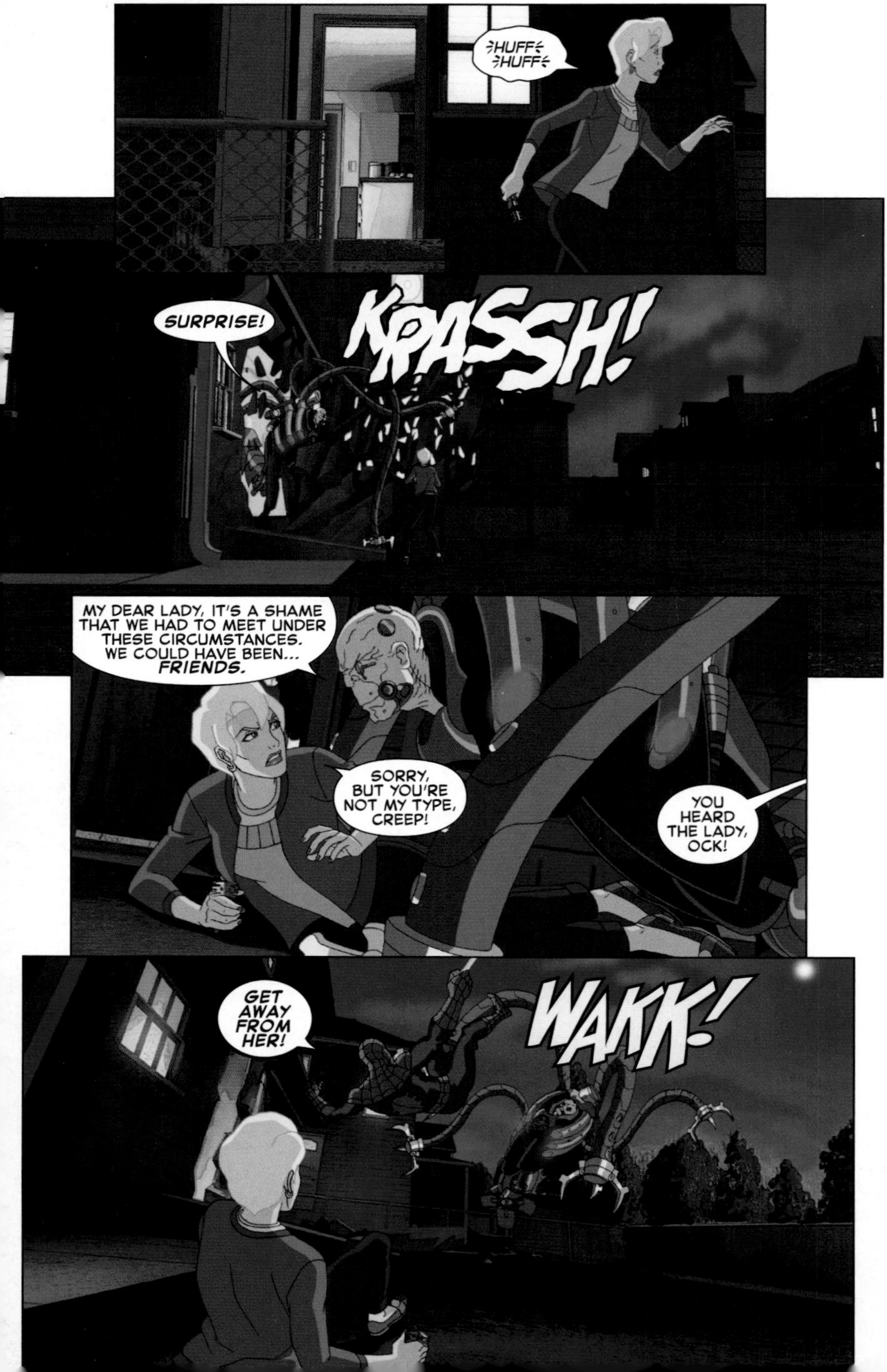

HUFF HUFF
SURPRISE!
KRASSH!
MY DEAR LADY, IT'S A SHAME THAT WE HAD TO MEET UNDER THESE CIRCUMSTANCES. WE COULD HAVE BEEN... FRIENDS.
SORRY, BUT YOU'RE NOT MY TYPE, CREEP!
YOU HEARD THE LADY, OCK!
GET AWAY FROM HER!
WAKK!

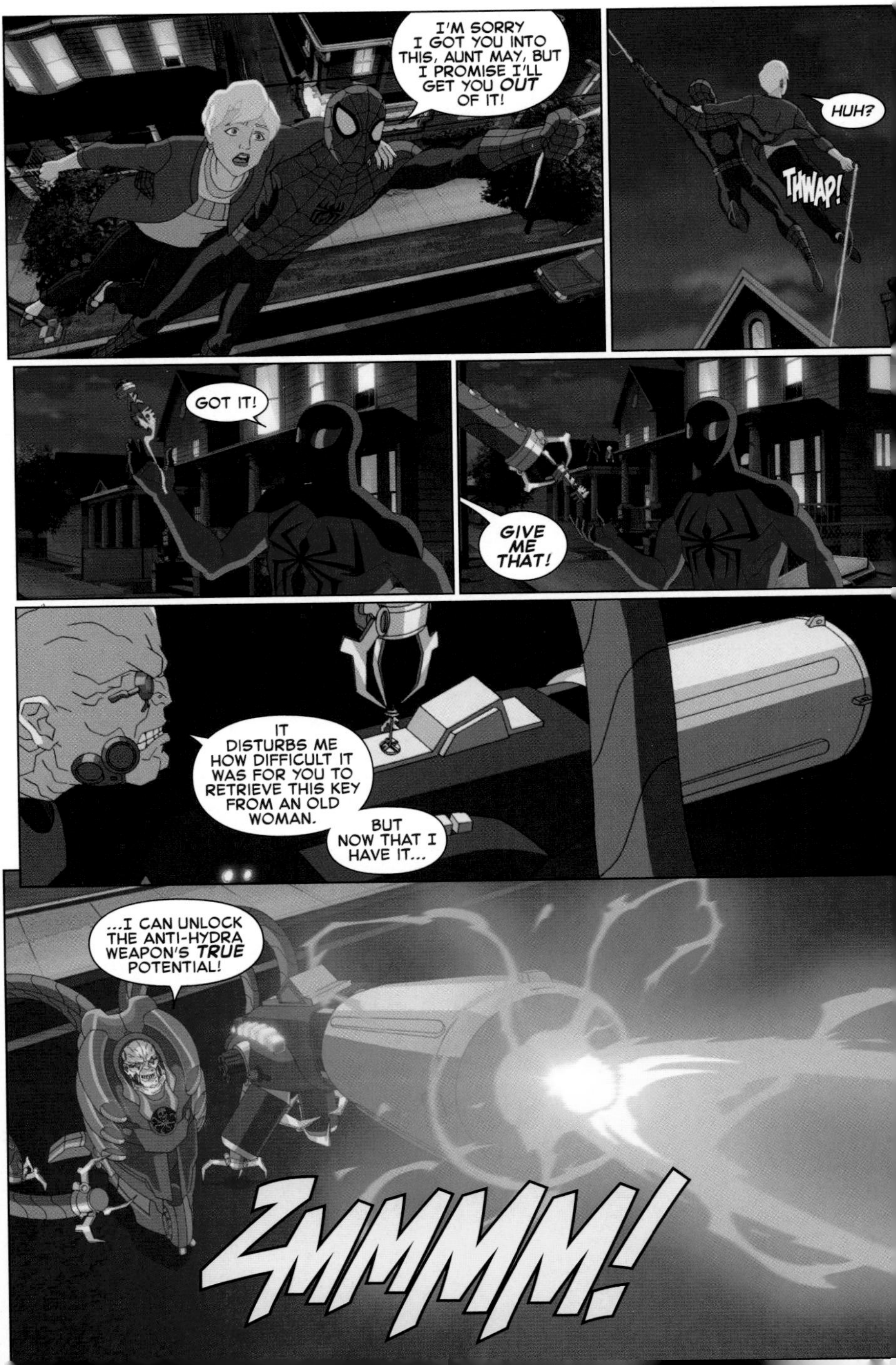

I'M SORRY I GOT YOU INTO THIS, AUNT MAY, BUT I PROMISE I'LL GET YOU *OUT* OF IT!
HUH?
THWAP!
GOT IT!
GIVE ME THAT!
IT DISTURBS ME HOW DIFFICULT IT WAS FOR YOU TO RETRIEVE THIS KEY FROM AN OLD WOMAN.
BUT NOW THAT I HAVE IT...
...I CAN UNLOCK THE ANTI-HYDRA WEAPON'S *TRUE* POTENTIAL!
ZMMMM!

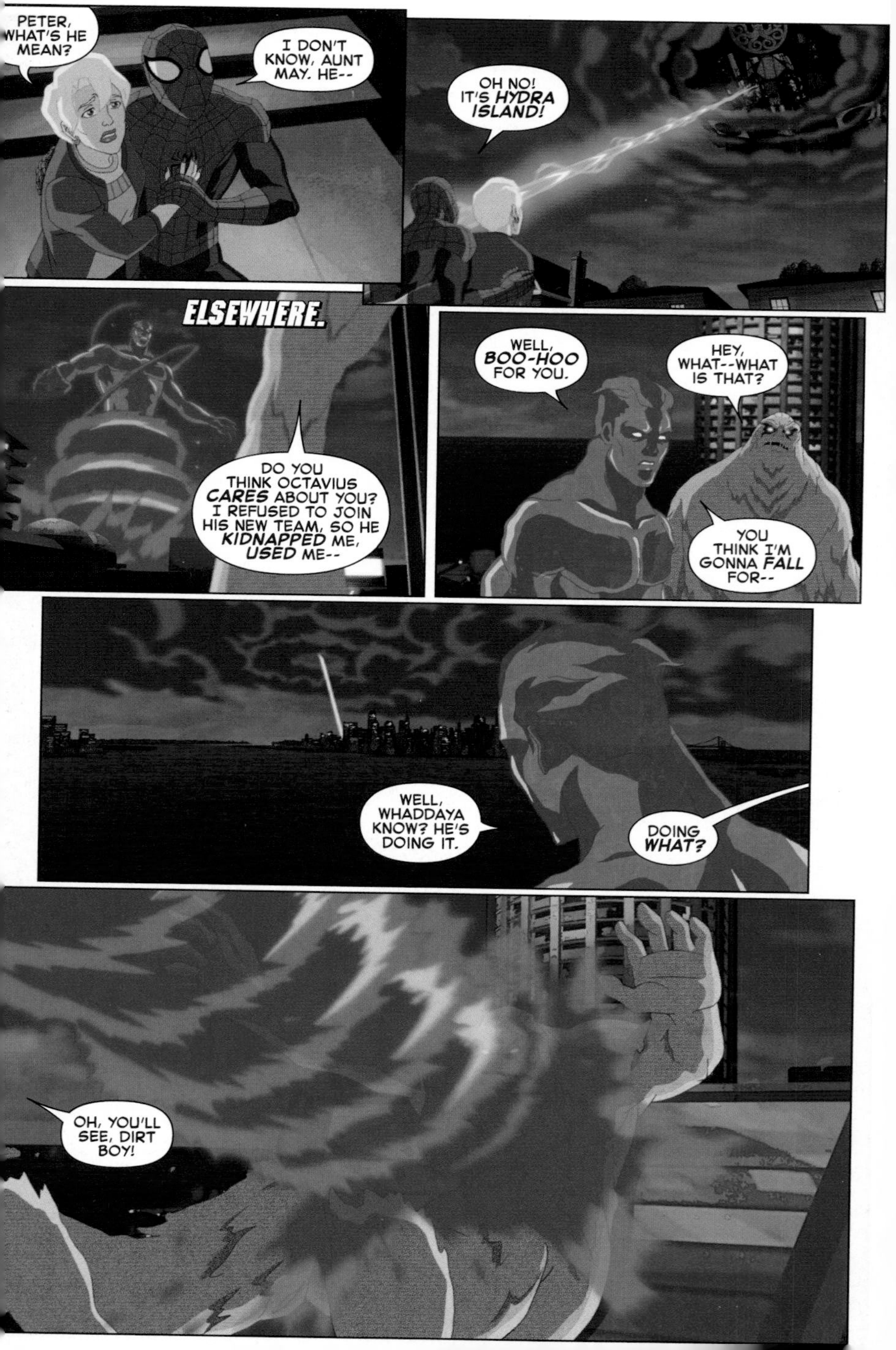
PETER, WHAT'S HE MEAN?
I DON'T KNOW, AUNT MAY. HE--
OH NO! IT'S HYDRA ISLAND!
ELSEWHERE.
DO YOU THINK OCTAVIUS CARES ABOUT YOU? I REFUSED TO JOIN HIS NEW TEAM, SO HE KIDNAPPED ME, USED ME--
WELL, BOO-HOO FOR YOU.
HEY, WHAT--WHAT IS THAT?
YOU THINK I'M GONNA FALL FOR--
WELL, WHADDAYA KNOW? HE'S DOING IT.
DOING WHAT?
OH, YOU'LL SEE, DIRT BOY!

THE ANTI-HYDRA WEAPON CAN MANIPULATE THE **NANOBOTS** THAT HYDRA USED TO CREATE HYDRA ISLAND.

I CAN BEND AND SHAPE THEM AT MY WLL.

BEHOLD--

¡¡OCTOPUS ISLAND!!

AND ITS *TENTACLES OF DESTRUCTION!*

HAHA!

BRKXM!

AAHH!

BEN, HOW CAN YOU JUST STAND THERE AND LET THIS HAPPEN?

OCK TOOK ME IN OFF THE STREET. *YOU*, OF *ALL* PEOPLE, SHOULD UNDERSTAND LOYALT--

KRMB!

SPIDER-MAN--

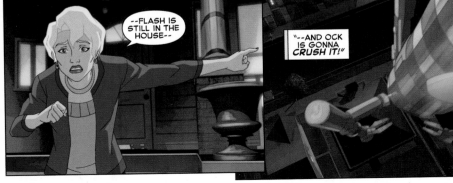

--FLASH IS STILL IN THE HOUSE--

"--AND OCK IS GONNA *CRUSH IT!*"

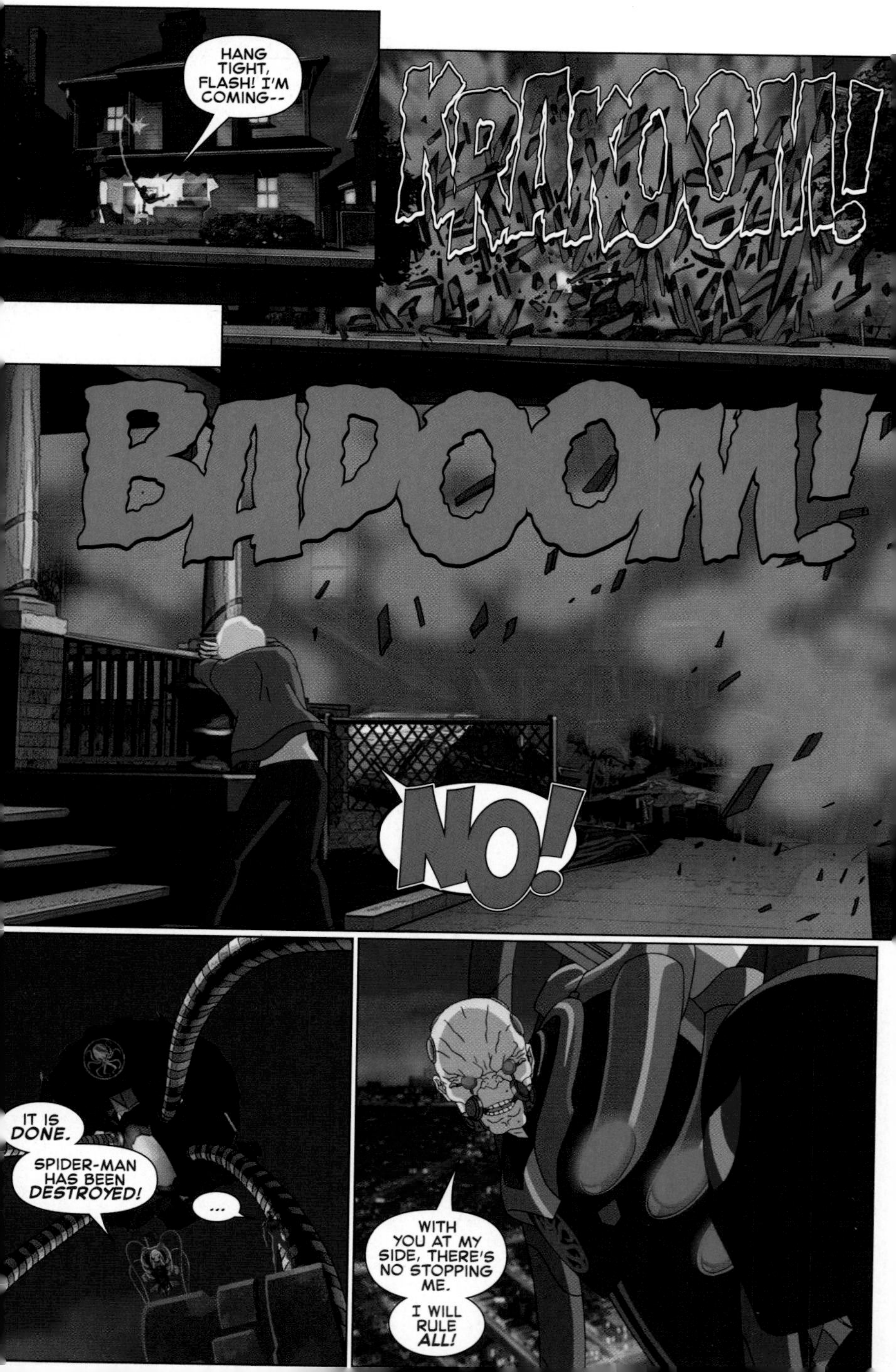
HANG TIGHT, FLASH! I'M COMING--
KRAKOOM!
BADOOM!
NO!
IT IS DONE.
SPIDER-MAN HAS BEEN DESTROYED!
...
WITH YOU AT MY SIDE, THERE'S NO STOPPING ME.
I WILL RULE ALL!

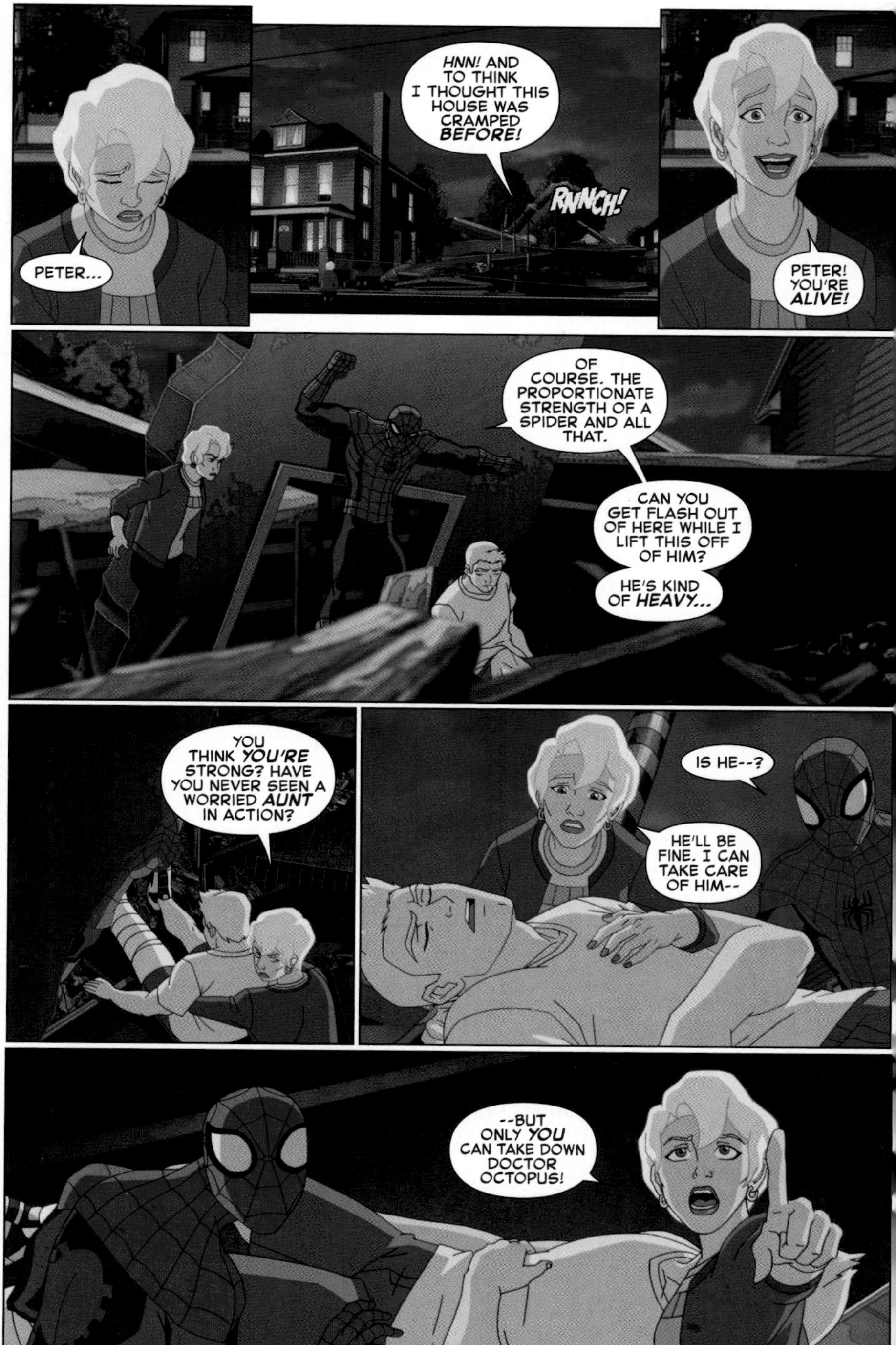
PETER...
HNN! AND TO THINK I THOUGHT THIS HOUSE WAS CRAMPED BEFORE!
RNNCH!
PETER! YOU'RE ALIVE!
OF COURSE. THE PROPORTIONATE STRENGTH OF A SPIDER AND ALL THAT.
CAN YOU GET FLASH OUT OF HERE WHILE I LIFT THIS OFF OF HIM?
HE'S KIND OF HEAVY...
YOU THINK YOU'RE STRONG? HAVE YOU NEVER SEEN A WORRIED AUNT IN ACTION?
IS HE--?
HE'LL BE FINE. I CAN TAKE CARE OF HIM--
--BUT ONLY YOU CAN TAKE DOWN DOCTOR OCTOPUS!

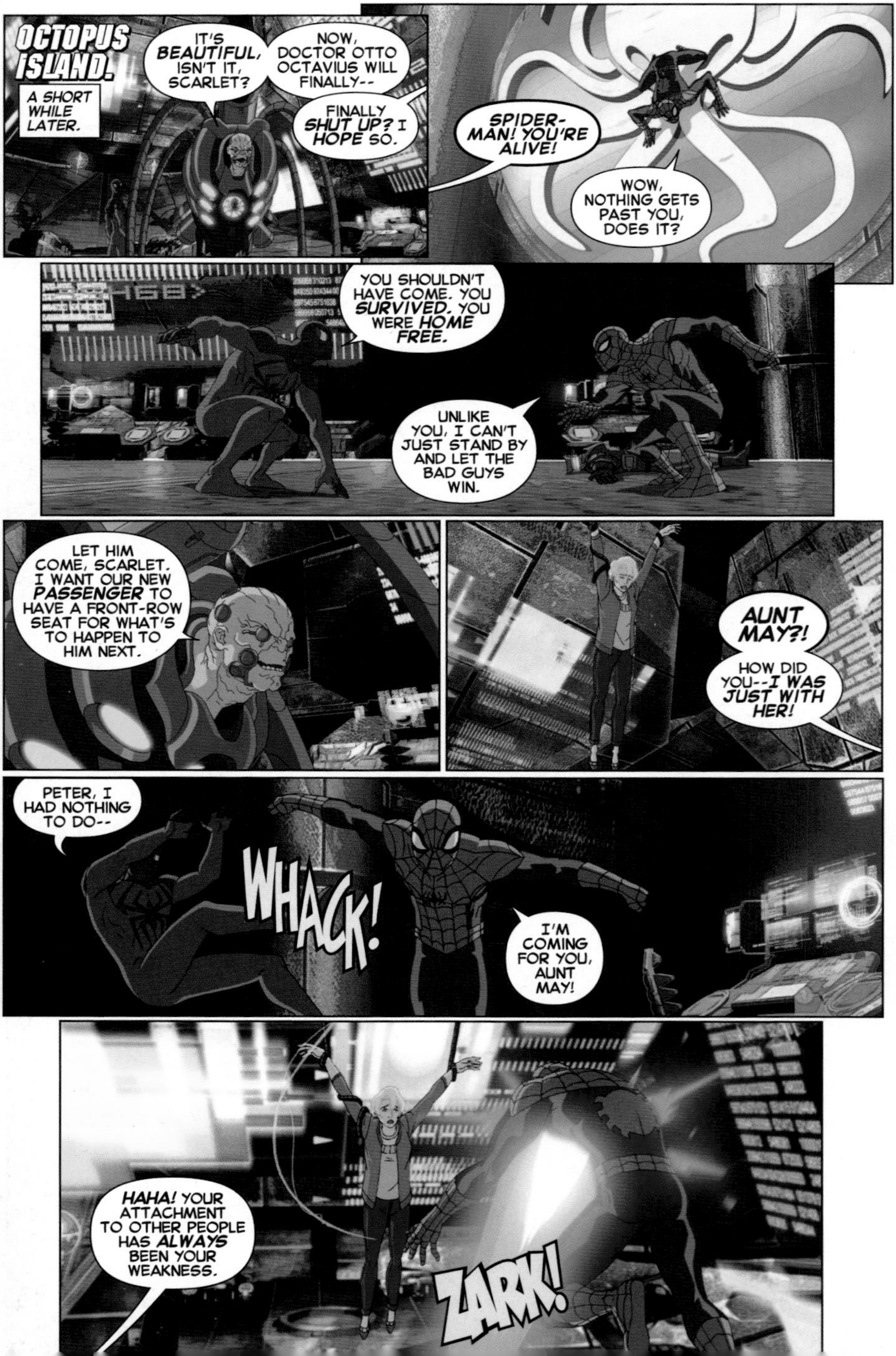
OCTOPUS ISLAND.
A SHORT WHILE LATER.
IT'S BEAUTIFUL, ISN'T IT, SCARLET?
NOW, DOCTOR OTTO OCTAVIUS WILL FINALLY--
FINALLY SHUT UP? I HOPE SO.
SPIDER-MAN! YOU'RE ALIVE!
WOW, NOTHING GETS PAST YOU, DOES IT?
YOU SHOULDN'T HAVE COME. YOU SURVIVED. YOU WERE HOME FREE.
UNLIKE YOU, I CAN'T JUST STAND BY AND LET THE BAD GUYS WIN.
LET HIM COME, SCARLET. I WANT OUR NEW PASSENGER TO HAVE A FRONT-ROW SEAT FOR WHAT'S TO HAPPEN TO HIM NEXT.
AUNT MAY?!
HOW DID YOU--I WAS JUST WITH HER!
PETER, I HAD NOTHING TO DO--
WHACK!
I'M COMING FOR YOU, AUNT MAY!
HAHA! YOUR ATTACHMENT TO OTHER PEOPLE HAS ALWAYS BEEN YOUR WEAKNESS.
ZARK!

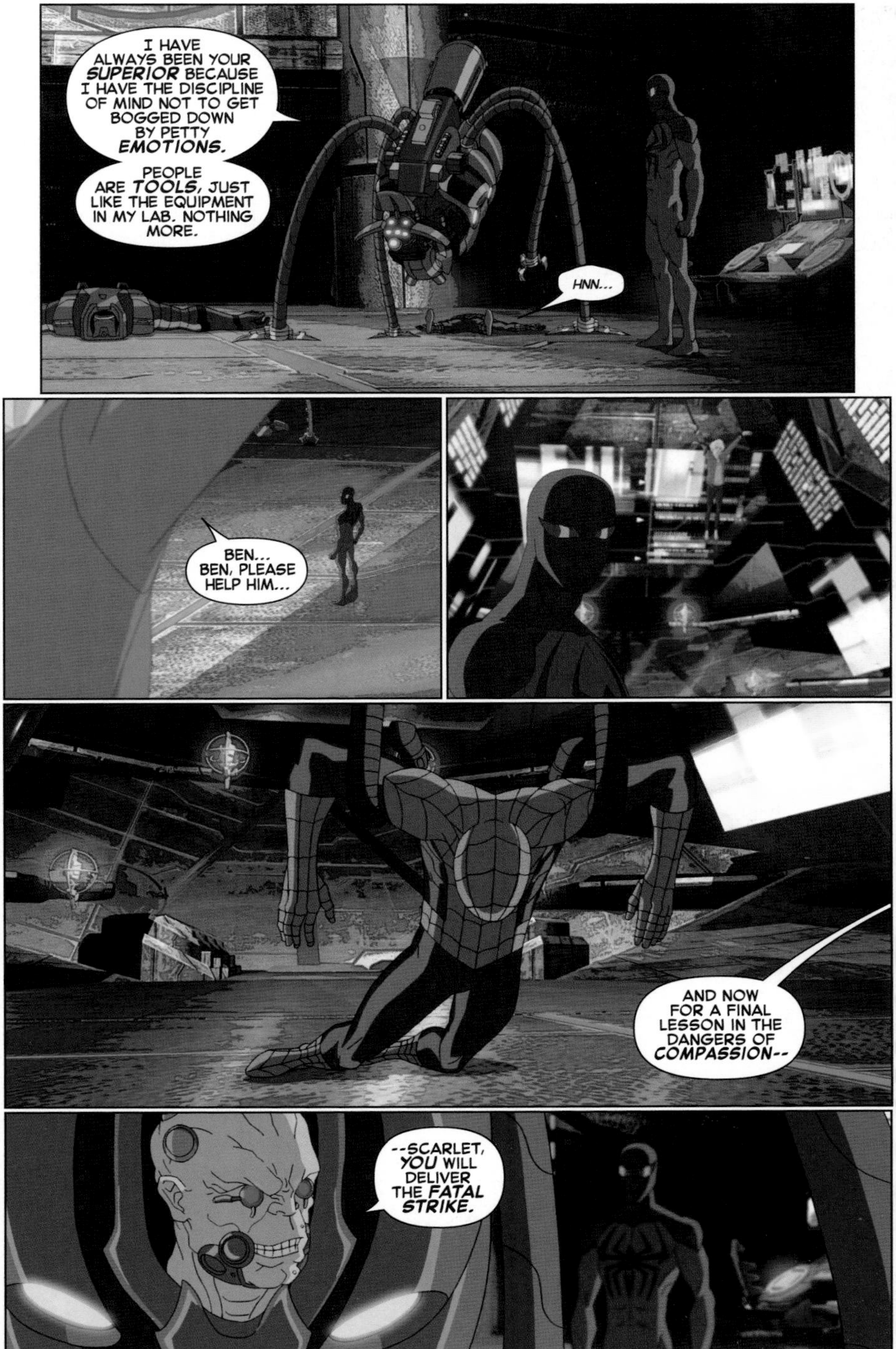
I HAVE ALWAYS BEEN YOUR SUPERIOR BECAUSE I HAVE THE DISCIPLINE OF MIND NOT TO GET BOGGED DOWN BY PETTY EMOTIONS.
PEOPLE ARE TOOLS, JUST LIKE THE EQUIPMENT IN MY LAB. NOTHING MORE.
HNN...
BEN... BEN, PLEASE HELP HIM...
AND NOW FOR A FINAL LESSON IN THE DANGERS OF COMPASSION--
--SCARLET, YOU WILL DELIVER THE FATAL STRIKE.

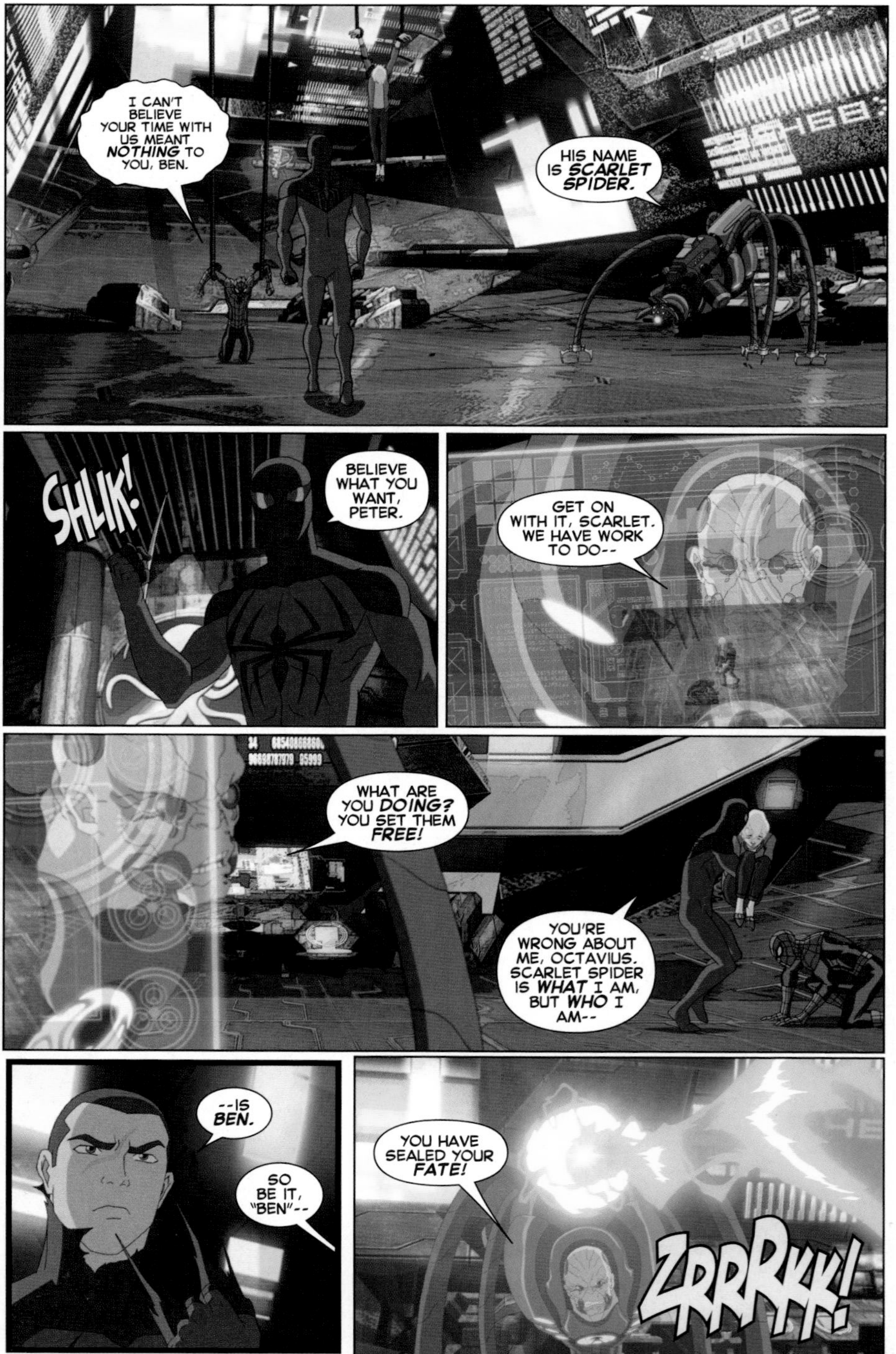
I CAN'T BELIEVE YOUR TIME WITH US MEANT NOTHING TO YOU, BEN.
HIS NAME IS SCARLET SPIDER.
SHLIK!
BELIEVE WHAT YOU WANT, PETER.
GET ON WITH IT, SCARLET. WE HAVE WORK TO DO--
WHAT ARE YOU DOING? YOU SET THEM FREE!
YOU'RE WRONG ABOUT ME, OCTAVIUS. SCARLET SPIDER IS WHAT I AM, BUT WHO I AM--
--IS BEN.
SO BE IT, "BEN"--
YOU HAVE SEALED YOUR FATE!
ZRRRKK!

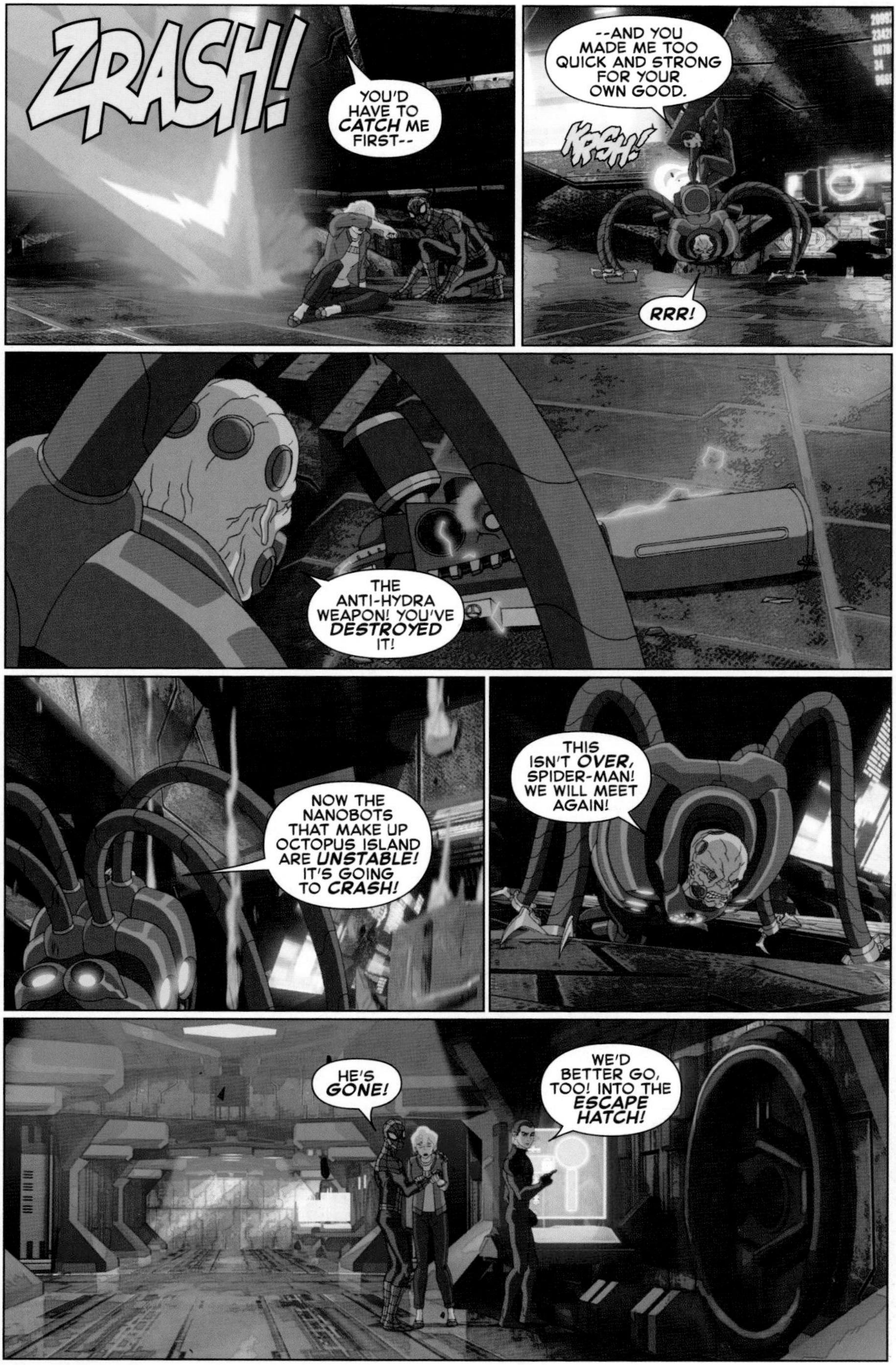
ZRASH!
YOU'D HAVE TO CATCH ME FIRST--
--AND YOU MADE ME TOO QUICK AND STRONG FOR YOUR OWN GOOD.
KRSH!
RRR!
THE ANTI-HYDRA WEAPON! YOU'VE DESTROYED IT!
NOW THE NANOBOTS THAT MAKE UP OCTOPUS ISLAND ARE UNSTABLE! IT'S GOING TO CRASH!
THIS ISN'T OVER, SPIDER-MAN! WE WILL MEET AGAIN!
HE'S GONE!
WE'D BETTER GO, TOO! INTO THE ESCAPE HATCH!

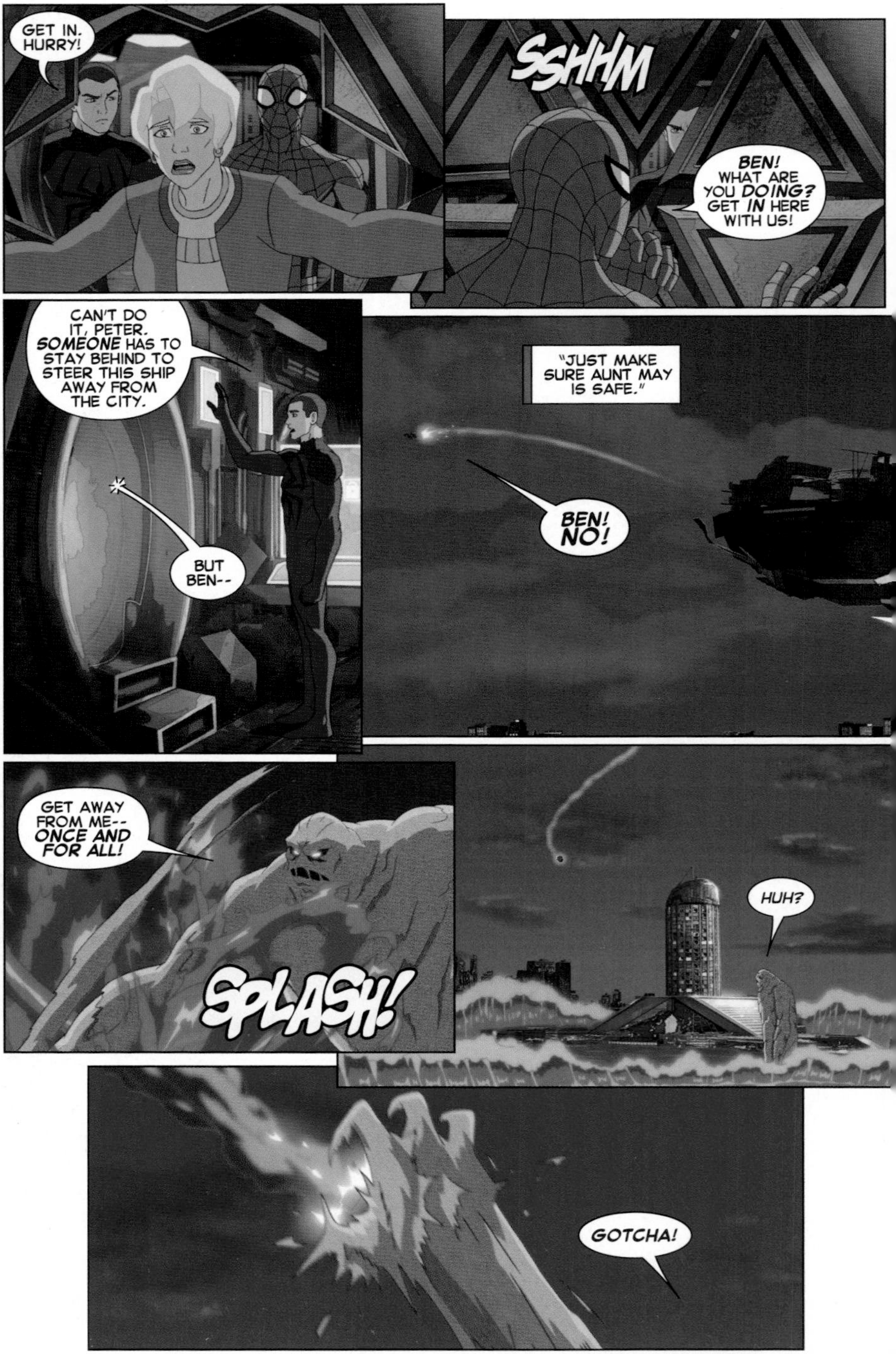
GET IN. HURRY!
SSHHM
BEN! WHAT ARE YOU DOING? GET IN HERE WITH US!
CAN'T DO IT, PETER. SOMEONE HAS TO STAY BEHIND TO STEER THIS SHIP AWAY FROM THE CITY.
BUT BEN--
"JUST MAKE SURE AUNT MAY IS SAFE."
BEN! NO!
GET AWAY FROM ME-- ONCE AND FOR ALL!
SPLASH!
HUH?
GOTCHA!

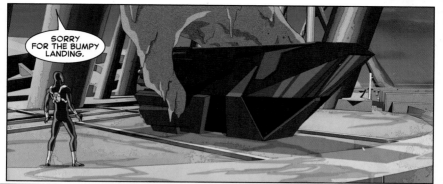

SORRY FOR THE BUMPY LANDING.

SPIDER-MAN! ARE YOU ALL RIGHT?

RRRNNCH

IRON SPIDER, GET THE *SPIDER-JET*! WE MIGHT STILL HAVE TIME!

"TIME FOR WHAT?"

TO SAVE *SCARLET SPIDER'S* LIFE!

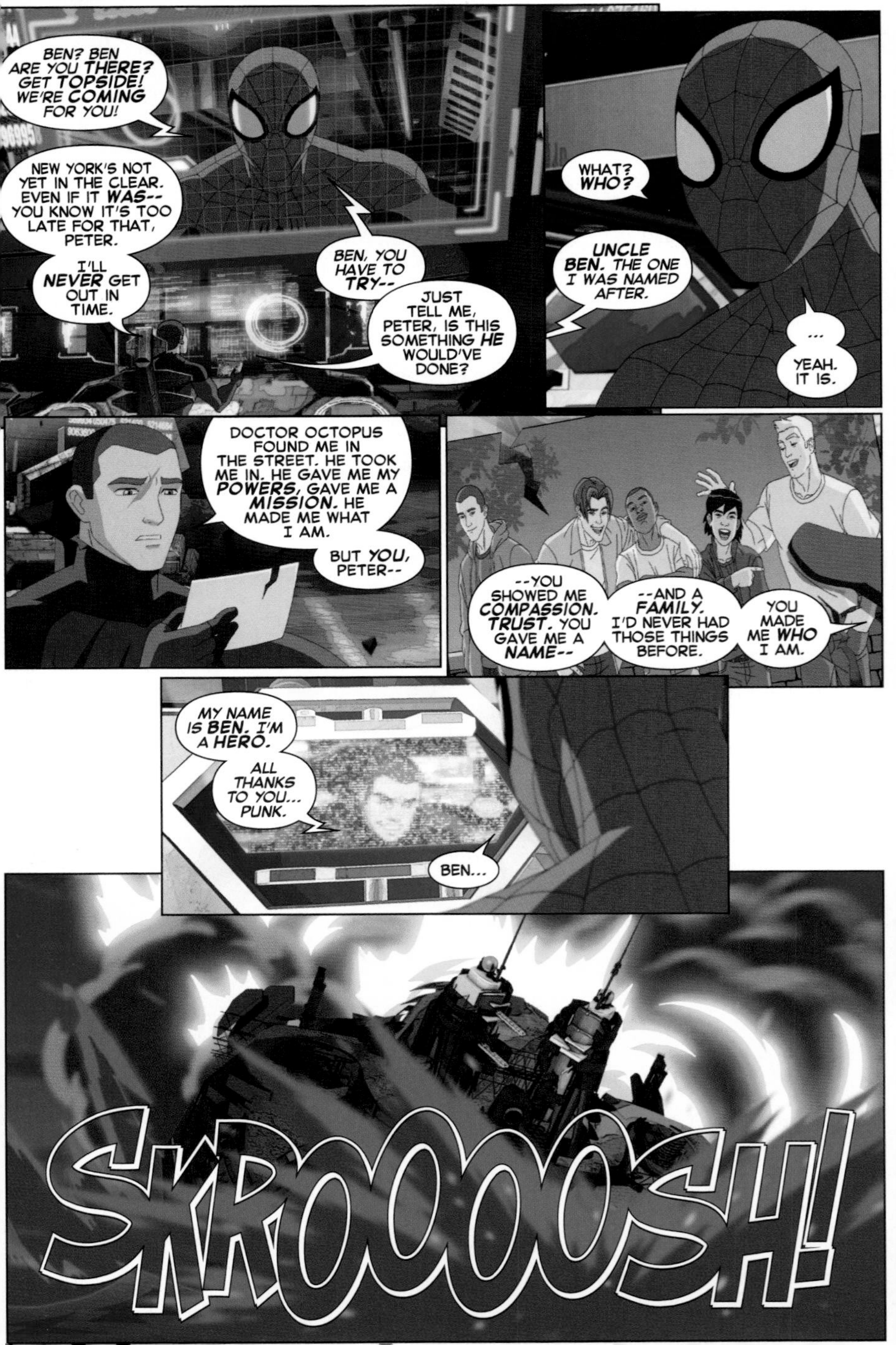
BEN? BEN ARE YOU THERE? GET TOPSIDE! WE'RE COMING FOR YOU!
NEW YORK'S NOT YET IN THE CLEAR. EVEN IF IT WAS-- YOU KNOW IT'S TOO LATE FOR THAT, PETER.
I'LL NEVER GET OUT IN TIME.
BEN, YOU HAVE TO TRY--
JUST TELL ME, PETER, IS THIS SOMETHING HE WOULD'VE DONE?
WHAT? WHO?
UNCLE BEN. THE ONE I WAS NAMED AFTER.
...
YEAH. IT IS.
DOCTOR OCTOPUS FOUND ME IN THE STREET. HE TOOK ME IN. HE GAVE ME MY POWERS, GAVE ME A MISSION. HE MADE ME WHAT I AM.
BUT YOU, PETER--
--YOU SHOWED ME COMPASSION. TRUST. YOU GAVE ME A NAME--
--AND A FAMILY. I'D NEVER HAD THOSE THINGS BEFORE.
YOU MADE ME WHO I AM.
MY NAME IS BEN. I'M A HERO.
ALL THANKS TO YOU... PUNK.
BEN...
SKROOOOSH!

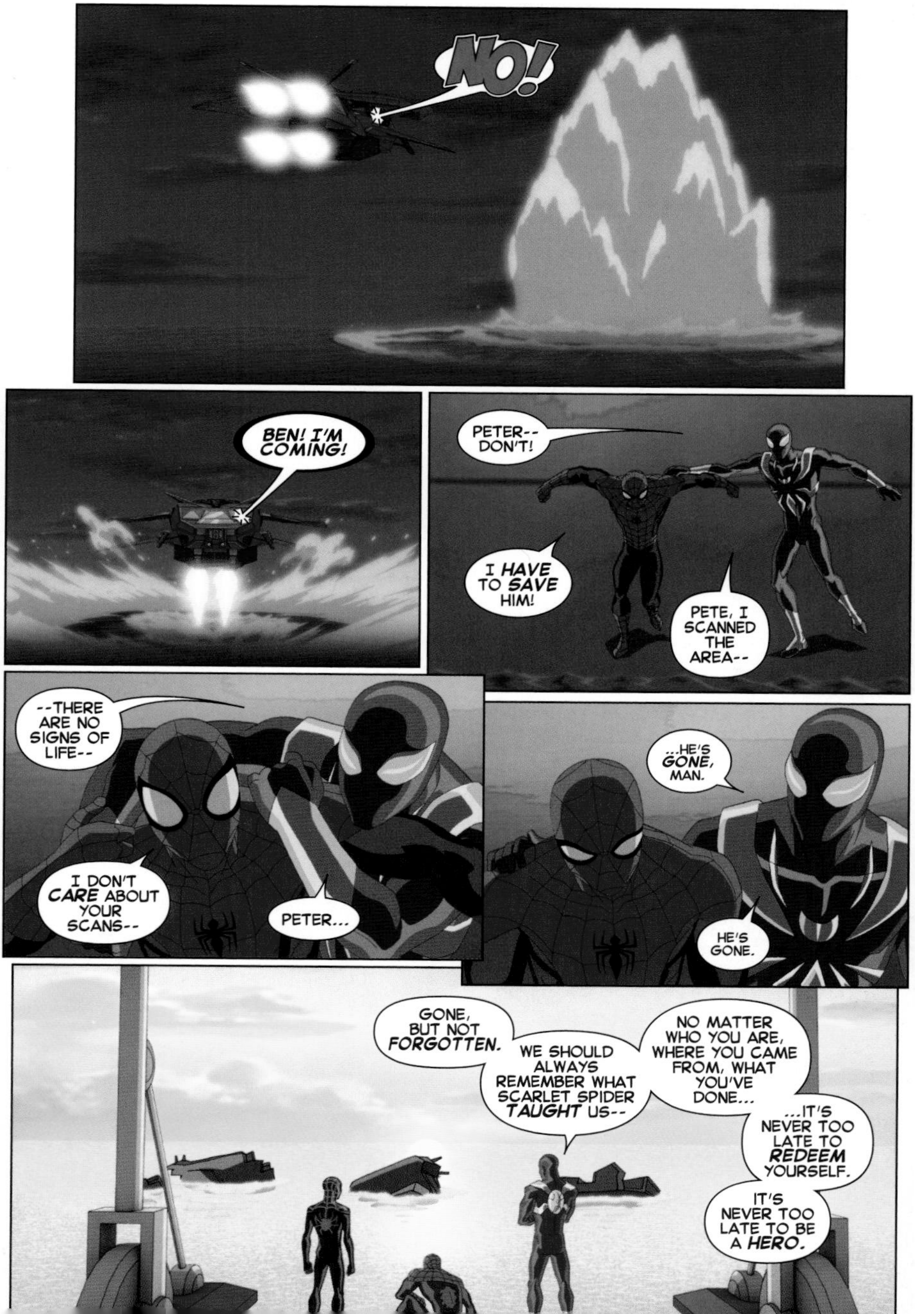
NO!
BEN! I'M COMING!
PETER-- DON'T!
I HAVE TO SAVE HIM!
PETE, I SCANNED THE AREA--
--THERE ARE NO SIGNS OF LIFE--
I DON'T CARE ABOUT YOUR SCANS--
PETER...
...HE'S GONE, MAN.
HE'S GONE.
GONE, BUT NOT FORGOTTEN.
WE SHOULD ALWAYS REMEMBER WHAT SCARLET SPIDER TAUGHT US--
NO MATTER WHO YOU ARE, WHERE YOU CAME FROM, WHAT YOU'VE DONE...
...IT'S NEVER TOO LATE TO REDEEM YOURSELF.
IT'S NEVER TOO LATE TO BE A HERO.

**MARVEL UNIVERSE
ULTIMATE SPIDER-MAN #1**

WHILE ATTENDING A DEMONSTRATION IN RADIOLOGY, HIGH SCHOOL STUDENT PETER PARKER WAS BITTEN BY A SPIDER THAT HAD ACCIDENTALLY BEEN EXPOSED TO RADIOACTIVE RAYS. THROUGH A MIRACLE OF SCIENCE, PETER SOON FOUND THAT HE HAD GAINED THE SPIDER'S POWERS...AND HAD, IN EFFECT, BECOME A HUMAN SPIDER! FROM THAT DAY ON, HE HAS ENDEAVORED TO BECOME THE...

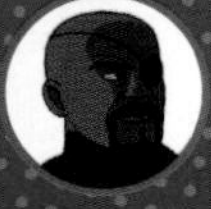

NICK FURY

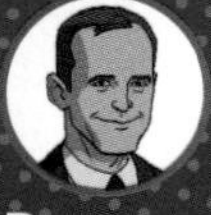

PRINCIPAL COULSON

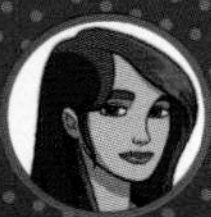

MARY JANE WATSON

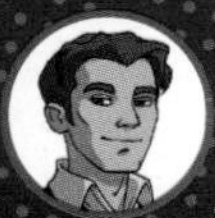

HARRY OSBORN

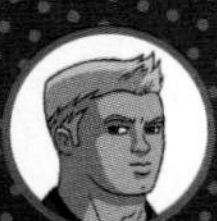

FLASH THOMPSON

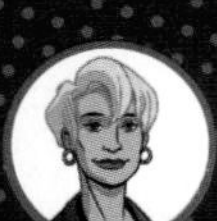

AUNT MAY

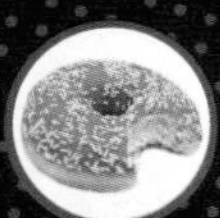

A DONUT (YUM!)

MARVEL ULTIMATE SPIDER-MAN™

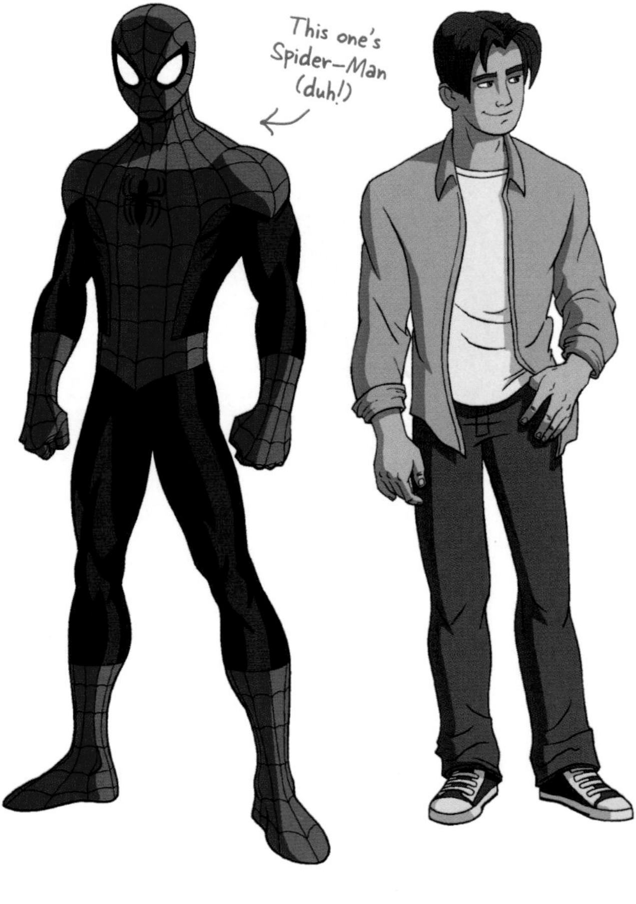
This one's Spider-Man (duh!)

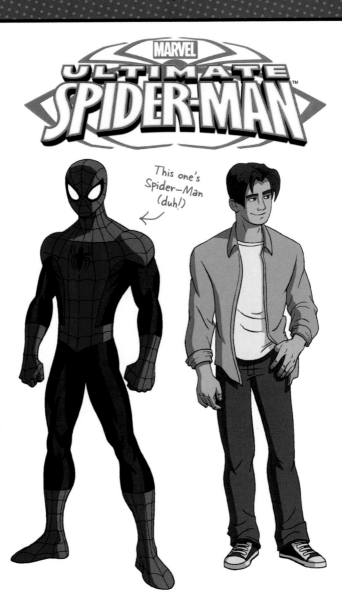

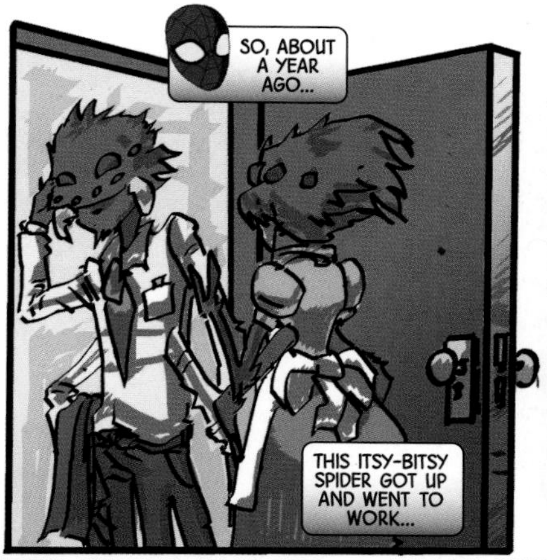
SO, ABOUT A YEAR AGO...
THIS ITSY-BITSY SPIDER GOT UP AND WENT TO WORK...

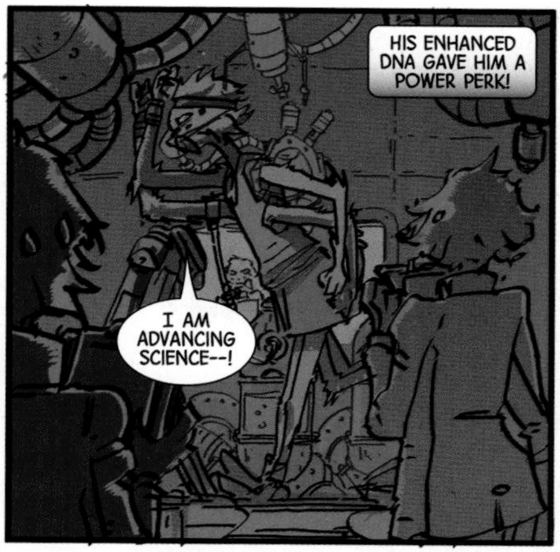
HIS ENHANCED DNA GAVE HIM A POWER PERK!
I AM ADVANCING SCIENCE--!

WRITTEN BY MAN OF ACTION ART BY NUNO PLATI LETTERS BY VC'S JOE CARAMAGNA

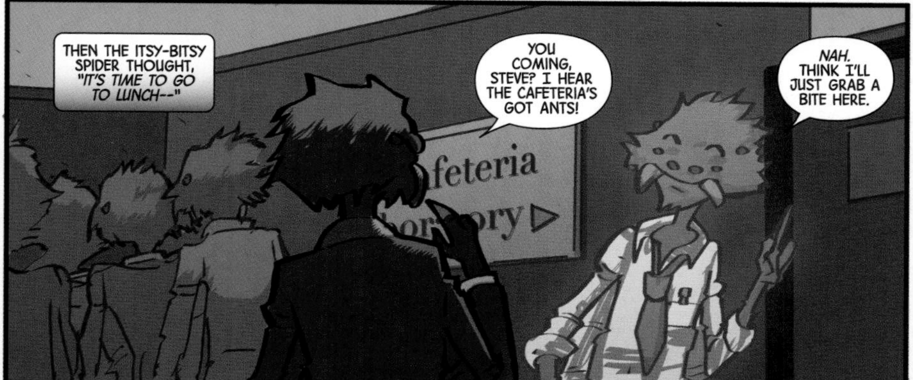
THEN THE ITSY-BITSY SPIDER THOUGHT, *"IT'S TIME TO GO TO LUNCH--"*
YOU COMING, STEVE? I HEAR THE CAFETERIA'S GOT ANTS!
NAH. THINK I'LL JUST GRAB A BITE HERE.

ASSISTANT EDITOR: ELLIE PYLE ASSOCIATE EDITOR: TOM BRENNAN EDITOR: STEPHEN WACKER

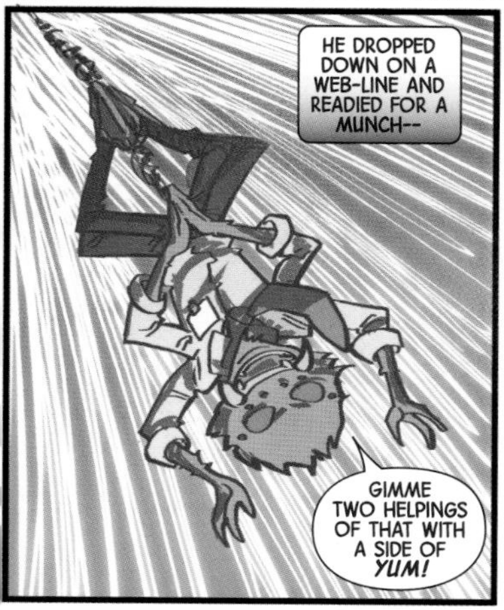
HE DROPPED DOWN ON A WEB-LINE AND READIED FOR A MUNCH--
GIMME TWO HELPINGS OF THAT WITH A SIDE OF *YUM!*

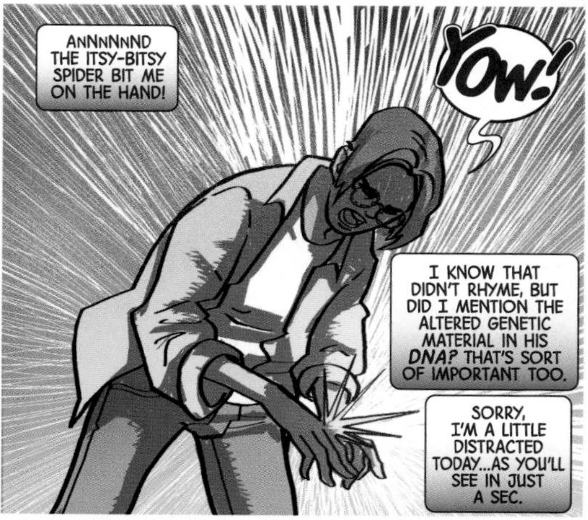
ANNNNNND THE ITSY-BITSY SPIDER BIT ME ON THE HAND!
YOW!
I KNOW THAT DIDN'T RHYME, BUT DID I MENTION THE ALTERED GENETIC MATERIAL IN HIS *DNA?* THAT'S SORT OF IMPORTANT TOO.
SORRY, I'M A LITTLE DISTRACTED TODAY...AS YOU'LL SEE IN JUST A SEC.

ALONSO, QUESADA, LOEB, BUCKLEY, FINE – THE BOSSES

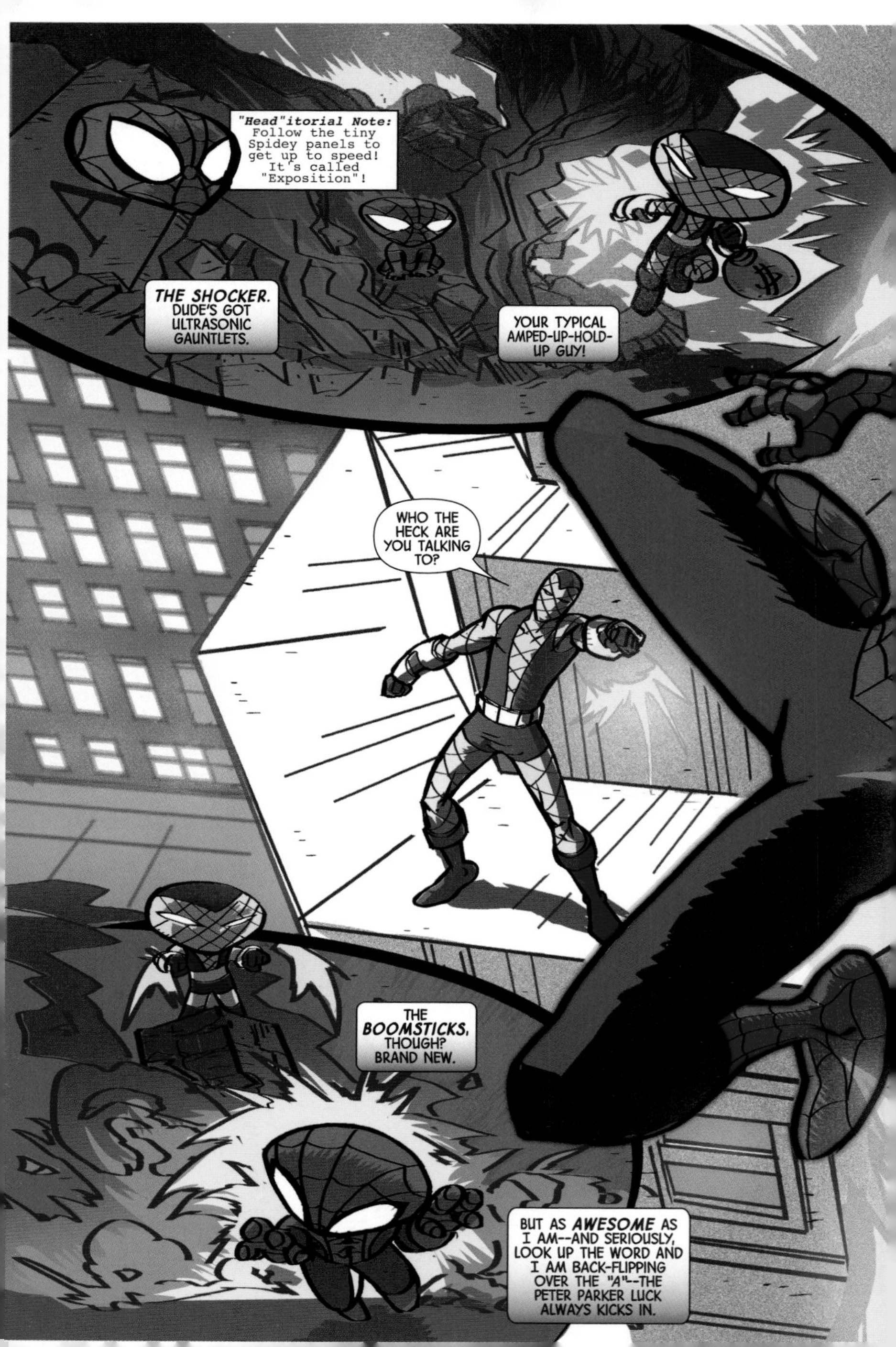
"Head"itorial Note: Follow the tiny Spidey panels to get up to speed! It's called "Exposition"!
THE SHOCKER. DUDE'S GOT ULTRASONIC GAUNTLETS.
YOUR TYPICAL AMPED-UP-HOLD-UP GUY!
WHO THE HECK ARE YOU TALKING TO?
THE BOOMSTICKS, THOUGH? BRAND NEW.
BUT AS AWESOME AS I AM--AND SERIOUSLY, LOOK UP THE WORD AND I AM BACK-FLIPPING OVER THE "A"--THE PETER PARKER LUCK ALWAYS KICKS IN.

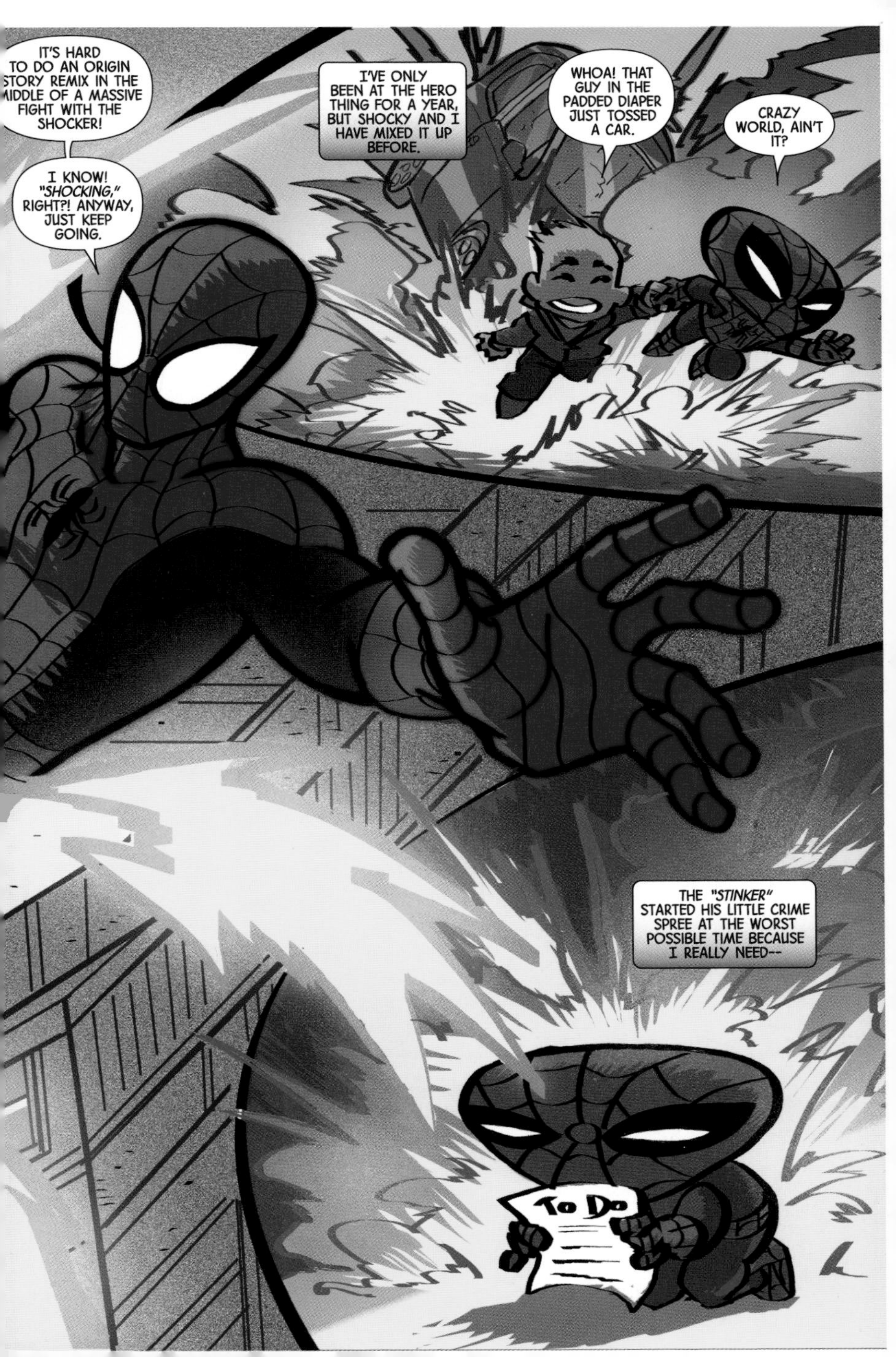
IT'S HARD TO DO AN ORIGIN STORY REMIX IN THE MIDDLE OF A MASSIVE FIGHT WITH THE SHOCKER!
I KNOW! "SHOCKING," RIGHT?! ANYWAY, JUST KEEP GOING.
I'VE ONLY BEEN AT THE HERO THING FOR A YEAR, BUT SHOCKY AND I HAVE MIXED IT UP BEFORE.
WHOA! THAT GUY IN THE PADDED DIAPER JUST TOSSED A CAR.
CRAZY WORLD, AIN'T IT?
THE "STINKER" STARTED HIS LITTLE CRIME SPREE AT THE WORST POSSIBLE TIME BECAUSE I REALLY NEED--
To Do

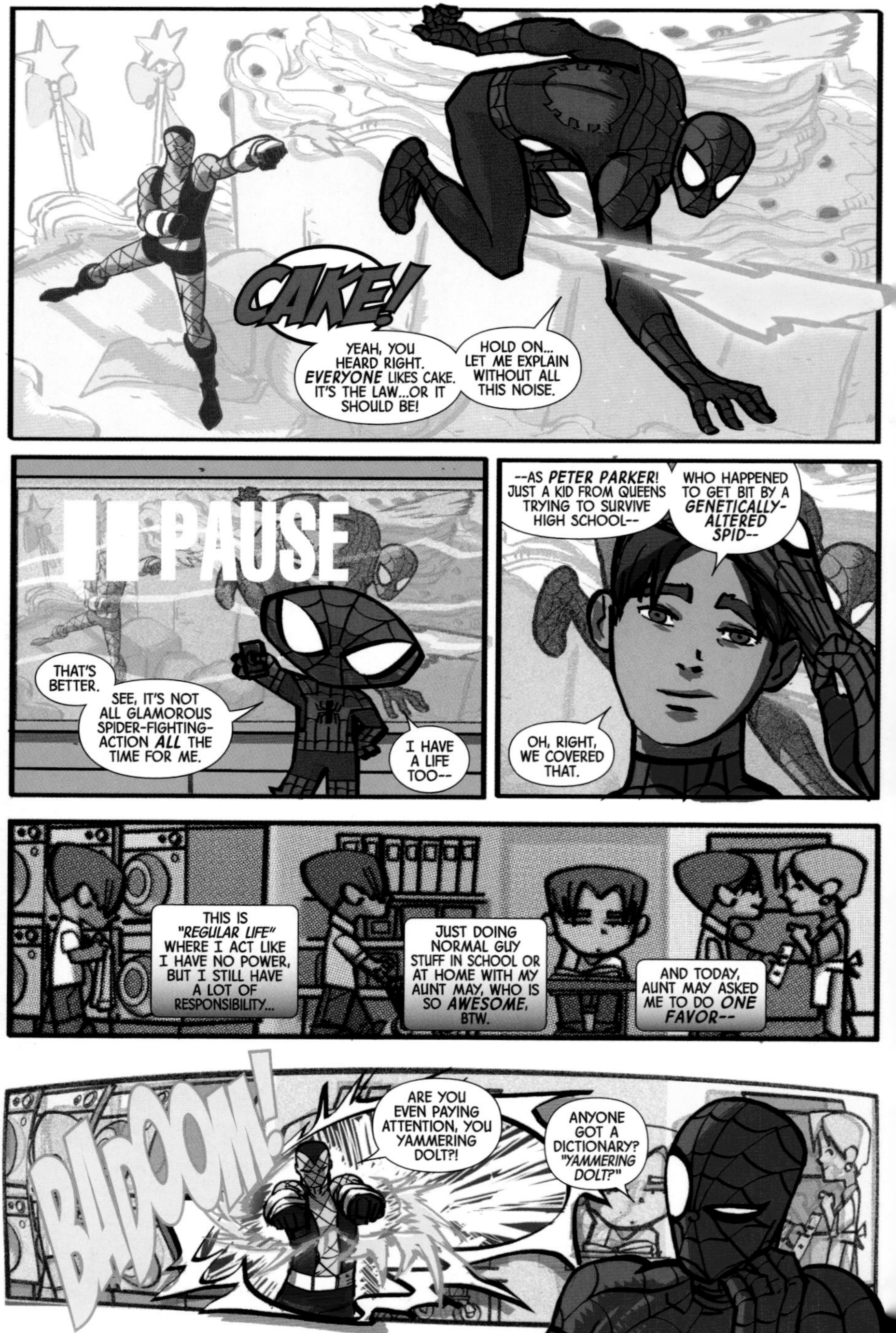
CAKE!
YEAH, YOU HEARD RIGHT. EVERYONE LIKES CAKE. IT'S THE LAW...OR IT SHOULD BE!
HOLD ON... LET ME EXPLAIN WITHOUT ALL THIS NOISE.
PAUSE
THAT'S BETTER.
SEE, IT'S NOT ALL GLAMOROUS SPIDER-FIGHTING-ACTION ALL THE TIME FOR ME.
I HAVE A LIFE TOO--
--AS PETER PARKER! JUST A KID FROM QUEENS TRYING TO SURVIVE HIGH SCHOOL--
WHO HAPPENED TO GET BIT BY A GENETICALLY-ALTERED SPID--
OH, RIGHT, WE COVERED THAT.
THIS IS "REGULAR LIFE" WHERE I ACT LIKE I HAVE NO POWER, BUT I STILL HAVE A LOT OF RESPONSIBILITY...
JUST DOING NORMAL GUY STUFF IN SCHOOL OR AT HOME WITH MY AUNT MAY, WHO IS SO AWESOME, BTW.
AND TODAY, AUNT MAY ASKED ME TO DO ONE FAVOR--
BADOOM!
ARE YOU EVEN PAYING ATTENTION, YOU YAMMERING DOLT?!
ANYONE GOT A DICTIONARY? "YAMMERING DOLT?"

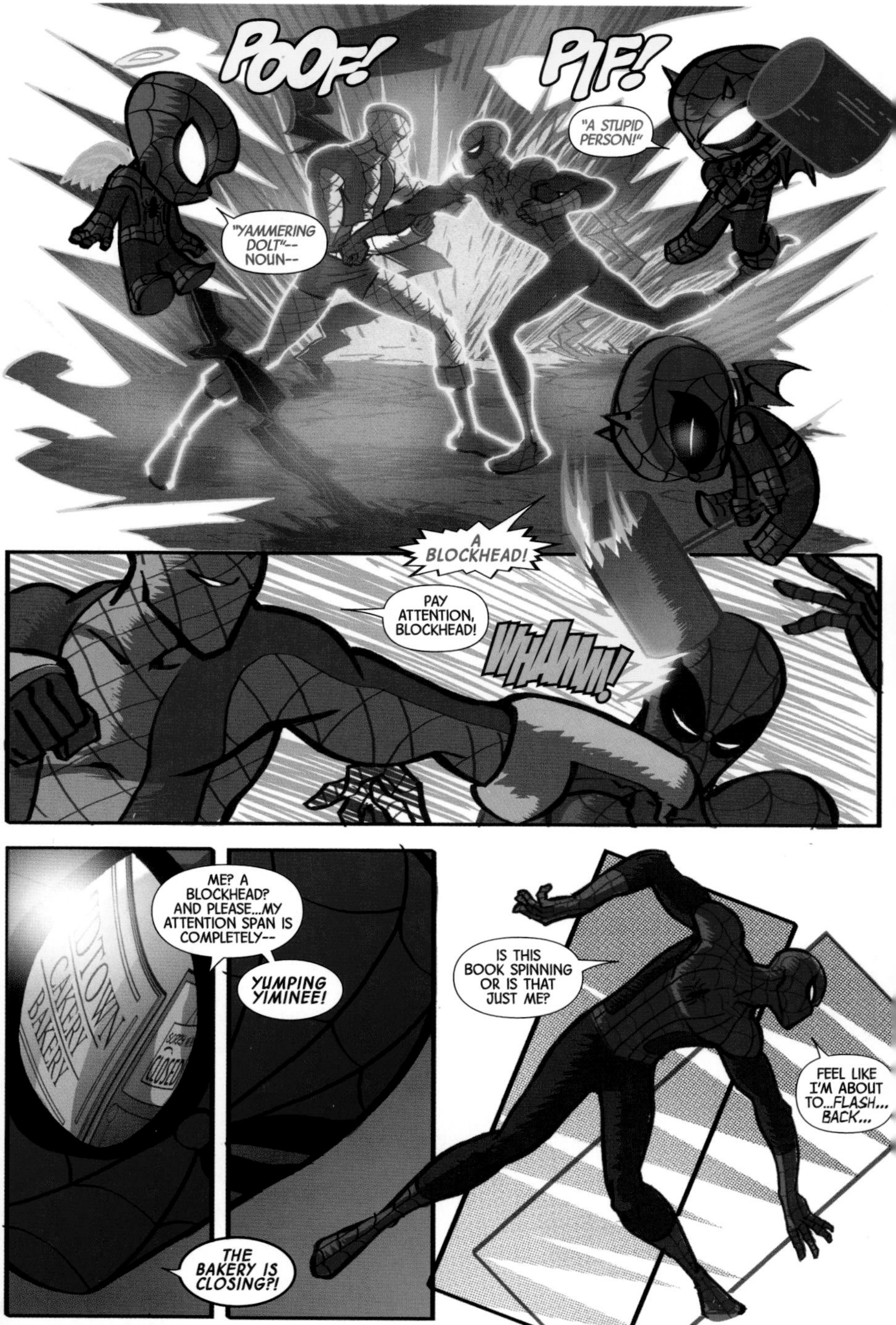
POOF!
PIF!
"A STUPID PERSON!"
"YAMMERING DOLT"-- NOUN--
A BLOCKHEAD!
PAY ATTENTION, BLOCKHEAD!
WHAMM!
ME? A BLOCKHEAD? AND PLEASE...MY ATTENTION SPAN IS COMPLETELY--
YUMPING YIMINEE!
CAKERY
BAKERY
CLOSED
THE BAKERY IS CLOSING?!
IS THIS BOOK SPINNING OR IS THAT JUST ME?
FEEL LIKE I'M ABOUT TO...FLASH... BACK...

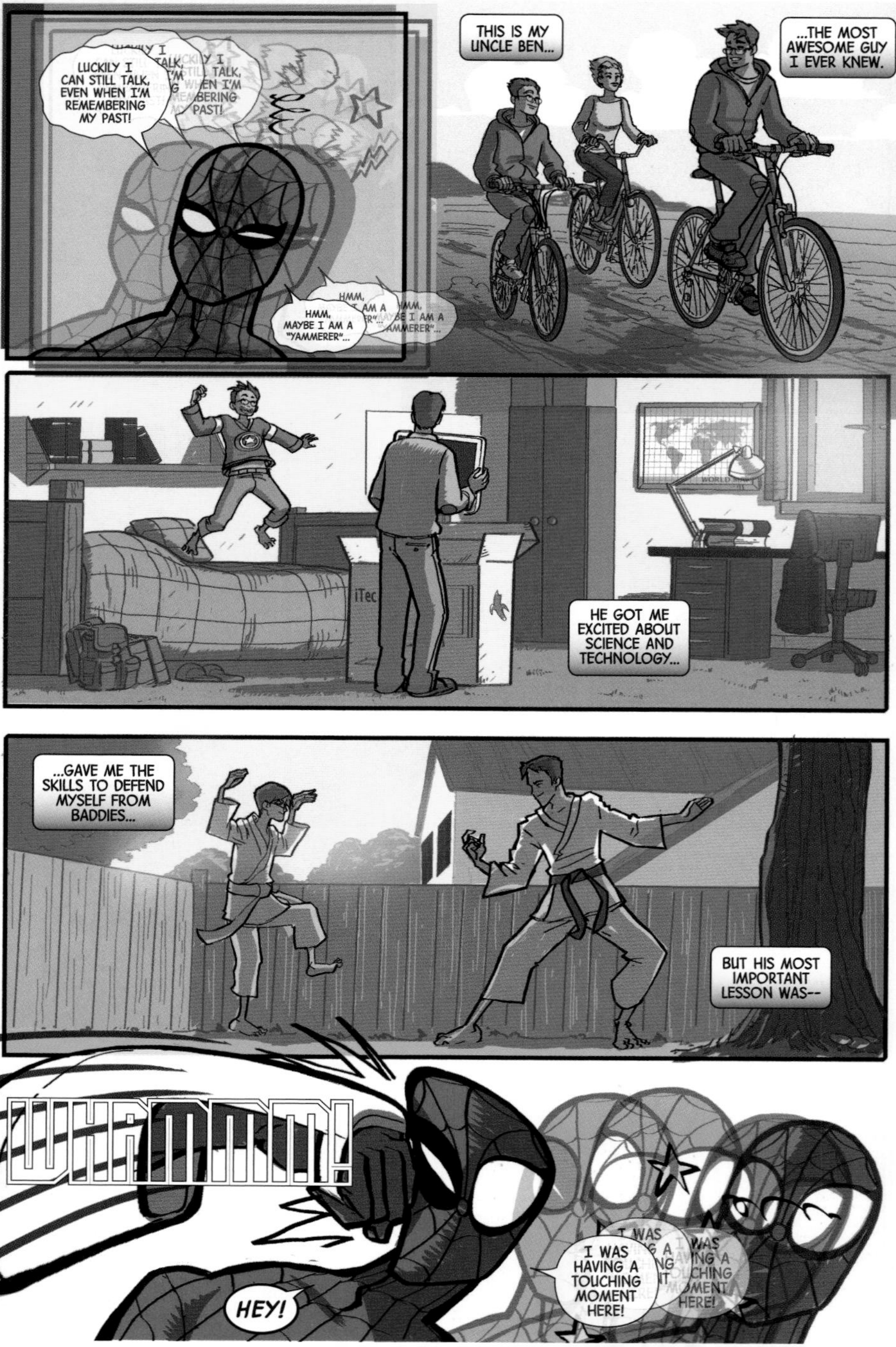
LUCKILY I CAN STILL TALK, EVEN WHEN I'M REMEMBERING MY PAST!
HMM, MAYBE I AM A "YAMMERER"...
THIS IS MY UNCLE BEN...
...THE MOST AWESOME GUY I EVER KNEW.
HE GOT ME EXCITED ABOUT SCIENCE AND TECHNOLOGY...
...GAVE ME THE SKILLS TO DEFEND MYSELF FROM BADDIES...
BUT HIS MOST IMPORTANT LESSON WAS--
WHAMMM!
HEY!
I WAS HAVING A TOUCHING MOMENT HERE!

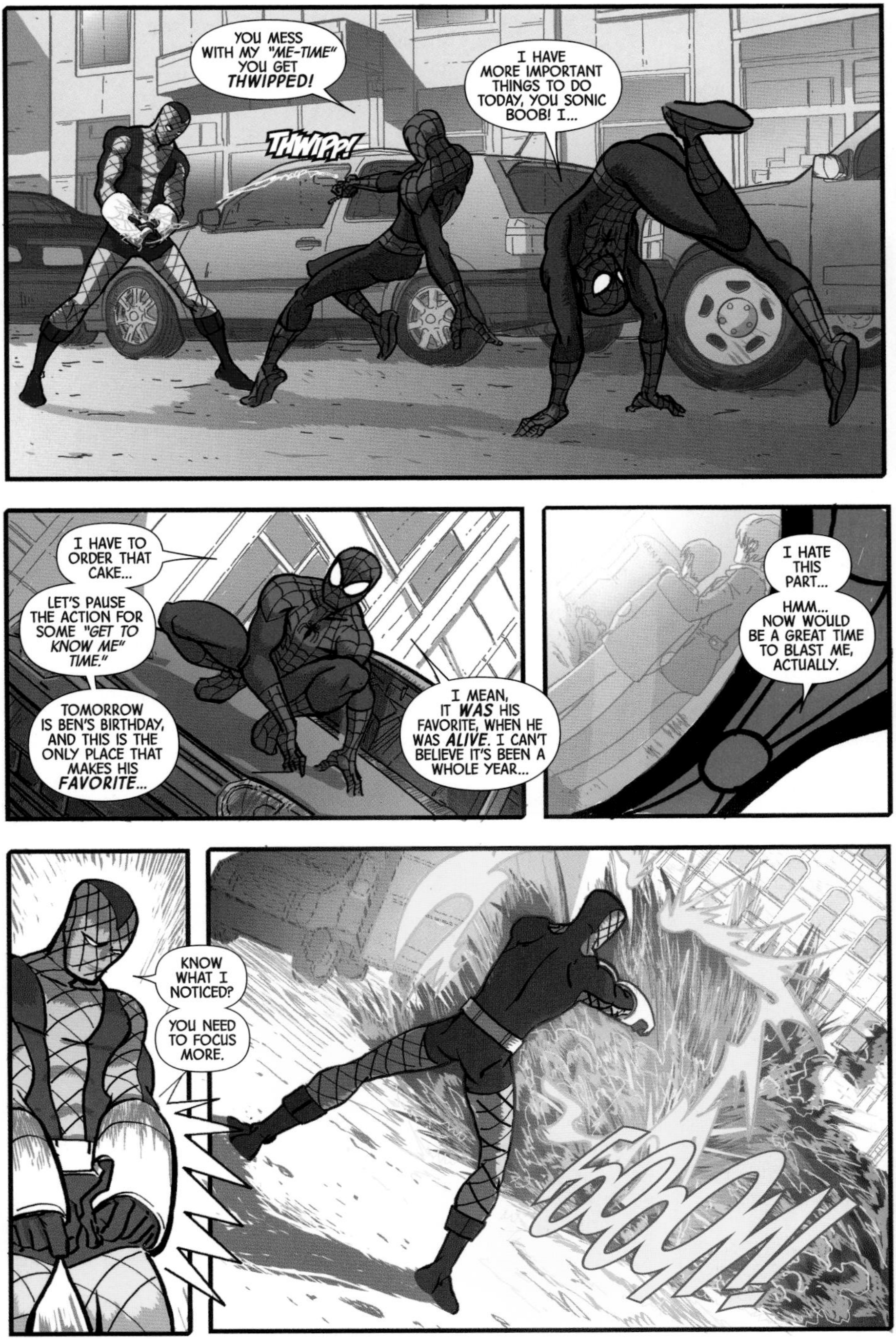
YOU MESS WITH MY "ME-TIME" YOU GET THWIPPED!
THWIPP!
I HAVE MORE IMPORTANT THINGS TO DO TODAY, YOU SONIC BOOB! I...
I HAVE TO ORDER THAT CAKE...
LET'S PAUSE THE ACTION FOR SOME "GET TO KNOW ME" TIME."
TOMORROW IS BEN'S BIRTHDAY, AND THIS IS THE ONLY PLACE THAT MAKES HIS FAVORITE...
I MEAN, IT WAS HIS FAVORITE, WHEN HE WAS ALIVE. I CAN'T BELIEVE IT'S BEEN A WHOLE YEAR...
I HATE THIS PART...
HMM... NOW WOULD BE A GREAT TIME TO BLAST ME, ACTUALLY.
KNOW WHAT I NOTICED?
YOU NEED TO FOCUS MORE.
BOOM!

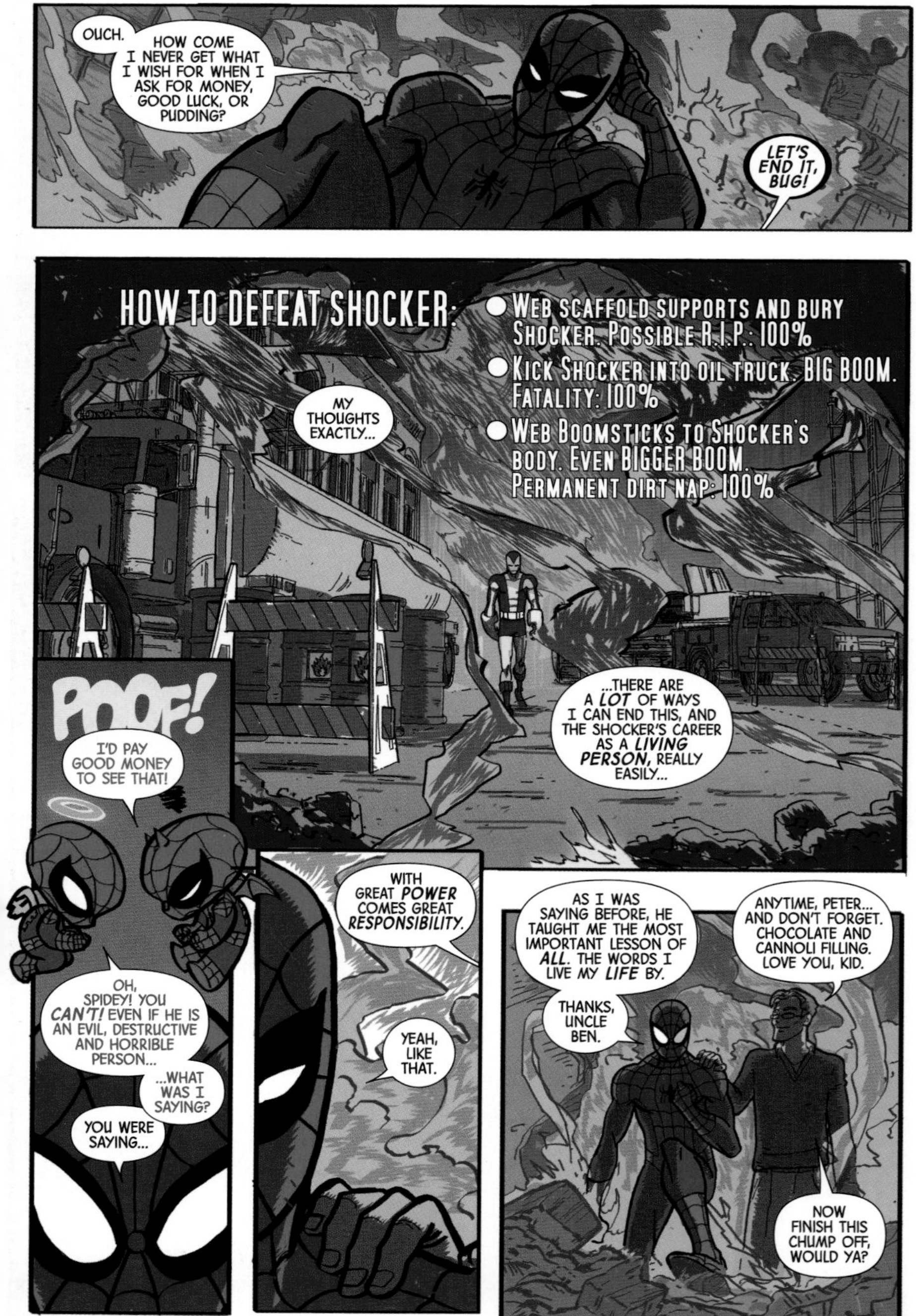
OUCH.
HOW COME I NEVER GET WHAT I WISH FOR WHEN I ASK FOR MONEY, GOOD LUCK, OR PUDDING?
LET'S END IT, BUG!
HOW TO DEFEAT SHOCKER:
Web scaffold supports and bury Shocker. Possible R.I.P.: 100%
Kick Shocker into oil truck. BIG BOOM. Fatality: 100%
Web Boomsticks to Shocker's body. Even BIGGER BOOM. Permanent dirt nap: 100%
MY THOUGHTS EXACTLY...
...THERE ARE A LOT OF WAYS I CAN END THIS, AND THE SHOCKER'S CAREER AS A LIVING PERSON, REALLY EASILY...
POOF!
I'D PAY GOOD MONEY TO SEE THAT!
OH, SPIDEY! YOU CAN'T! EVEN IF HE IS AN EVIL, DESTRUCTIVE AND HORRIBLE PERSON...
...WHAT WAS I SAYING?
YOU WERE SAYING...
WITH GREAT POWER COMES GREAT RESPONSIBILITY.
YEAH, LIKE THAT.
AS I WAS SAYING BEFORE, HE TAUGHT ME THE MOST IMPORTANT LESSON OF ALL. THE WORDS I LIVE MY LIFE BY.
THANKS, UNCLE BEN.
ANYTIME, PETER... AND DON'T FORGET. CHOCOLATE AND CANNOLI FILLING. LOVE YOU, KID.
NOW FINISH THIS CHUMP OFF, WOULD YA?

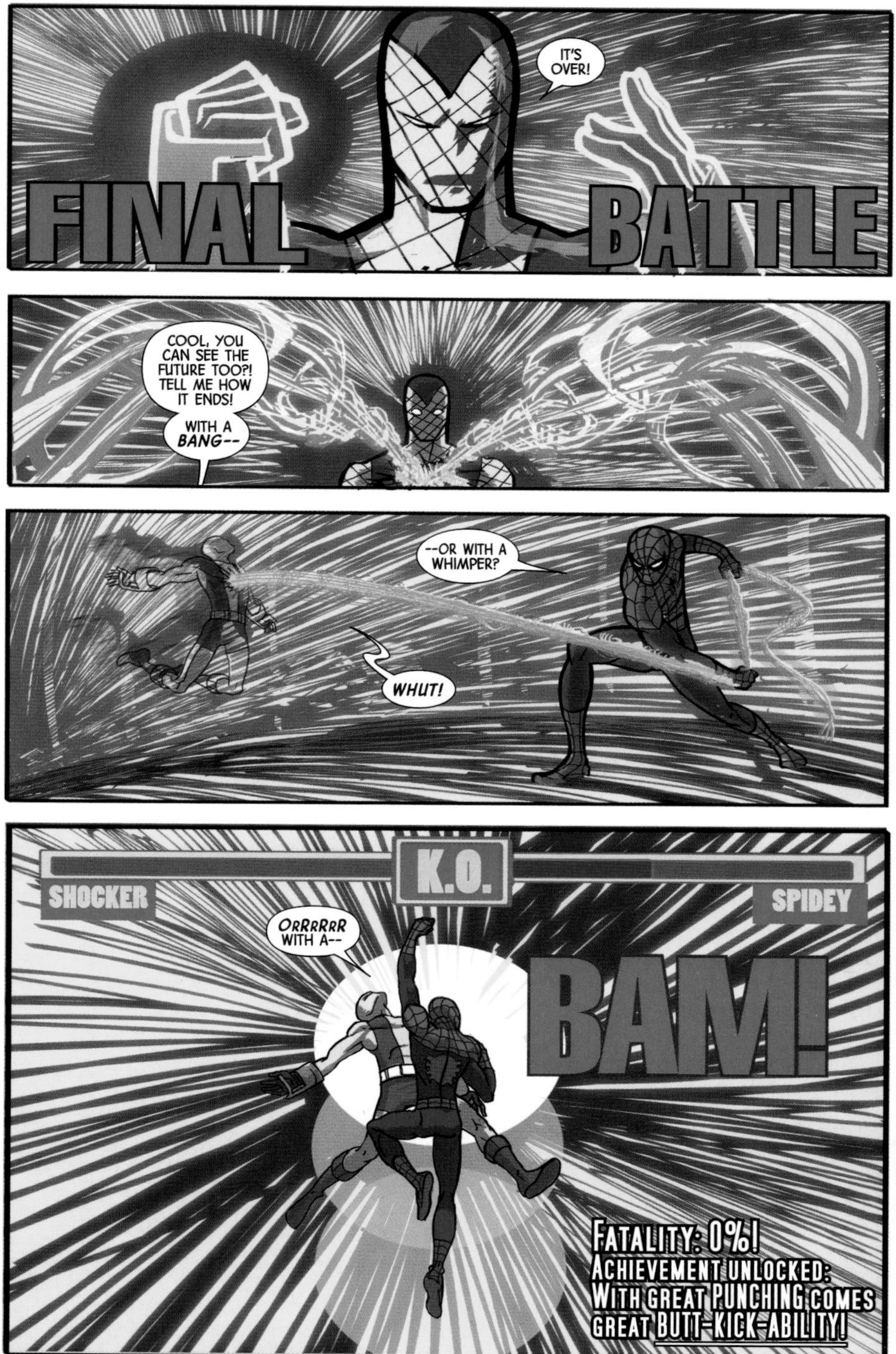
IT'S OVER!
FINAL BATTLE
COOL, YOU CAN SEE THE FUTURE TOO?! TELL ME HOW IT ENDS!
WITH A *BANG*--
--OR WITH A WHIMPER?
WHUT!
K.O.
SHOCKER
SPIDEY
ORRRRRR WITH A--
BAM!
FATALITY: 0%!
ACHIEVEMENT UNLOCKED:
WITH GREAT PUNCHING COMES
GREAT BUTT-KICK-ABILITY!

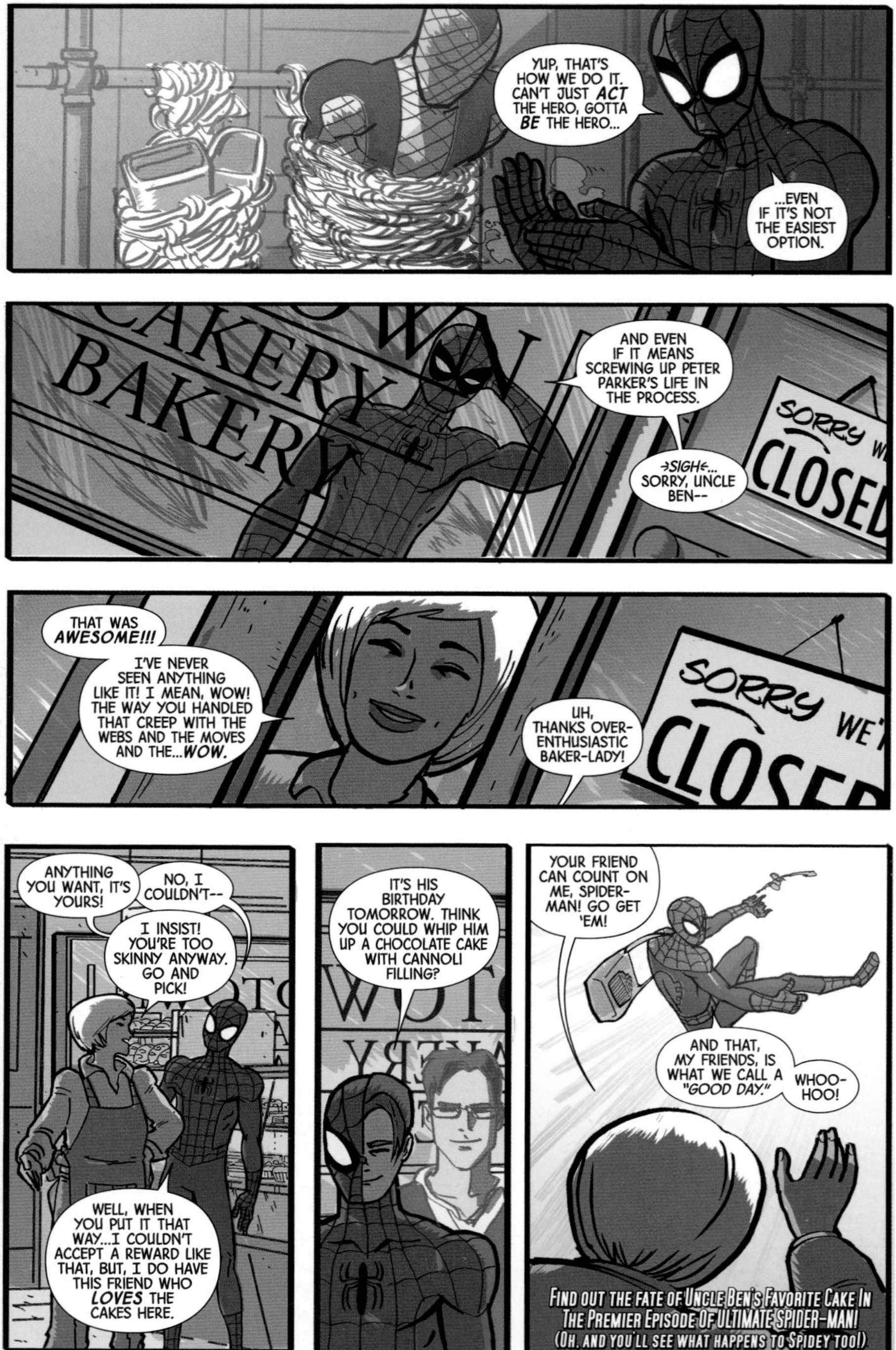
YUP, THAT'S HOW WE DO IT. CAN'T JUST *ACT* THE HERO, GOTTA *BE* THE HERO...
...EVEN IF IT'S NOT THE EASIEST OPTION.
CAKERY
BAKERY
AND EVEN IF IT MEANS SCREWING UP PETER PARKER'S LIFE IN THE PROCESS.
→SIGH←... SORRY, UNCLE BEN--
SORRY WE
CLOSED
THAT WAS *AWESOME!!!*
I'VE NEVER SEEN ANYTHING LIKE IT! I MEAN, WOW! THE WAY YOU HANDLED THAT CREEP WITH THE WEBS AND THE MOVES AND THE...*WOW.*
UH, THANKS OVER-ENTHUSIASTIC BAKER-LADY!
SORRY WE'
CLOSE
ANYTHING YOU WANT, IT'S YOURS!
NO, I COULDN'T--
I INSIST! YOU'RE TOO SKINNY ANYWAY. GO AND PICK!
WELL, WHEN YOU PUT IT THAT WAY...I COULDN'T ACCEPT A REWARD LIKE THAT, BUT, I DO HAVE THIS FRIEND WHO *LOVES* THE CAKES HERE.
IT'S HIS BIRTHDAY TOMORROW. THINK YOU COULD WHIP HIM UP A CHOCOLATE CAKE WITH CANNOLI FILLING?
YOUR FRIEND CAN COUNT ON ME, SPIDER-MAN! GO GET 'EM!
AND THAT, MY FRIENDS, IS WHAT WE CALL A *"GOOD DAY."*
WHOO-HOO!
FIND OUT THE FATE OF UNCLE BEN'S FAVORITE CAKE IN THE PREMIER EPISODE OF ULTIMATE SPIDER-MAN!
(OH, AND YOU'LL SEE WHAT HAPPENS TO SPIDEY TOO!)

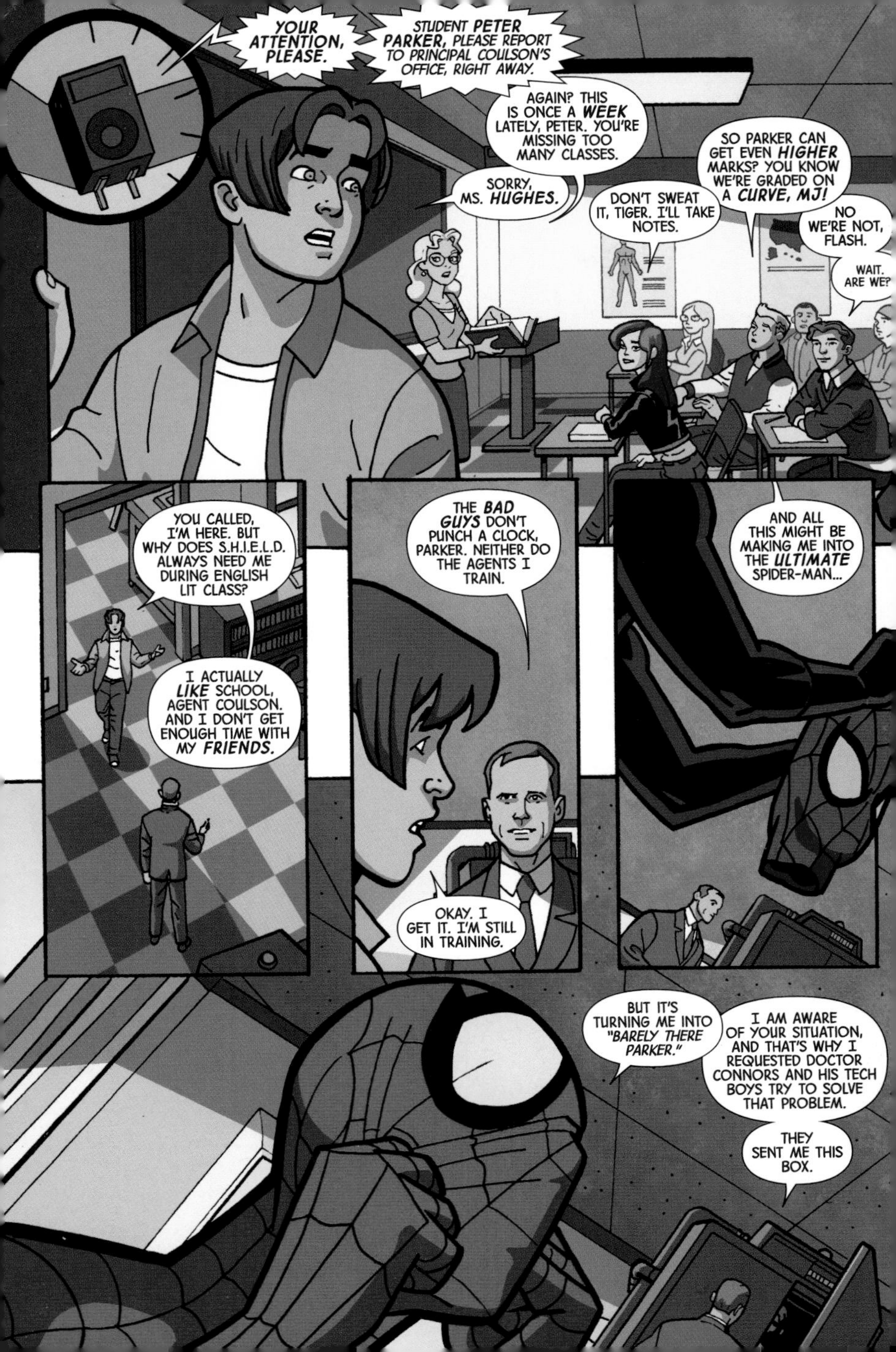
YOUR ATTENTION, PLEASE.
STUDENT PETER PARKER, PLEASE REPORT TO PRINCIPAL COULSON'S OFFICE, RIGHT AWAY.
AGAIN? THIS IS ONCE A WEEK LATELY, PETER. YOU'RE MISSING TOO MANY CLASSES.
SORRY, MS. HUGHES.
DON'T SWEAT IT, TIGER. I'LL TAKE NOTES.
SO PARKER CAN GET EVEN HIGHER MARKS? YOU KNOW WE'RE GRADED ON A CURVE, MJ!
NO WE'RE NOT, FLASH.
WAIT. ARE WE?
YOU CALLED, I'M HERE. BUT WHY DOES S.H.I.E.L.D. ALWAYS NEED ME DURING ENGLISH LIT CLASS?
I ACTUALLY LIKE SCHOOL, AGENT COULSON. AND I DON'T GET ENOUGH TIME WITH MY FRIENDS.
THE BAD GUYS DON'T PUNCH A CLOCK, PARKER. NEITHER DO THE AGENTS I TRAIN.
OKAY. I GET IT. I'M STILL IN TRAINING.
AND ALL THIS MIGHT BE MAKING ME INTO THE ULTIMATE SPIDER-MAN...
BUT IT'S TURNING ME INTO "BARELY THERE PARKER."
I AM AWARE OF YOUR SITUATION, AND THAT'S WHY I REQUESTED DOCTOR CONNORS AND HIS TECH BOYS TRY TO SOLVE THAT PROBLEM.
THEY SENT ME THIS BOX.

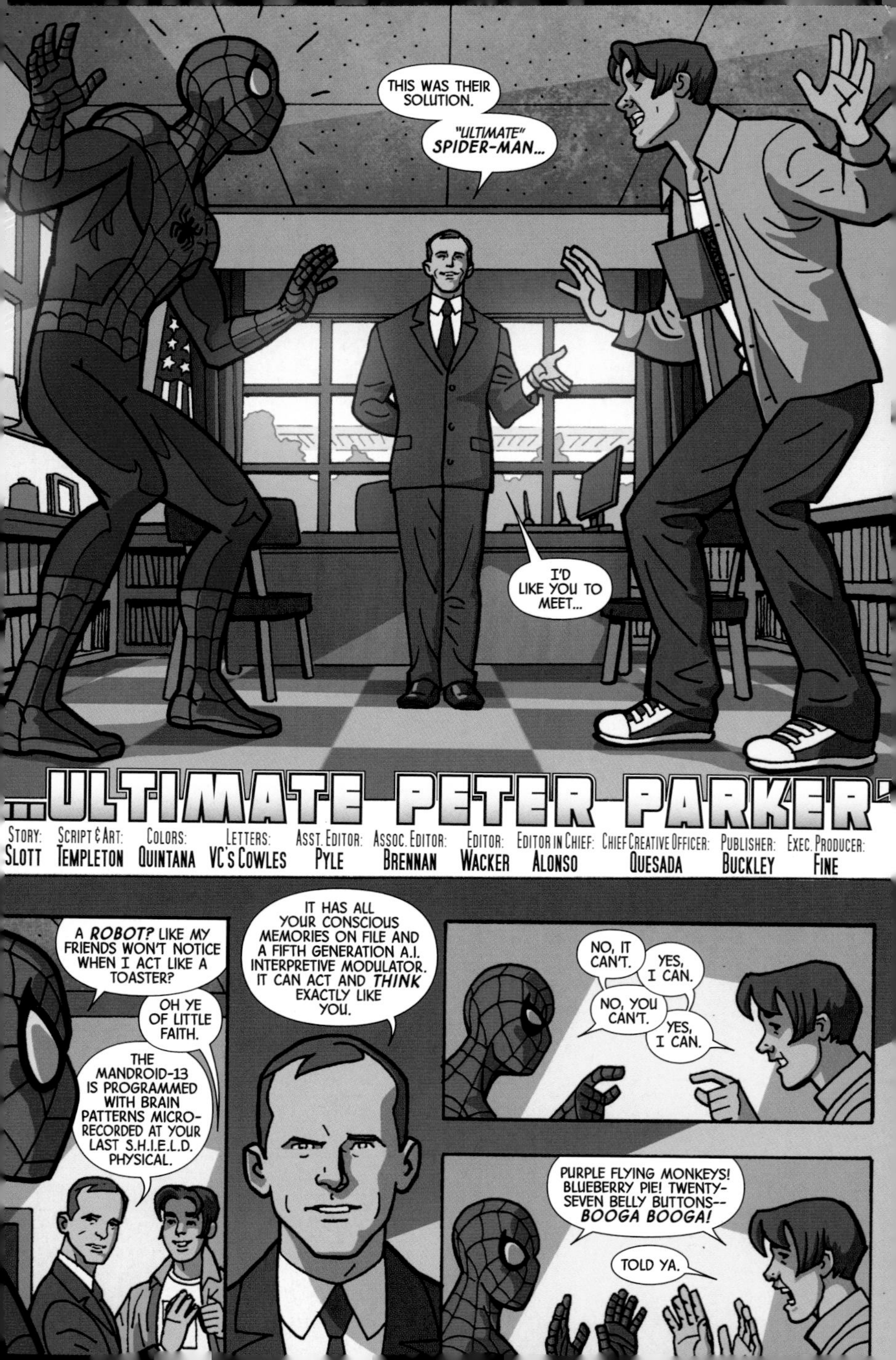
THIS WAS THEIR SOLUTION.
"ULTIMATE" SPIDER-MAN...
I'D LIKE YOU TO MEET...
...ULTIMATE PETER PARKER'
STORY: SLOTT
SCRIPT & ART: TEMPLETON
COLORS: QUINTANA
LETTERS: VC'S COWLES
ASST. EDITOR: PYLE
ASSOC. EDITOR: BRENNAN
EDITOR: WACKER
EDITOR IN CHIEF: ALONSO
CHIEF CREATIVE OFFICER: QUESADA
PUBLISHER: BUCKLEY
EXEC. PRODUCER: FINE
A ROBOT? LIKE MY FRIENDS WON'T NOTICE WHEN I ACT LIKE A TOASTER?
OH YE OF LITTLE FAITH.
THE MANDROID-13 IS PROGRAMMED WITH BRAIN PATTERNS MICRO-RECORDED AT YOUR LAST S.H.I.E.L.D. PHYSICAL.
IT HAS ALL YOUR CONSCIOUS MEMORIES ON FILE AND A FIFTH GENERATION A.I. INTERPRETIVE MODULATOR. IT CAN ACT AND THINK EXACTLY LIKE YOU.
NO, IT CAN'T.
YES, I CAN.
NO, YOU CAN'T.
YES, I CAN.
PURPLE FLYING MONKEYS! BLUEBERRY PIE! TWENTY-SEVEN BELLY BUTTONS-- BOOGA BOOGA!
TOLD YA.

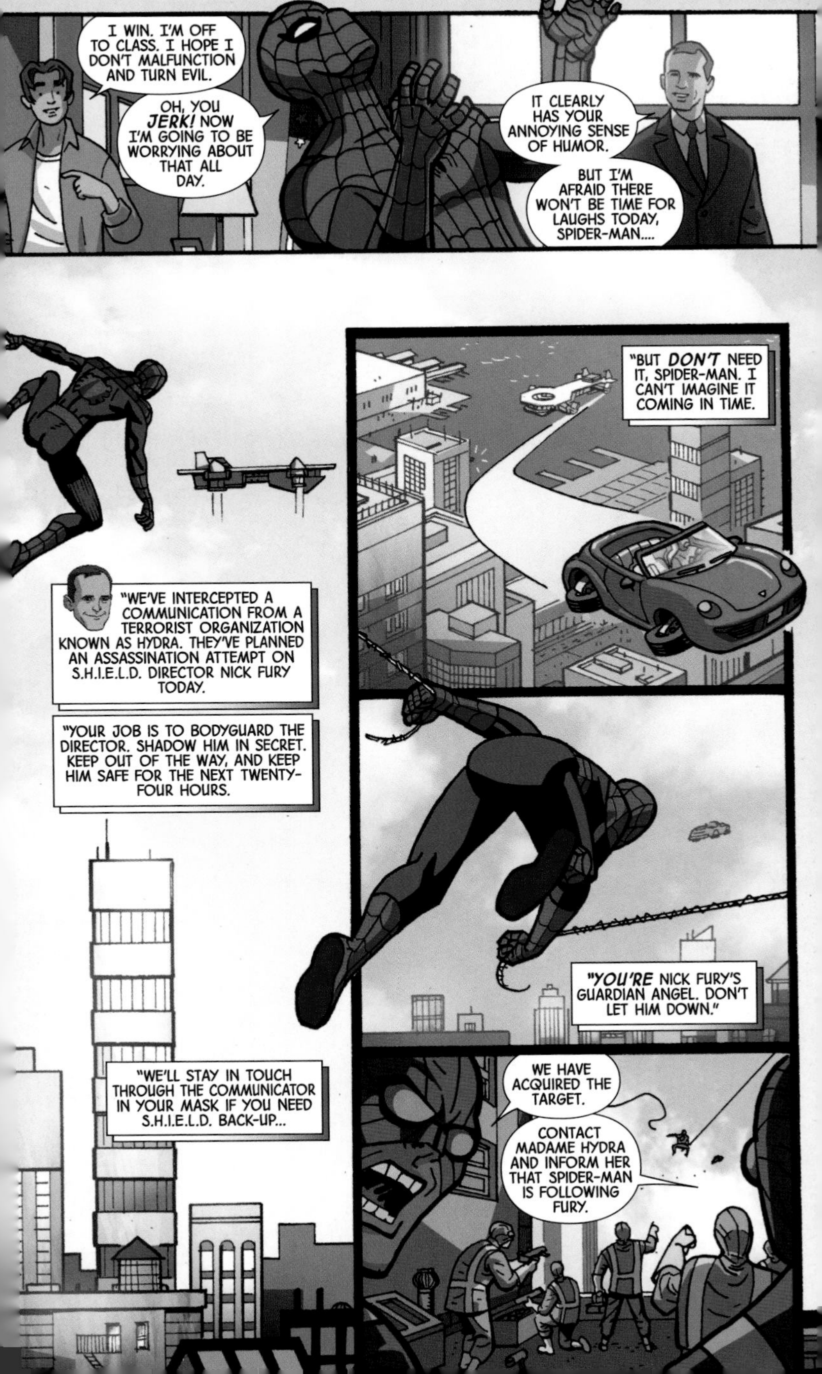
I WIN. I'M OFF TO CLASS. I HOPE I DON'T MALFUNCTION AND TURN EVIL.
OH, YOU JERK! NOW I'M GOING TO BE WORRYING ABOUT THAT ALL DAY.
IT CLEARLY HAS YOUR ANNOYING SENSE OF HUMOR.
BUT I'M AFRAID THERE WON'T BE TIME FOR LAUGHS TODAY, SPIDER-MAN....
"WE'VE INTERCEPTED A COMMUNICATION FROM A TERRORIST ORGANIZATION KNOWN AS HYDRA. THEY'VE PLANNED AN ASSASSINATION ATTEMPT ON S.H.I.E.L.D. DIRECTOR NICK FURY TODAY.
"YOUR JOB IS TO BODYGUARD THE DIRECTOR. SHADOW HIM IN SECRET. KEEP OUT OF THE WAY, AND KEEP HIM SAFE FOR THE NEXT TWENTY-FOUR HOURS.
"WE'LL STAY IN TOUCH THROUGH THE COMMUNICATOR IN YOUR MASK IF YOU NEED S.H.I.E.L.D. BACK-UP...
"BUT DON'T NEED IT, SPIDER-MAN. I CAN'T IMAGINE IT COMING IN TIME.
"YOU'RE NICK FURY'S GUARDIAN ANGEL. DON'T LET HIM DOWN."
WE HAVE ACQUIRED THE TARGET.
CONTACT MADAME HYDRA AND INFORM HER THAT SPIDER-MAN IS FOLLOWING FURY.

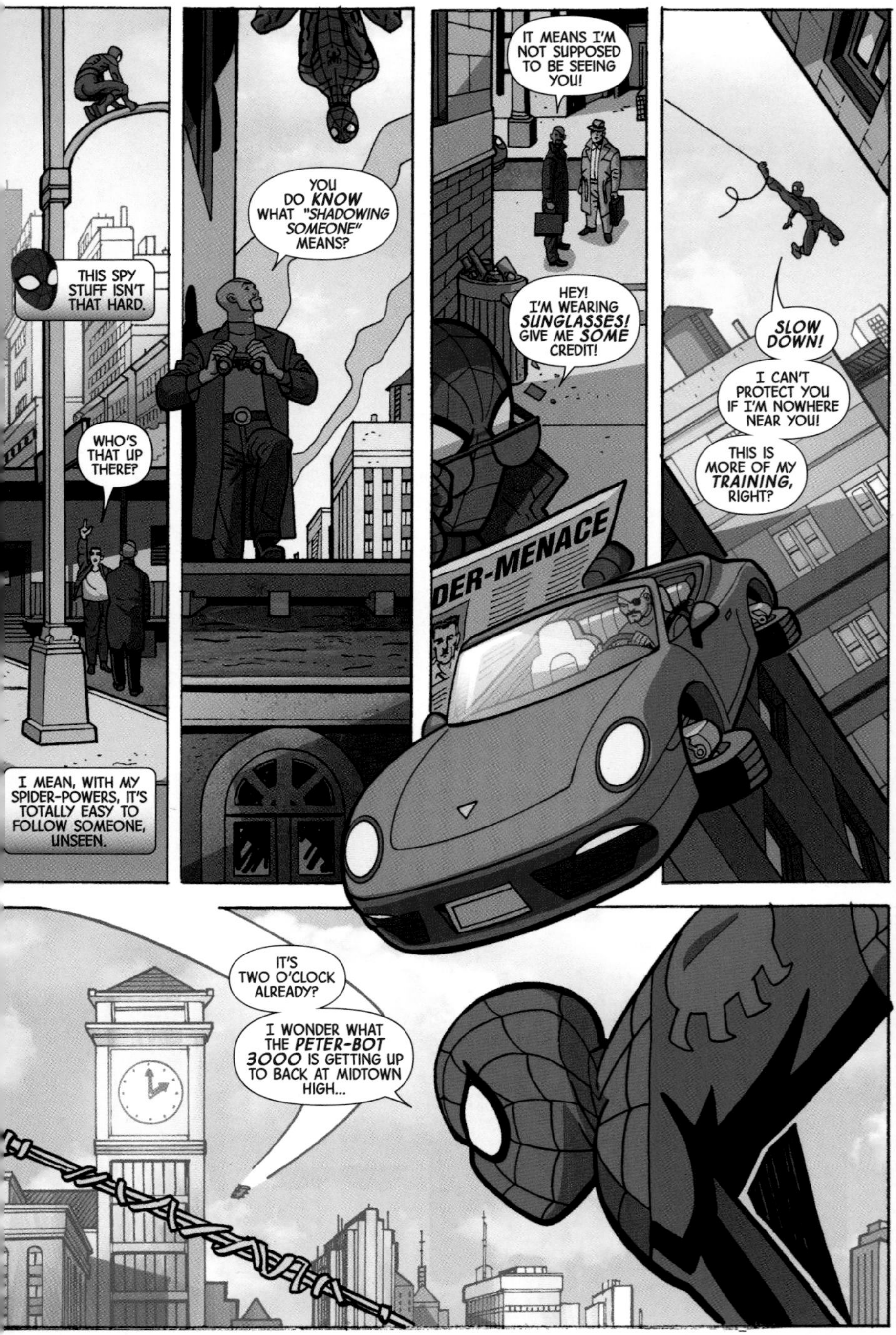
THIS SPY STUFF ISN'T THAT HARD.
WHO'S THAT UP THERE?
I MEAN, WITH MY SPIDER-POWERS, IT'S TOTALLY EASY TO FOLLOW SOMEONE, UNSEEN.
YOU DO KNOW WHAT "SHADOWING SOMEONE" MEANS?
IT MEANS I'M NOT SUPPOSED TO BE SEEING YOU!
HEY! I'M WEARING SUNGLASSES! GIVE ME SOME CREDIT!
DER-MENACE
SLOW DOWN!
I CAN'T PROTECT YOU IF I'M NOWHERE NEAR YOU!
THIS IS MORE OF MY TRAINING, RIGHT?
IT'S TWO O'CLOCK ALREADY?
I WONDER WHAT THE PETER-BOT 3000 IS GETTING UP TO BACK AT MIDTOWN HIGH...

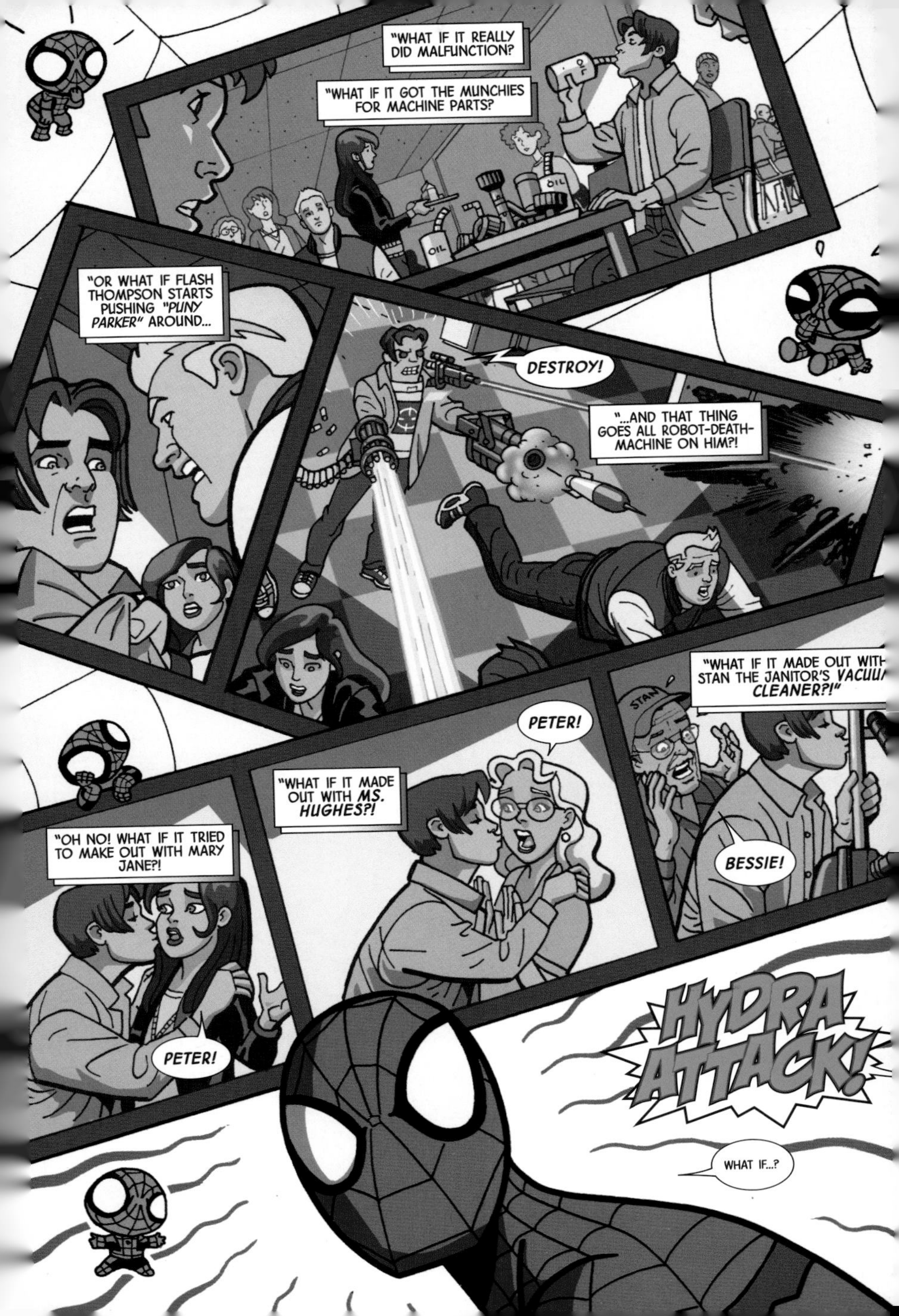

"WHAT IF IT REALLY DID MALFUNCTION?
"WHAT IF IT GOT THE MUNCHIES FOR MACHINE PARTS?
OIL
OIL
OIL
"OR WHAT IF FLASH THOMPSON STARTS PUSHING "PUNY PARKER" AROUND...
DESTROY!
"...AND THAT THING GOES ALL ROBOT-DEATH-MACHINE ON HIM?!
"OH NO! WHAT IF IT TRIED TO MAKE OUT WITH MARY JANE?!
PETER!
"WHAT IF IT MADE OUT WITH MS. HUGHES?!
PETER!
"WHAT IF IT MADE OUT WITH STAN THE JANITOR'S VACUUM CLEANER?!"
STAN
BESSIE!
HYDRA ATTACK!
WHAT IF...?

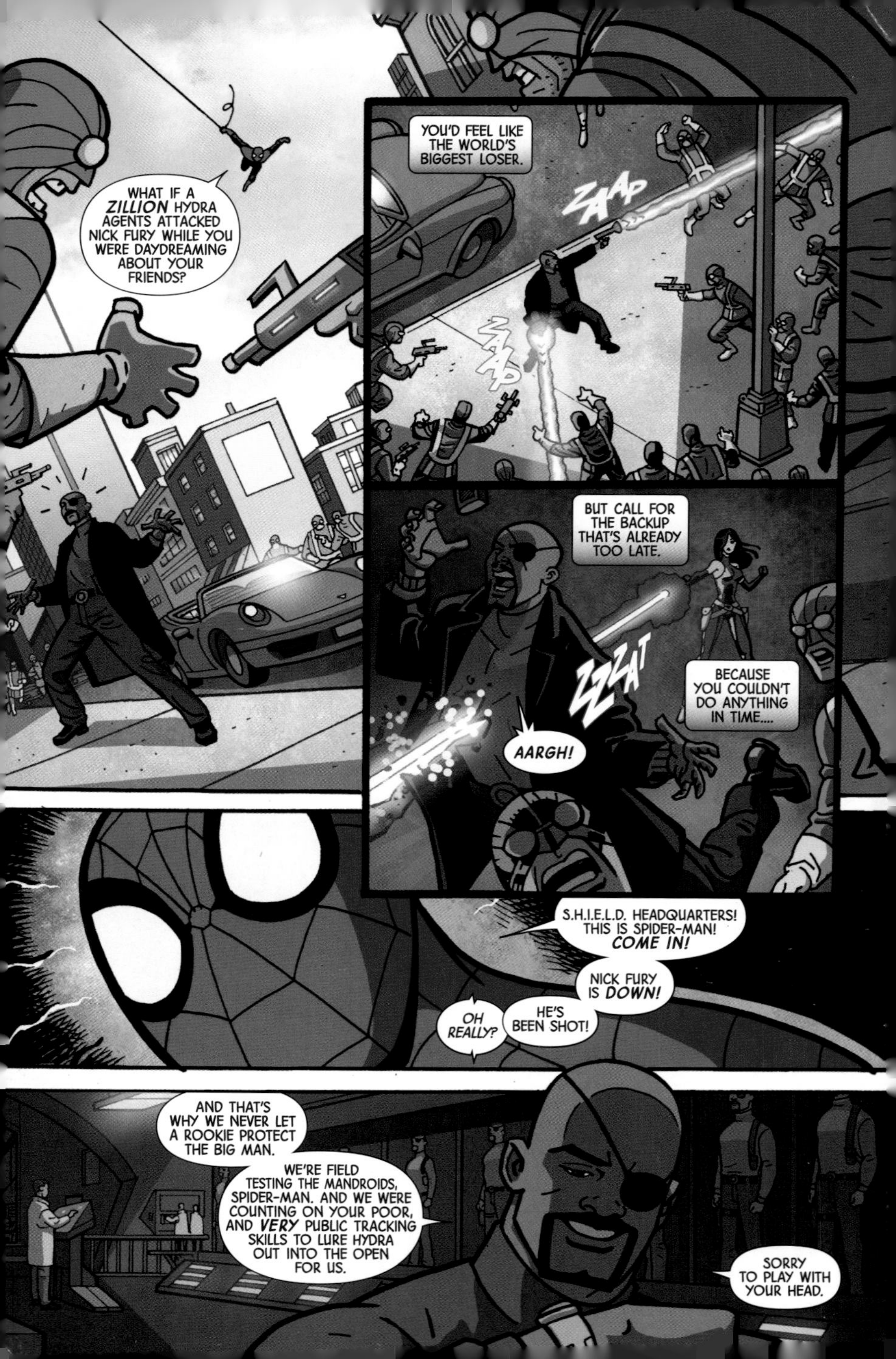
WHAT IF A ZILLION HYDRA AGENTS ATTACKED NICK FURY WHILE YOU WERE DAYDREAMING ABOUT YOUR FRIENDS?
YOU'D FEEL LIKE THE WORLD'S BIGGEST LOSER.
ZAAP
ZAAP
BUT CALL FOR THE BACKUP THAT'S ALREADY TOO LATE.
ZZZAT
BECAUSE YOU COULDN'T DO ANYTHING IN TIME....
AARGH!
S.H.I.E.L.D. HEADQUARTERS! THIS IS SPIDER-MAN! COME IN!
NICK FURY IS DOWN!
HE'S BEEN SHOT!
OH REALLY?
AND THAT'S WHY WE NEVER LET A ROOKIE PROTECT THE BIG MAN.
WE'RE FIELD TESTING THE MANDROIDS, SPIDER-MAN. AND WE WERE COUNTING ON YOUR POOR, AND VERY PUBLIC TRACKING SKILLS TO LURE HYDRA OUT INTO THE OPEN FOR US.
SORRY TO PLAY WITH YOUR HEAD.

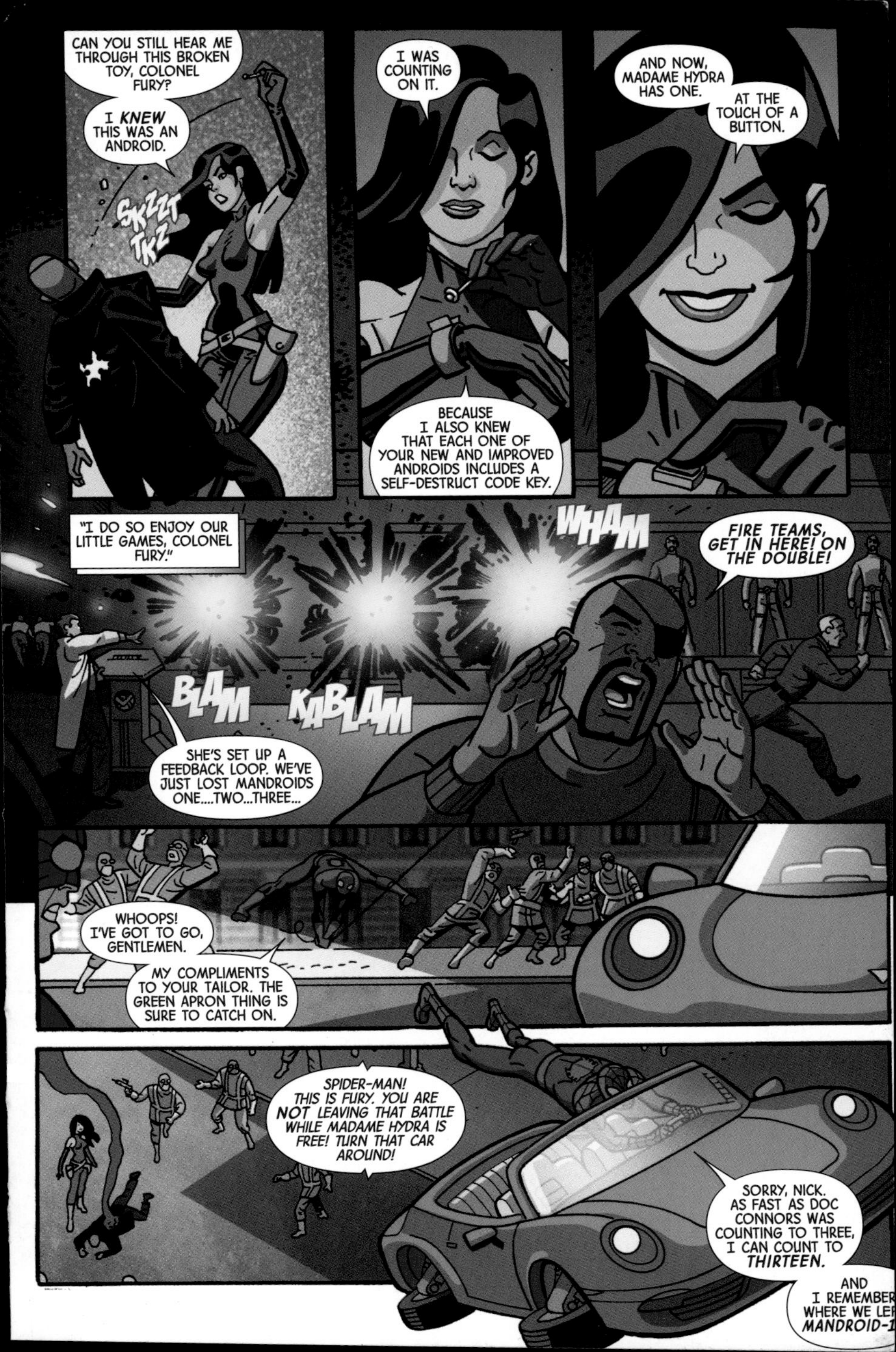
CAN YOU STILL HEAR ME THROUGH THIS BROKEN TOY, COLONEL FURY?
I *KNEW* THIS WAS AN ANDROID.
SKZZT TKZ
I WAS COUNTING ON IT.
BECAUSE I ALSO KNEW THAT EACH ONE OF YOUR NEW AND IMPROVED ANDROIDS INCLUDES A SELF-DESTRUCT CODE KEY.
AND NOW, MADAME HYDRA HAS ONE.
AT THE TOUCH OF A BUTTON.
"I DO SO ENJOY OUR LITTLE GAMES, COLONEL FURY."
WHAM
FIRE TEAMS, GET IN HERE! ON THE DOUBLE!
BLAM
KABLAM
SHE'S SET UP A FEEDBACK LOOP. WE'VE JUST LOST MANDROIDS ONE....TWO...THREE...
WHOOPS! I'VE GOT TO GO, GENTLEMEN.
MY COMPLIMENTS TO YOUR TAILOR. THE GREEN APRON THING IS SURE TO CATCH ON.
SPIDER-MAN! THIS IS FURY. YOU ARE *NOT* LEAVING THAT BATTLE WHILE MADAME HYDRA IS FREE! TURN THAT CAR AROUND!
SORRY, NICK. AS FAST AS DOC CONNORS WAS COUNTING TO THREE, I CAN COUNT TO *THIRTEEN*.
AND I REMEMBER WHERE WE LE *MANDROID-1*

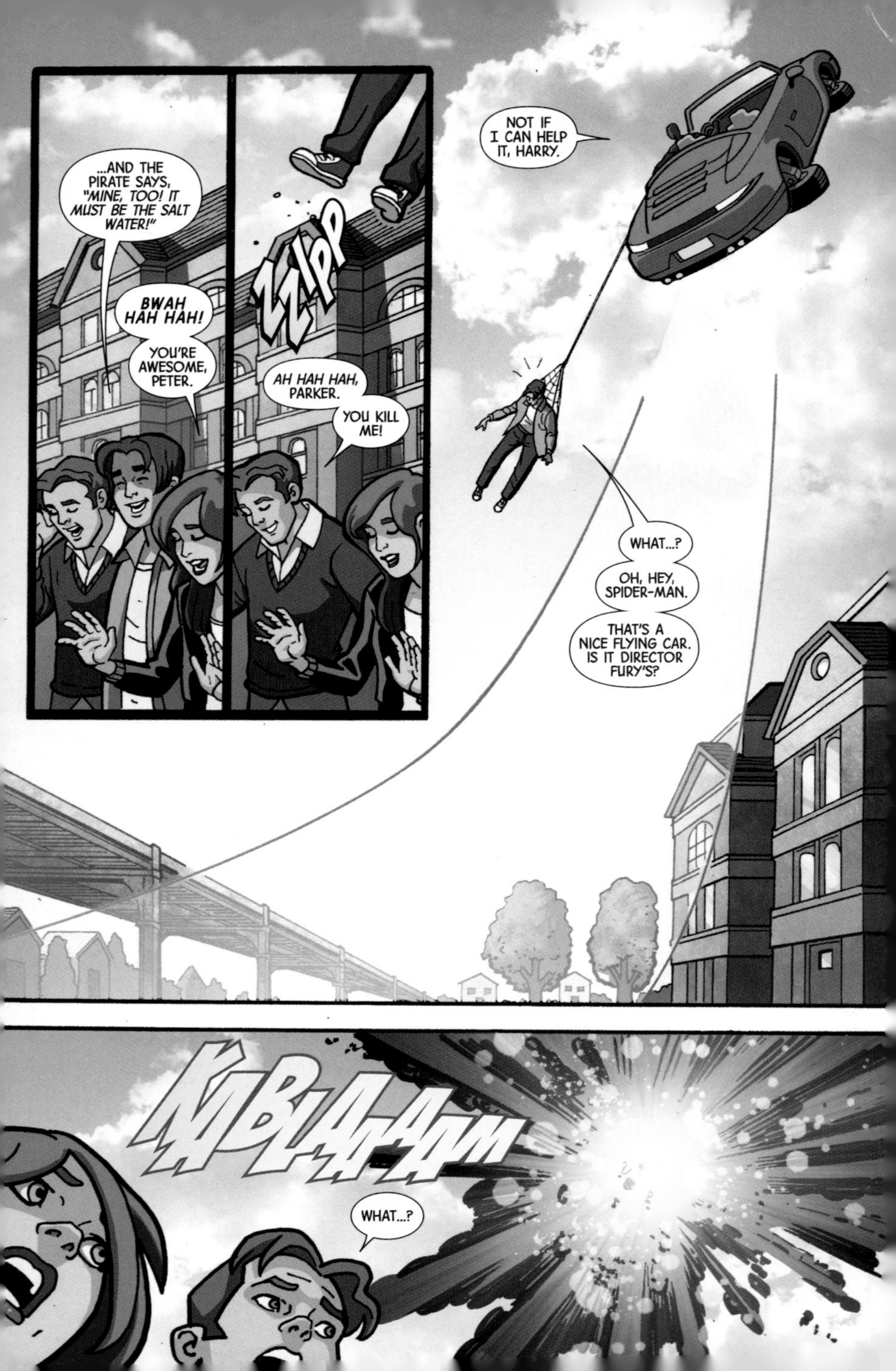
...AND THE PIRATE SAYS, "MINE, TOO! IT MUST BE THE SALT WATER!"
BWAH HAH HAH!
YOU'RE AWESOME, PETER.
ZZIPP
AH HAH HAH, PARKER.
YOU KILL ME!
NOT IF I CAN HELP IT, HARRY.
WHAT...?
OH, HEY, SPIDER-MAN.
THAT'S A NICE FLYING CAR. IS IT DIRECTOR FURY'S?
KABLAAAM
WHAT...?

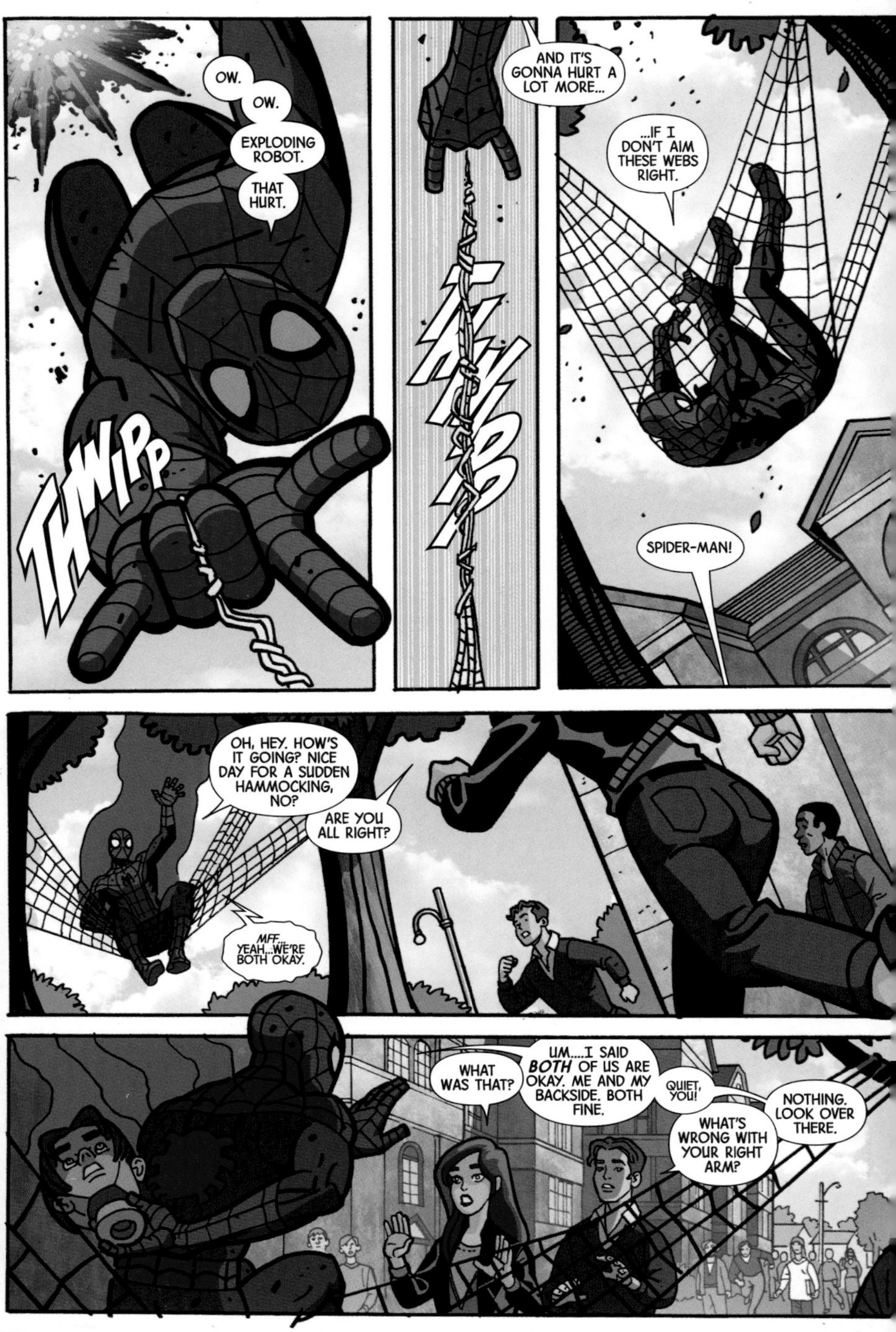
OW.
OW.
EXPLODING ROBOT.
THAT HURT.
THWIPP
AND IT'S GONNA HURT A LOT MORE...
...IF I DON'T AIM THESE WEBS RIGHT.
SPIDER-MAN!
OH, HEY. HOW'S IT GOING? NICE DAY FOR A SUDDEN HAMMOCKING, NO?
ARE YOU ALL RIGHT?
MFF... YEAH...WE'RE BOTH OKAY.
WHAT WAS THAT?
UM....I SAID *BOTH* OF US ARE OKAY. ME AND MY BACKSIDE. BOTH FINE.
QUIET, YOU!
NOTHING. LOOK OVER THERE.
WHAT'S WRONG WITH YOUR RIGHT ARM?

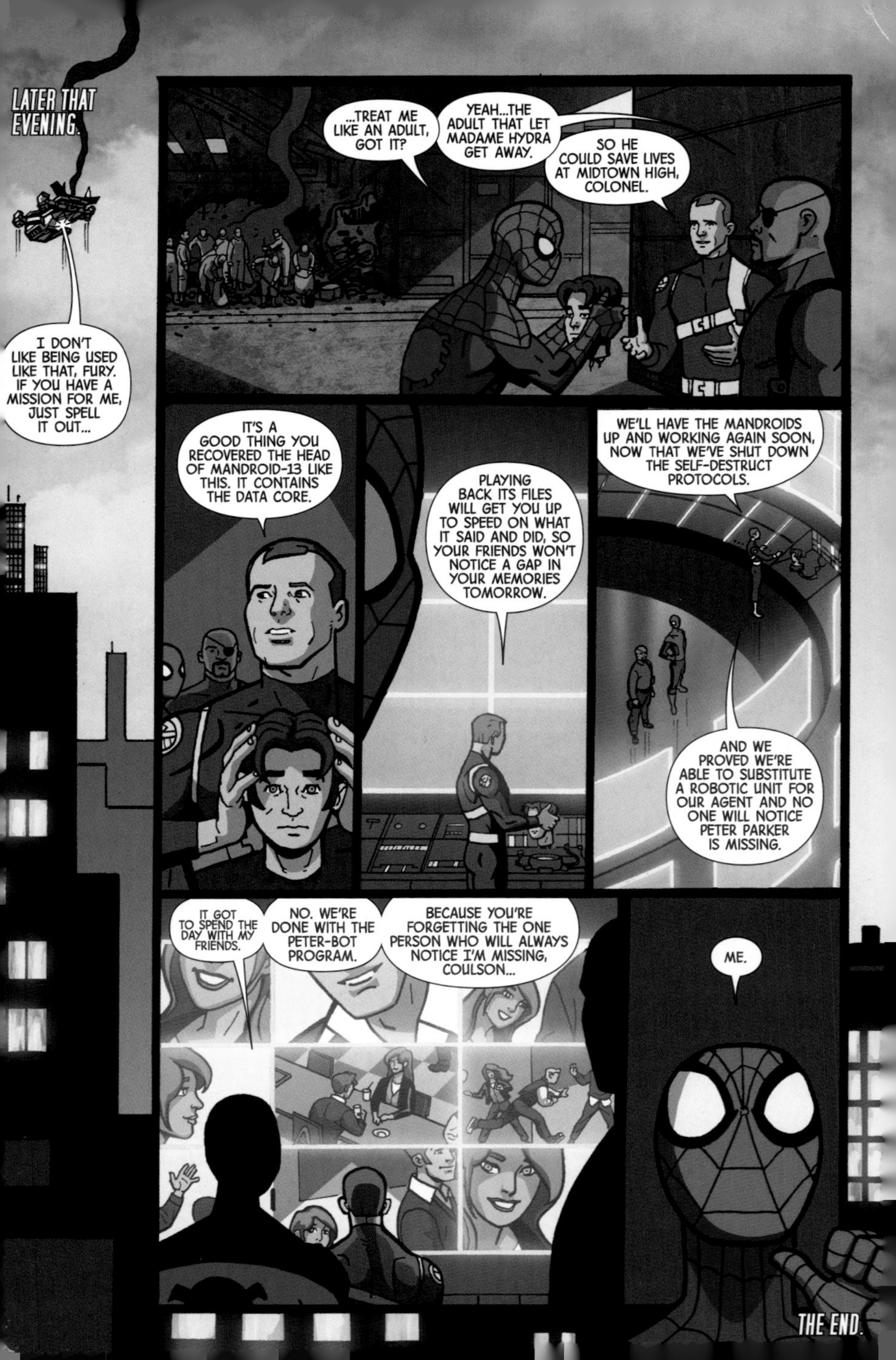
LATER THAT EVENING.
I DON'T LIKE BEING USED LIKE THAT, FURY. IF YOU HAVE A MISSION FOR ME, JUST SPELL IT OUT...
...TREAT ME LIKE AN ADULT, GOT IT?
YEAH...THE ADULT THAT LET MADAME HYDRA GET AWAY.
SO HE COULD SAVE LIVES AT MIDTOWN HIGH, COLONEL.
IT'S A GOOD THING YOU RECOVERED THE HEAD OF MANDROID-13 LIKE THIS. IT CONTAINS THE DATA CORE.
PLAYING BACK ITS FILES WILL GET YOU UP TO SPEED ON WHAT IT SAID AND DID, SO YOUR FRIENDS WON'T NOTICE A GAP IN YOUR MEMORIES TOMORROW.
WE'LL HAVE THE MANDROIDS UP AND WORKING AGAIN SOON, NOW THAT WE'VE SHUT DOWN THE SELF-DESTRUCT PROTOCOLS.
AND WE PROVED WE'RE ABLE TO SUBSTITUTE A ROBOTIC UNIT FOR OUR AGENT AND NO ONE WILL NOTICE PETER PARKER IS MISSING.
IT GOT TO SPEND THE DAY WITH MY FRIENDS.
NO. WE'RE DONE WITH THE PETER-BOT PROGRAM.
BECAUSE YOU'RE FORGETTING THE ONE PERSON WHO WILL ALWAYS NOTICE I'M MISSING, COULSON...
ME.
THE END.

LIVE! ON PAPER! IT'S TIME AGAIN FOR... MARVEL MASH-UP

COMICS YOU LOVE...REWRITTEN BY THE PEOPLE YOU DON'T!

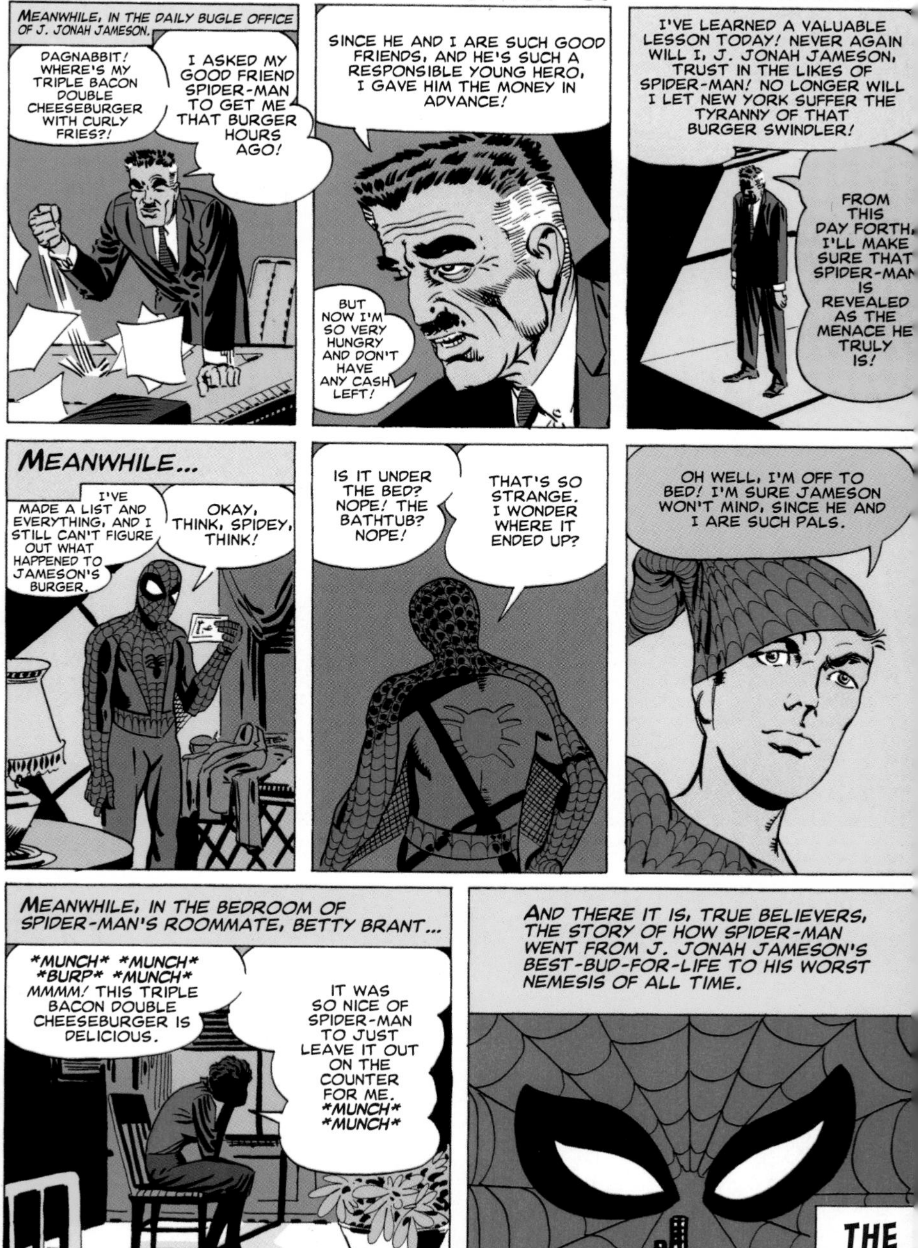
MEANWHILE, IN THE DAILY BUGLE OFFICE OF J. JONAH JAMESON.
DAGNABBIT! WHERE'S MY TRIPLE BACON DOUBLE CHEESEBURGER WITH CURLY FRIES?!
I ASKED MY GOOD FRIEND SPIDER-MAN TO GET ME THAT BURGER HOURS AGO!
SINCE HE AND I ARE SUCH GOOD FRIENDS, AND HE'S SUCH A RESPONSIBLE YOUNG HERO, I GAVE HIM THE MONEY IN ADVANCE!
BUT NOW I'M SO VERY HUNGRY AND DON'T HAVE ANY CASH LEFT!
I'VE LEARNED A VALUABLE LESSON TODAY! NEVER AGAIN WILL I, J. JONAH JAMESON, TRUST IN THE LIKES OF SPIDER-MAN! NO LONGER WILL I LET NEW YORK SUFFER THE TYRANNY OF THAT BURGER SWINDLER!
FROM THIS DAY FORTH, I'LL MAKE SURE THAT SPIDER-MAN IS REVEALED AS THE MENACE HE TRULY IS!
MEANWHILE...
I'VE MADE A LIST AND EVERYTHING, AND I STILL CAN'T FIGURE OUT WHAT HAPPENED TO JAMESON'S BURGER.
OKAY, THINK, SPIDEY, THINK!
IS IT UNDER THE BED? NOPE! THE BATHTUB? NOPE!
THAT'S SO STRANGE. I WONDER WHERE IT ENDED UP?
OH WELL, I'M OFF TO BED! I'M SURE JAMESON WON'T MIND, SINCE HE AND I ARE SUCH PALS.
MEANWHILE, IN THE BEDROOM OF SPIDER-MAN'S ROOMMATE, BETTY BRANT...
MUNCH *MUNCH* *BURP* *MUNCH* MMMM! THIS TRIPLE BACON DOUBLE CHEESEBURGER IS DELICIOUS.
IT WAS SO NICE OF SPIDER-MAN TO JUST LEAVE IT OUT ON THE COUNTER FOR ME. *MUNCH* *MUNCH*
22
AND THERE IT IS, TRUE BELIEVERS, THE STORY OF HOW SPIDER-MAN WENT FROM J. JONAH JAMESON'S BEST-BUD-FOR-LIFE TO HIS WORST NEMESIS OF ALL TIME.
THE END... FOR NOW.

ORIGINAL BY STAN LEE & STEVE DITKO

NEW DIALOGUE BY HARRISON WILCOX

LETTERED BY VC'S CLAYTON COWLES

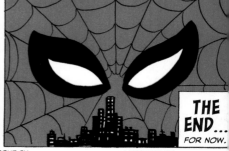

LIVE! ON PAPER! IT'S TIME AGAIN FOR... MARVEL MASH-UP

COMICS YOU LOVE...REWRITTEN BY THE PEOPLE YOU DON'T!

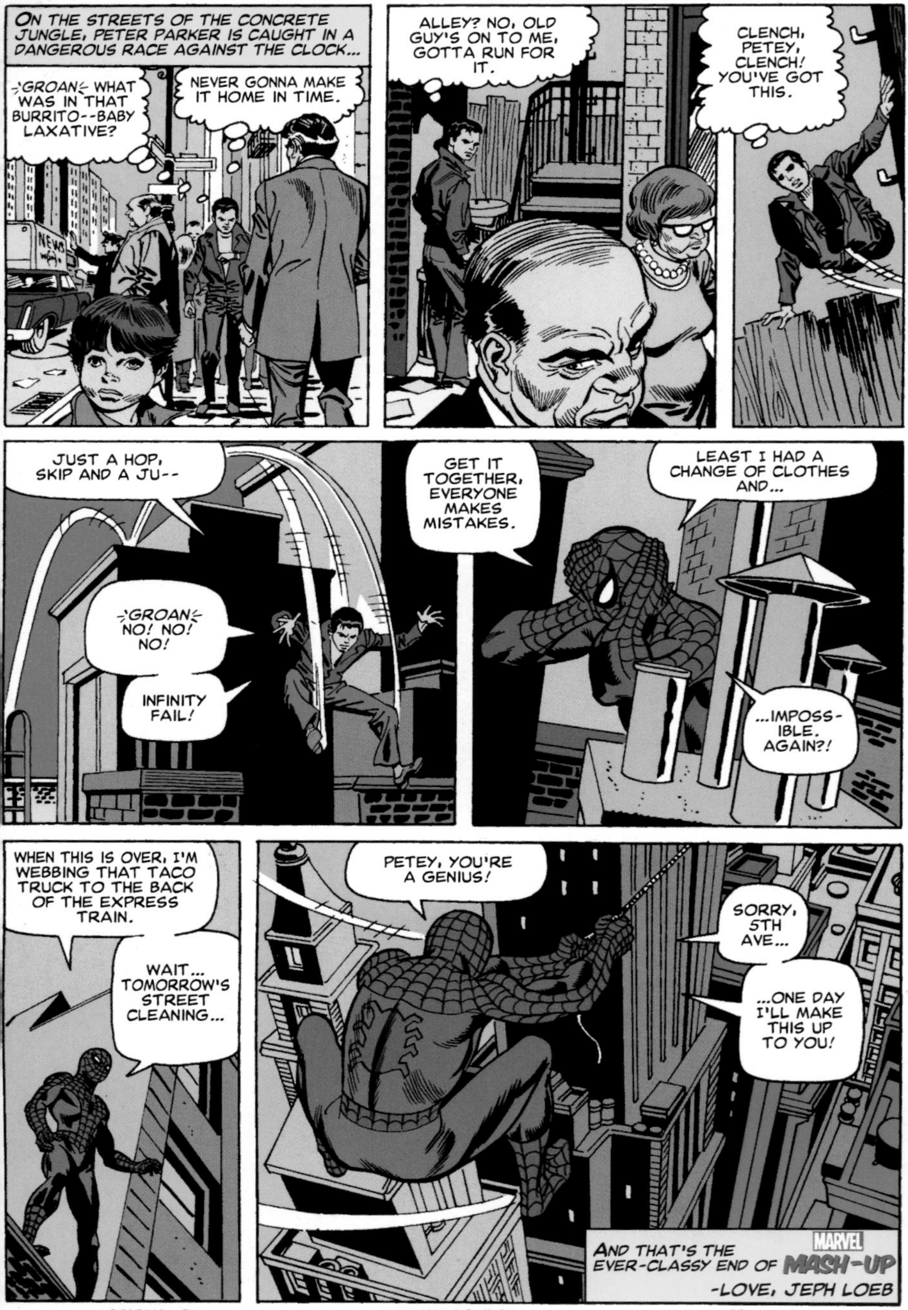
ON THE STREETS OF THE CONCRETE JUNGLE, PETER PARKER IS CAUGHT IN A DANGEROUS RACE AGAINST THE CLOCK...
GROAN WHAT WAS IN THAT BURRITO--BABY LAXATIVE?
NEVER GONNA MAKE IT HOME IN TIME.
NEWS
ALLEY? NO, OLD GUY'S ON TO ME, GOTTA RUN FOR IT.
CLENCH, PETEY, CLENCH! YOU'VE GOT THIS.
JUST A HOP, SKIP AND A JU--
GROAN NO! NO! NO!
INFINITY FAIL!
GET IT TOGETHER, EVERYONE MAKES MISTAKES.
LEAST I HAD A CHANGE OF CLOTHES AND...
...IMPOSS-IBLE. AGAIN?!
WHEN THIS IS OVER, I'M WEBBING THAT TACO TRUCK TO THE BACK OF THE EXPRESS TRAIN.
WAIT... TOMORROW'S STREET CLEANING...
PETEY, YOU'RE A GENIUS!
SORRY, 5TH AVE...
...ONE DAY I'LL MAKE THIS UP TO YOU!
AND THAT'S THE EVER-CLASSY END OF MARVEL MASH-UP
-LOVE, JEPH LOEB

ORIGINAL BY STAN LEE & STEVE DITKO

NEW DIALOGUE BY TODD CASEY

LETTERED BY VC'S CLAYTON COWLES

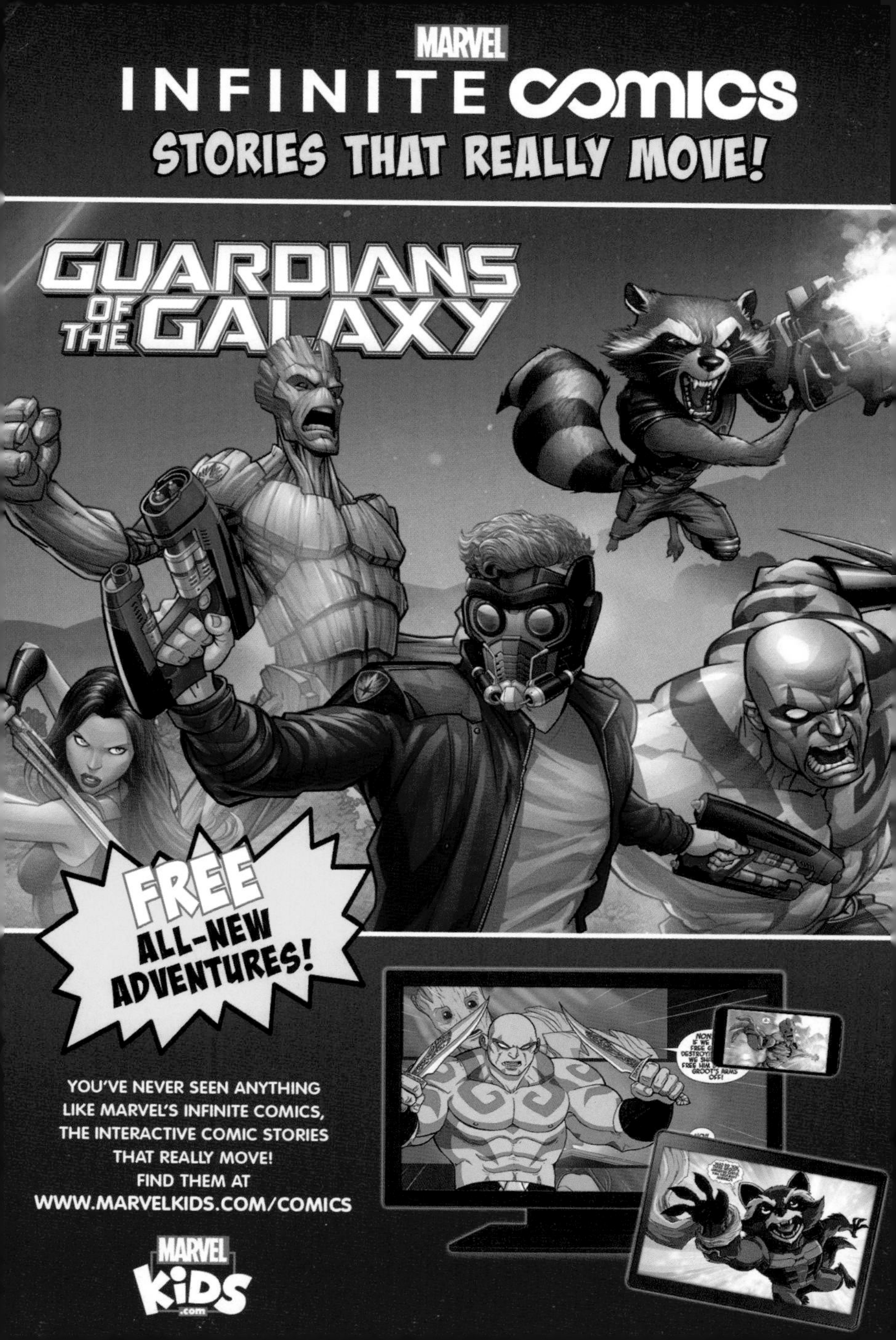
MARVEL
INFINITE COMICS
STORIES THAT REALLY MOVE!
GUARDIANS OF THE GALAXY
FREE ALL-NEW ADVENTURES!
YOU'VE NEVER SEEN ANYTHING LIKE MARVEL'S INFINITE COMICS, THE INTERACTIVE COMIC STORIES THAT REALLY MOVE!
FIND THEM AT
WWW.MARVELKIDS.COM/COMICS
MARVEL KIDS .com